Praise for Leslie Gould

"*When They Met Again* is a tender friends-to-more love story that will delight fans of Amish fiction."

Beth Wiseman, bestselling and award-winning author

"Gould expertly builds the relationship between her leads, blending gently comedic moments with emotional depth as the pair's irritation with one another slowly gives way to genuine affection. This charms."

Publishers Weekly on *The Shop Down the Lane*

"Leslie Gould's *The Shop Down the Lane* is a touching Amish romance of second chances. Lois Yoder, pressured to marry for convenience, finds her life upended by Moses Lantz—her new landlord and the man who once broke her heart. An anonymous connection through bird-watching letters leads to a tender, unexpected journey of healing and true love."

Suzanne Woods Fisher, bestselling author of *A Season on the Wind* and avid birder

"*The Shop Down the Lane* is a sweet, tender story about two people nursing their own 'broken wings' who find renewed love through grace, friendship, and faith. A must read for fans of Amish fiction and bird lovers alike."

Kathleen Fuller, *USA Today* bestselling author

"She's quirky and accident prone, and he's broken her heart once already. A delightfully entertaining Amish twist on *You've Got Mail*. This book has a sweet cast of characters who leave your heart overflowing and keep you turning the pages. Leslie Gould never disappoints!"

Patricia Johns, *Publishers Weekly*
bestselling author of *Green Pastures* on
The Shop Down the Lane

When They Met Again

Books by Leslie Gould

The Courtships of Lancaster County

Courting Cate

Adoring Addie

Minding Molly

Becoming Bea

Neighbors of Lancaster County

Amish Promises

Amish Sweethearts

Amish Weddings

The Sisters of Lancaster County

A Plain Leaving

A Simple Singing

A Faithful Gathering

Plain Patterns

Piecing It All Together

A Patchwork Past

Threads of Hope

Amish Memories

A Brighter Dawn

This Passing Hour

By Evening's Light

Letters from Lancaster County

The Shop Down the Lane

When They Met Again

An Amish Family Christmas:
An Amish Christmas Kitchen *Novella*

LETTERS *from*
LANCASTER COUNTY

When They Met Again

LESLIE GOULD

BETHANYHOUSE
a division of Baker Publishing Group
Minneapolis, Minnesota

Published by Bethany House Publishers
Minneapolis, Minnesota
BethanyHouse.com

Bethany House Publishers is a division of
Baker Publishing Group, Grand Rapids, Michigan

Printed in the United States of America

ISBN 9780764244230 (paper)
ISBN 9780764246111 (casebound)
ISBN 9781493452514 (ebook)

Library of Congress Cataloging-in-Publication Control Number: 2025045224

Scripture quotations are from the King James Version of the Bible.

Cover design by LOOK Design Studio, Peter Glöege

The author is represented by the literary agency of Browne & Miller Literary Associates.

Baker Publishing Group publications use paper produced from sustainable forestry practices and postconsumer waste whenever possible.

26 27 28 29 30 31 32   7 6 5 4 3 2 1

For my grandchildren,
Harlow and Teza.
I love and adore you, beyond measure.

1

The moment the ladybug landed on her arm, Joanna Grebel decided she wouldn't go to her cousin's wedding after all. She'd been cutting flowers for the bride, but now she couldn't seem to move. Why had she thought going away for a night was a good idea?

The sound of a vehicle approached, and she turned toward it. A van slowed as it came up the driveway, and the passenger window lowered as Ike Slaybaugh called out, "Joanna! Get your grandparents. We have a long drive ahead of us." His silver beard blew in the wind.

As the van stopped, the side door swung open and a dark-haired boy—young man, rather—jumped down. It was Adam Slaybaugh, Ike's grandson. He wore a blue shirt, black pants, and no hat. His wavy hair was too long. He was new to the community, but her friend Mandy already had a crush on him.

Mammi Lu stepped onto the back porch carrying a basket of food. "Joanna, grab your bag."

Adam started toward the house, asking Mammi Lu if he could help.

"*Denki*. The bags are in the kitchen." Mammi nodded toward the door, where *Dawdi* Marcus struggled to come through the screen door with his bag and Mammi's.

Joanna brushed the ladybug against the columbine. Then she added the flowers—dianthus, lupine, and baptisia—to the ones in the bucket and carried it and the clippers out the gate and to the back porch. Dawdi Marcus hadn't made it through the door yet, but it wouldn't do for her to take one of the bags. Instead Adam hurried past her, brushing his hand against Joanna's arm as he did.

"Sorry." He grinned as he sped by.

She rubbed her arm. He took both bags from her grandfather.

Mammi Lu waited at the bottom of the steps as the men continued on to the van. Again, she said, "Grab your bag."

Joanna loved her grandparents' place with its garden, red barn, and two-story house with a wraparound back porch. She told her grandmother, "I'm not leaving."

"Why do you want to stay?"

Joanna shrugged.

"I don't think you should."

"Why?" Joanna was nineteen. And more than trustworthy.

"Your father wouldn't approve."

"He's in Maine."

Mammi's eyes shone. "Emily is expecting you."

"She won't notice if I'm not there." They hadn't seen each other for several years.

Mammi's expression softened. "Joanna." Her voice was

just above a whisper. "I can't let you stay here alone. Please grab your bag."

Joanna shifted her gaze toward the van. Ike and Becky Slaybaugh stood beside it. They and Adam and Dawdi all waited in a semicircle, watching her. She turned her attention to Mammi Lu, locking eyes with her. "I can ask Mandy to spend the night."

Mammi shook her head. "Both stoves are cold, I promise. Dawdi and I each checked. And I know you did too—several times."

Joanna's face warmed. Was she that obvious?

"We do our best to make sure our home is safe," Mammi Lu said, "but then we have to trust the Lord."

Joanna took a deep breath, exhaled slowly, and then handed the bucket of flowers to her grandmother. "I'll get my bag."

She sat in the back of the van, ignoring the chatter and laughter of the others as they left Strasburg Township. Too anxious to read the book she'd brought, she stared at Becky's snow-white bun right in front of her. It was so white—as pure as her bleached *Kapp*—that it looked as if she used a rinse on her hair, but Joanna knew that couldn't be true.

When they stopped for a picnic dinner at a park a couple of hours later, Adam sat across from Joanna and said, "So how are you related to Noah?"

"Noah?"

Adam smiled. "The groom."

"Oh." Joanna frowned. "I'm not. Emily is my cousin."

"First?"

"Second." She paused. "Maybe third. They left Lancaster County a few years ago."

Joanna wanted to retrieve her *Buch* from her bag and read, but Adam kept talking. There was something endearing about his chatter, in an annoying sort of way. "I've known Noah since we were kids, when I moved to Spartansburg."

Joanna forced a smile.

Adam asked, "Do you live close to your grandparents?"

Joanna answered, "I live with them."

He leaned closer. "I'm living with my grandparents too, as of two weeks ago."

Joanna already knew that. Becky and Ike lived a half mile away. Mammi and Becky had been best friends since they were girls.

Soon they were back on the road, and Joanna fell asleep. Three hours later they arrived in Spartansburg, near both the Ohio and New York borders. The *Englisch* middle-aged driver, whose name was Nick, dropped Joanna and her grandparents off at a relative's farm first.

"See you tomorrow," Adam called out from the van.

Mammi turned toward Joanna as they walked to the front door. "He's such a nice young man, don't you think?"

Joanna forced a smile. "He and Mandy are interested in each other."

Mammi narrowed her eyes. "Really?"

~

They arrived at the wedding the next morning early enough to help with the chores and to set up the chairs and tables. Joanna didn't see Emily until breakfast. Her cousin acted surprised to see her, asking, "You came all the way from Maine?"

"*Nee*. I'm living with Mammi and Dawdi in Lancaster County."

Emily's eyes widened. "Your parents didn't force you to move?"

Joanna shook her head.

Emily leaned forward. "I miss Lancaster County."

Joanna could only imagine. Yet that was only part of her reason for staying behind. Her mother wrote each week, saying Joanna's father wanted her to join them in Maine. Joanna was running out of excuses not to.

Unlike weddings in Lancaster County, decorations were nonexistent for Emily's wedding. The only flowers were the ones from Mammi Lu's garden. During the wedding dinner, Adam, whose hair had been cut since yesterday, was everywhere. Teasing the groom. First avoiding a pretty young woman wearing a bright blue dress and then later talking with her. Both looked sad and the girl wiped at her eyes and walked away. Later, he was helping move benches while Joanna helped Mammi and Becky wash dishes in the kitchen.

When they finished, Becky said, "We'll leave in about a half hour."

A woman approached Becky and said, "Leroy and I are having second thoughts about Adam staying in Lancaster County."

As Mammi and Joanna walked out the back door, Mammi said, "That's Adam's mother, Elizabeth."

Joanna turned her head. The woman appeared to be in her late thirties.

In the distance, at the door to the shed, Adam and Ike now talked with a middle-aged man. "And that's Adam's stepfather, Leroy," Mammi said.

"What happened to his *Dat*?"

"He died when Adam was small."

"Oh." Joanna's family had lived across Lancaster County from her maternal grandparents, Mammi Lu and Dawdi Marcus, who resided in Strasburg Township. Joanna had been living with them for three months now, but she was just learning the stories of the people who lived near them.

Adam threw up his hands and Ike put his arm around him, pulling him close. Joanna hadn't seen a grandfather touch his grandson in an affectionate way before. The stepfather's brows furrowed. Joanna couldn't stop watching Adam. There was definitely something attractive about him. His smile. The curl of his dark hair at his neck. His bright blue eyes. The way he constantly interacted with others.

Two younger boys ran up to the group and the stepfather put his hands on their shoulders and spoke with them for a moment, but then Nick pulled the van up the driveway, waved, and parked on the other side of the shed.

"Nick's early," Mammi Lu said.

"It's a long way home." Joanna smelled smoke and turned her head, trying not to panic. A group of *Youngie* had gathered around a pit and started a fire. She took a deep breath and then exhaled slowly. She was okay. Everything was fine.

Beyond them, Adam gave his stepfather a quick wave and started toward the van.

The man called out, "Tell your *Mamm* goodbye."

Adam veered toward the house, toward Joanna. He gave her a smile as he passed. A minute later he passed her again and practically bounced to the van. He seemed more than ready to leave Spartansburg.

Joanna followed. By the time she reached the van, Adam was sitting in the back seat. Her seat. Dawdi was in the front. The grandmothers sat in the first bench seat and Ike sat in the third. Joanna could sit by Ike, whom she didn't really know, or by Adam.

She continued to the back bench, pulling her Buch from her purse as she did.

~

It wasn't until night fell that Adam began to talk. Ike had fallen asleep. Joanna was sure of it because every once in a while a snore escaped. Mammi and Becky seemed to be sleeping too. By the soft murmur of voices from the front, it seemed Dawdi and Nick were deep in conversation, although Joanna couldn't make out what they were saying. She'd come to understand over the last two days that Ike and Becky's remodeling company owned the van and Nick had worked for them full-time for the last ten years.

Joanna put her Buch in her purse when the light waned enough that she couldn't make out the words.

"What book were you reading?" Adam asked.

"*Little Women* by Louisa May Alcott."

"Is it good?"

She nodded. "Very." She had only a few chapters left, but she'd read it before. She loved the sense of home in the story and thought of it as she worked in her grandmother's home and now, again, as she reread *Little Women*. That's what she wanted—a happy home. She'd found it for now with Mammi Lu and Dawdi Marcus.

"Are you allowed to read whatever you want?" Adam grinned. "I mean *were* you, when you were younger?"

"My parents didn't pay much attention. A librarian where I grew up recommended a lot of classics," Joanna said. "And Mammi Lu has quite a few books I can read."

"My stepdad was strict about what I could read." Adam turned toward her. "I heard you're new to Lancaster County too."

"Not to the county." Joanna stared straight ahead. "But to the Strasburg area, *jah*. I moved in with Mammi Lu and Dawdi Marcus a few months ago." She gave him a sly glance. "I'm friends with Mandy."

Adam's voice lowered. "Mandy?"

Joanna rolled her eyes. "The girl you went on a date with."

He laughed and brushed his bangs, which were still a little long, out of his eyes. "I didn't. Caleb did." Adam continued talking. "I had ice cream with the two of them last week, that's all."

Joanna's face grew warm. Thankfully it was dark enough she doubted Adam would notice if she had turned red. Had Mandy lied? Or had Joanna misunderstood her?

"What were you talking to the girl in the blue dress about?"

"Ruthie?"

Joanna nodded. She hadn't seen any other girls in blue dresses. Most of the others were wearing dark green. Except Emily, who had on a purple dress.

"Not much," Adam responded.

"It looked serious. Did you break up with her?"

After a moment's hesitation he said, "Jah. I don't want a long-distance relationship."

"Wait, so you went out on a date with Mandy while you were still courting Ruthie?" Joanna needed to stay away from Adam.

"*Nee*," he said. He leaned back against the bench seat. "Mandy's not my type."

"How about Miriam?" Joanna asked. "Is she your type?"

"Miriam?" He was bluffing. No one forgot Miriam.

Joanna played along. "Mandy's twin."

He laughed. "Oh, her. Definitely not. She's too wild for me."

Miriam was too wild for Joanna too. The twins were as opposite as possible, even though they were identical. Miriam made Joanna nervous—she reminded Joanna of her Dat.

For the next couple of hours Joanna and Adam talked, first about *Little Women*, which Adam said he'd like to read. She asked what it was like to grow up in Spartansburg and he told her—lots of freedom to fish, hunt, and ride horses. He didn't mention his stepfather, his younger brothers, or his mother. He said he moved to Lancaster County to learn more about the remodeling business from his grandfather.

"You don't want to be a farmer?"

Adam smiled wryly. "There's no farm for me to farm." The tone of his voice made Joanna wonder if one of his younger brothers would inherit the family land.

Joanna wasn't sure when it had happened, but Adam was closer to her than when they'd started the journey. He must have inched across the seat as they talked. She squinted. He wasn't wearing his seatbelt. "You need to buckle up." She patted the strap across her shoulder. "Mammi Lu said your grandparents are strict about safety in their work van." Mammi Lu had mentioned that one time when they were riding in another Amish driver's van together.

Adam hesitated.

Joanna leaned toward him until their noses were an inch apart. She smelled a hint of aftershave, which distracted her for a moment. But then she said, "I wasn't joking about you putting on your seatbelt." Jah, she was concerned about his safety, but also about Mandy. Joanna wasn't sure that Mandy *didn't* like Adam. She wasn't going to betray her friend by encouraging him.

Adam smiled broadly, but retreated and did as she said. As he clicked the buckle, he shifted the conversation back to Mandy. "I don't know why Mandy would have said we went on a date."

Joanna didn't want to speak for her friend. "Well, sometimes information becomes misconstrued."

"Misconstrued?" He laughed. "What kind of *Vatt* is that?"

Joanna smiled. "An I-don't-want-to-talk-about-why-she-would-have-said-what-she-did kind of word."

He put his hand over his heart. "Ouch. You got me." He leaned toward her. "Who are *you* courting?"

Joanna wasn't courting anyone, but she didn't want to tell Adam. She ignored him.

The van began to slow, taking the exit to a rest area. Streetlights lit up the interior of the van as Nick parked the vehicle. The two sets of grandparents began to talk as they stepped out of the van. Joanna admired how close they all seemed. She wanted that someday—good friends and a strong community.

In the restroom, Becky asked Joanna if she'd found a job.

"Not yet," Joanna answered. "I've been doing chores and weeding Mammi's gardens." Mammi Lu sold flowers to tourists in a stand by the highway. Besides growing daffodils and tulips and her spring perennials, Mammi grew peonies, bachelor's buttons, black-eyed Susans, cosmos, zinnias, salvia, dahlias, gladioli, bellflowers, sunflowers, and more.

Becky took a tube from her purse and ran it over her lips.

Was it tinted? Nee. Just more expensive than the drugstore lip balm Joanna used. When she'd finished, Becky said, "I'm looking for someone to organize the warehouse, clean our two vacation rentals, and wash the linens. That sort of thing. Would you be interested?"

"Jah." If she had a job, maybe her Dat would stop pressuring her to move to Maine.

"*Wunderbar*!" Becky beamed at Joanna in the mirror. "Come into the office Monday morning." Becky put the tube back in her purse and then patted the top of her Kapp as she said, "We'll talk." Becky was Mammi Lu's age—sixty-four—but she was spry and stylish and still beautiful, with curves that showed because she, or someone, had tailored her cape dress with purposefully placed pleats and tucks. She also wore a sleek black cardigan that Joanna guessed was made out of cashmere. Jah, Becky was old—but still beautiful.

Mammi Lu was pretty too, but in a soft, squishy sort of way.

Joanna linked her arm through Mammi Lu's as they walked back to the van. Sometimes her grandmother had balance issues, and Joanna didn't want her to trip. That was Joanna's excuse. Really, she just liked to be close to Mammi Lu.

When they reached the van, Ike and Dawdi had switched seats but otherwise everyone was in the same place. Joanna stepped to the back.

Adam followed her and immediately fastened his seatbelt.

"So." He picked up the bag of chips in the middle of the seat that he must have purchased at the mini-mart. "Who *are* you courting?" He passed the bag to her.

As Joanna read the ingredients she asked, "Why do you care?" She popped a chip into her mouth and chewed slowly.

Adam leaned toward her. "Are you evading my question?"

She smiled. "I'm barely nineteen."

"I think the point is, you *are* nineteen. Most Amish Youngie start courting by our ages."

"How old are you?"

He squared his shoulders. "Twenty."

"You might be ready to court—but I'm not."

"I don't believe you. The right person hasn't come along is all." He sat tall. "I could be that person, that man." He leaned closer. "Let me take you out for ice cream at the creamery for our first date."

She forced herself to laugh. Was he serious? "We just met. We have plenty of time. Let's just be friends." She brushed her hand on her apron and then extended it to him because, regardless of how forward he was, she still found him appealing. "Friends?"

He crossed his arms over his chest. "Men and women can't just be friends."

Adam was annoying—but he was also handsome and talkative, in a good way. Plus he listened. And he also smelled good. Perhaps they could be more than friends, someday.

Adam turned forward and leaned back against the seat. "I think you'll change your mind."

Joanna pulled her hand back, feeling conflicted. "Time will tell." Him asking her to court when they'd only just met seemed impulsive, a red flag for Joanna. And yet, he had a lot of good qualities.

She passed the bag of chips back to him. Joanna let out a

sigh of relief as the van turned down Mammi Lu and Dawdi Marcus's driveway. The house was intact. So was the barn.

"Do you plan to go to the Youngie gathering tomorrow evening at the bishop's farm?" Adam asked.

"Jah."

"*Gut*." He grinned. "I'll see you there."

2

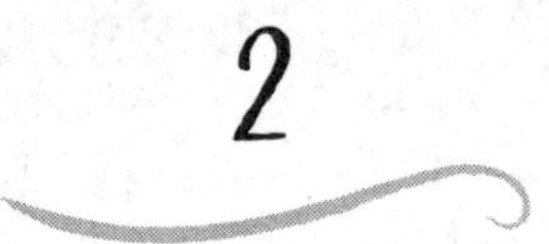

The next day was an off Sunday for church. In the afternoon Mandy stopped by, and she and Joanna sat on the porch drinking lemonade. Mandy had a little bit of makeup on, lip gloss and mascara, which made her brown eyes pop. Miriam often wore makeup, but this was the first time Joanna had seen Mandy with any on. The identical twins had blond hair and dark brows. Both were striking but Miriam, with her sparkling personality, stood out more.

After Joanna described the trip to Spartansburg and back, leaving out any mention of Adam, Mandy said, her voice a little wobbly, "Caleb—" Mandy gave Joanna an apologetic look—"asked to give me a ride home tonight after the ice cream social."

Joanna smiled, happy for her friend. But that meant Joanna would need to find a ride home. "*Ach*, don't worry about it." Adam had been telling the truth about Caleb and Mandy after all. "I don't need to go."

"Nee, you definitely need to." Mandy met Joanna's gaze again. "Can't you take your Dawdi's buggy?"

"I don't do very well with his horse."

"How about your scooter?"

"Mammi doesn't like me riding it after dark." Honestly, Joanna didn't either. Vehicles whizzed by on the highway, often without any thought to pedestrians or scooters.

"How about Adam Slaybaugh?" Mandy asked. "He lives practically next door. I can stop by and ask him to give both of us a ride there—and you a ride home."

Joanna didn't want Adam to think she was interested in him after what she'd said the night before. "Only if you tell him I only want a ride because you and I are friends—not for any other reason."

"Why? He's cute. And funny. Not to mention Becky and Ike's grandson. You two would be a perfect match." Her eyebrows arched. "Your grandmothers would be over the moon."

Joanna was beginning to figure out the dynamics in Mammi Lu's friend group. She and Becky were best friends. Mandy's grandmother Elaine was friends with both of them. Weirdly, Joanna's paternal grandmother, Mammi Rhoda, was part of the friend group too. But she lived on the other side of the county, where Joanna used to live. Also, it seemed Becky was the ringleader.

"Joanna?" Mandy was staring at her. "I asked why you wouldn't be interested in Adam?"

"I'm not ready to court," Joanna answered. "I'm only nineteen." Mandy and Miriam were both twenty.

"Well, don't wait too long." Mandy smiled, a little patronizingly.

Maybe Joanna *should* think about courting someone sooner

than she intended to—if she could get a job working for Becky and Ike *and* start courting, surely her Dat wouldn't expect her to move to Maine. Maybe she should say yes to Adam's ice cream date offer after all.

Mandy stood. "I'll go ask Adam about a ride. I'm sure he'll say yes. We'll pick you up at five thirty."

"What about Miriam? Does she need a ride?"

"Nee," Mandy said. "She's going to ride her scooter. She said she'll find a ride home."

Joanna smiled. "With?"

Mandy rolled her eyes. "Who knows. I'm definitely not my sister's keeper."

Because Elaine was Mandy and Miriam's grandmother, Mammi Lu used to arrange playdates when Joanna visited. She and Mandy clicked immediately, more so than she did with Miriam. But she liked Miriam too.

Joanna didn't have many friends that were girls. The district she grew up in was small and had more boys. Her family had more boys than girls too—she was outnumbered six to one. She relished spending time with Mandy and Miriam when she visited Mammi Lu. Best of all, she'd already had friends when she'd arrived in Strasburg Township, hopefully to stay.

~

Mandy and Miriam's grandfather, Daniel, was the bishop of their district, and he and Elaine were hosting the ice cream social.

Joanna noticed a stranger—a man—who was tall, muscular, and handsome with sandy hair and deep brown eyes. She didn't recognize him, and she tried not to stare.

After the singing, the guys took turns cranking the ice cream freezer and showing off their muscles. The stranger had a five o'clock shadow and appeared a few years older than most of the Youngie. As they all stood around in groups eating the ice cream, Caleb introduced him to Joanna and Mandy. "This is Jacob Byer," he said. Miriam stepped into the circle. Caleb continued. "Jacob is new to our—"

"Hallo!" Miriam said, interrupting Caleb. "Welcome to Strasburg Township."

Jacob took a step backward but then smiled. "Denki. And who are you?"

"Miriam." She grinned and then swept her hand toward Mandy. "This is my twin." She nodded toward Joanna. "And our friend Joanna."

Forcing herself to be outgoing, Joanna asked Jacob, "Where are you from?"

"Ohio. Holmes County." Jacob took a step closer to Joanna. He towered over her, even though she was five eight. "I have an uncle who lives here. Enoch Byer."

Joanna spoke as confidently as she could. "Are you visiting Lancaster County or do you plan to stay?"

Jacob's eyes twinkled as his gaze met hers. "I'm staying."

Someone called out, "Joanna!" She turned. Adam sauntered toward them. "Are you ready to leave?"

She wasn't.

"I hope I'll see you soon." Jacob gave her a charming smile that left her feeling flustered. Miriam was now standing beside him.

Joanna gave Jacob, and everyone, a wave and turned around slowly. She didn't want to hurry and make Jacob think she was courting Adam. Nor did she want to go too slowly and risk having Adam say something embarrassing in front of Jacob. Her heart beat faster. Perhaps she hadn't met the right person yet—until now.

On the way home as Adam chatted away about the ice cream, about Mandy and Caleb, and about his grandparents' business that he was excited to learn, Joanna thought about Jacob. About how tall he was. And how handsome with his square jaw and deep brown eyes. And his charming smile. Compared to Adam, who seemed to be an open book, Jacob was quiet and mysterious. She couldn't *stop* thinking about him.

When they reached Mammi Lu's, Joanna thanked Adam for the ride and started to open the buggy door.

"Wait!" Adam set the brake and jumped to the ground. "I need to do that for you."

Joanna waited, a little impatiently. When Adam appeared at her door he extended his hand to her as he grinned.

She took his hand and jumped down. "Denki." She started toward the back door. Mammi Lu had left a battery-operated lantern hanging to light her way.

"Wait," he said again but not as enthusiastically as before. "Aren't you going to ask me to stay? Lemonade on the porch? Maybe a cookie."

Joanna turned toward him at the bottom of the steps. "I'm tired. From the trip and everything."

"Oh." He took off his hat and ran his hand through his dark hair. "I wanted to talk about the trip. About sitting in the back of the van together. Don't tell me you didn't feel something."

Annoyed, Joanna said, "I didn't feel anything." But she

had. Although it paled when compared with what she was feeling for Jacob.

His face fell. "Well, I'll see you tomorrow. At the office, right? You're coming by to talk to Mammi about a job."

"Jah." Joanna momentarily regretted not asking him to stay. But not enough to change her mind. "See you tomorrow." If she got the job, she and Adam would have a chance to get to know each other. Perhaps she'd want to court him eventually—unless Jacob Byer asked her out first.

~

The next morning, Joanna watched Becky run dishwater into the kitchen sink in the warehouse. As she added soap, she said, "Apparently the boys couldn't wash their own mugs on Friday." All of the mugs were white and matched. The kitchen consisted of a counter with a stovetop, a sink, a drying rack, and a small fridge.

Becky put the mugs into the soapy water as she chatted with Joanna. "Business has picked up, plus we have two vacation rentals—the apartment above the shop and a house. We're renovating one property and looking to buy another one to flip. I need an assistant and Ike needs a couple more men. You'd be supporting the team too." She began washing one of the cups.

"The team?"

She dunked the cup in the rinse water. "That's what we call our crew. Have you ever heard the saying 'Teamwork divides the effort and multiplies the effect'?"

Joanna nodded as she picked up a towel to dry. Mammi Lu sometimes said that when they tackled a big job together.

"Teamwork is one of our top values." Becky put the mug

in the rack and began washing a second mug. "I'd need you to shop, clean and stock the rentals, launder the linens, and help with decorating the houses we renovate. Nothing big. Just enough to make possible buyers take notice, if you like that sort of work."

The mug slipped a couple of inches through Joanna's hand before she caught it. She loved that sort of work. She'd wanted to decorate her parents' house but was never allowed to. Mammi Lu had let her do some painting and other projects, however.

"Are you interested?"

"Absolutely." Joanna placed the dry mug in the cupboard. "When can I start?"

"How about today? Nick can take you into Lancaster. I have a list of supplies we need." Becky grinned. "Welcome to the team. It's wonderful *gut* that you want to join us."

Joanna couldn't stop smiling as she spent the morning shopping in Lancaster. Nor as she cleaned the vacation apartment that afternoon. After work, as she recorded her hours on her time sheet, Adam approached her. She was happy to see him, but then in the distance Jacob waved.

She smiled past Adam to Jacob. Adam turned, nodded at Jacob, and faced Joanna again. A forlorn expression settled on his face as he stopped at the counter and picked up a pen.

"Joanna." Jacob stopped when he reached her. "What are you doing here?"

"Working."

"Nice," Adam muttered. She noted he had a book under his arm.

Jacob grinned.

"You work here too?" Joanna asked him, now ignoring Adam.

"Jah." Jacob flashed his charming smile. "Ike hired me this afternoon."

Adam groaned, and Jacob gave Joanna a wave as he headed to the other side of the warehouse.

Joanna stepped closer to Adam. She couldn't keep herself from asking, "What Buch are you reading?"

Without smiling Adam held up the book. *Little Women.* "It's my Mammi Becky's copy."

~

Tuesday morning as they clocked in, Jacob asked Joanna to go with him for ice cream that evening.

"How about if we meet there?" His brown eyes shone. "After supper."

Joanna surprised herself by immediately saying, "I'd like that." She noted Adam stood by the office door. Had he heard her exchange with Jacob? Flustered, she thought of how she'd rejected Adam's invitation to ice cream just three days before. And then refused to serve him lemonade and cookies Sunday evening, which hadn't been very hospitable.

She spent her morning cleaning the vacation rental house. In the afternoon, she and Becky organized the warehouse. After dinner Joanna scootered to the creamery. Jacob already waited in a line of tourists. She joined him, ordering one scoop of chocolate ice cream. Jacob ordered and then devoured a banana split—and then ordered a second one.

As he ate, he told her about growing up in Ohio. "This

is hard to talk about," he said, "but my Dat left our family when I was six for an Englisch woman."

Empathy washed through Joanna. In comparison to Jacob, she'd had a happy childhood. "I'm sorry," she said. "That must have been really hard."

"Jah," he said. "I don't talk about it much—I haven't told anyone here what happened to my family."

Joanna was touched he'd told her. "I won't tell anyone. I don't gossip."

As he smiled his eyes shimmered, sending a wave of warmth through her. "You don't seem to be the type who would." He took another bite of ice cream and then said, "Anyway, that's why I came here to live with my uncle. I'll farm his land someday."

"That's fortunate."

Jacob nodded. "It's a relief to have a plan. In the meantime, I'll work for Ike and Becky."

While they chatted, Miriam approached on her scooter. "Joanna! Jacob!" She hopped off and yanked it up onto the sidewalk. She grinned at Jacob. "What are you doing here?"

"We're celebrating our new jobs." Jacob explained both he and Joanna had been hired by Ike and Becky.

Miriam tilted her head and turned her gaze to Joanna. "Lucky you." Then she chuckled, a little ruefully. "Must be nice to be the granddaughter of Becky's best friend."

Joanna's face grew warm. If Miriam thought that was why she'd been hired, which was most likely true, nothing Joanna could say would make a difference. She stayed quiet.

"Well, nice to see you, but I've gotta go." Miriam jumped

back on her scooter, dodging an Englisch couple as she maneuvered from the sidewalk back to the street and around the corner.

Jacob grimaced. "Is she always so blunt?"

"Oh, she's fine." Joanna wasn't going to speak badly of the bishop's granddaughter—or of anyone, she hoped. Besides, Miriam really was her friend, even if they were very different.

Fifteen minutes later, as they readied to leave, Jacob looked Joanna in the eye and said, "I'd like to be your friend, to get to know you. Out of all the girls at the singing last night, you're the one who caught my attention. You seem the most interesting."

Joanna had never been so flattered in her life. He'd chosen her, even over Miriam. And he wanted to be her friend, meaning she could get to know him before any thought of courting. She said, her voice barely above a whisper, "I'd like to be your friend too."

The next morning, Becky appeared tired as she sat at her desk with her head down. She jotted something on a legal pad.

Joanna took a step closer to the desk. "*Guder Mariye.*"

Becky lifted her head, showing red-rimmed eyes.

Alarmed, Joanna asked, "What's the matter?"

Becky brushed at her eyes. "Adam left for Florida."

Joanna stepped closer. "Pinecraft?"

Becky nodded. "Two friends of his from Spartansburg have construction jobs waiting there. They stopped by last night and convinced him to go with them. Although it didn't take much talking on their part for Adam to decide to leave."

As she thought of Adam's forlorn expression the previous afternoon, Joanna suppressed a pang of regret. She should have been nicer to Adam. "For how long?"

Becky shrugged. "I have no idea. For a while, I'm guessing." Her eyes grew watery. "Maybe for good."

3

Joanna was a homebody and didn't like leaving her grandparents' place for one night, let alone for two weeks. Even more so, she didn't want to leave Jacob. But Mandy's grandparents—Elaine and Daniel—were going to Florida for the last two weeks of January and had invited Mandy and Joanna to go with them before Mandy married Caleb in March.

Mammi Lu told Joanna she'd never regret going to Florida. Mammi and Dawdi had vacationed in Pinecraft a few years before but didn't feel up to going now. That was okay with Joanna. She didn't think they should all be away from home at the same time.

Joanna left with Mandy and her grandparents and arrived at the shopping center parking lot in Lancaster just after noon on Monday. They all wore long coats and boots, which they wouldn't need in Florida.

Her heart pounded as the bus turned into the parking lot. Joanna and Jacob had just started courting. Their ice cream date in May had led to conversations on their lunch breaks.

But by the end of June, he was giving Miriam rides home from church and activities. Joanna had been disappointed but remained composed.

Nevertheless, she couldn't stop thinking about Jacob, and honestly, she had been jealous of Miriam. But it was no surprise. Miriam was pretty and outgoing and a lot of fun.

But for some reason Miriam and Jacob's relationship had ended in September. Mandy said Miriam had decided Jacob wasn't right for her, but when Jacob began chatting with Joanna more at work he'd said Miriam was too wild for him. That endeared Jacob to her again. She wasn't surprised he'd been attracted to Miriam initially, but he'd seen things for what they were. Miriam wasn't right for him after all.

In November, he went back to Ohio for Thanksgiving. Joanna feared he wouldn't return, but he did. In early December he asked to drive her home from the Youngie singing. Then he asked to drive her home from church. Soon, Joanna's favorite place to be was in Jacob's courting buggy.

Sunday before last, Jacob had pulled her close. "We've been friends long enough, don't you think?"

All Joanna could do was nod. She didn't exactly think of him as a friend—she didn't know him well enough yet—but she wasn't as convinced that she needed to be friends before courting him as she once was.

Her mother once said that she hadn't known Joanna's father very well before they married, and Joanna believed that showed in their relationship. But she could get to know Jacob as they courted just as well—she wouldn't rush into a serious relationship. If she'd learned one thing from her parents' relationship, it was to take her time. And Jacob didn't seem to be the type to rush into anything either.

Being with Jacob made her feel seen. Others in the community took notice of her because of him. She'd observed him working hard, cooperating with the team, and learning from Ike. He was ambitious—he'd mentioned once, in private, that he'd like to buy Ike and Becky's business, once they were ready to retire, and also run his uncle's farm.

Maybe she knew Jacob as well as she needed to.

His face had fallen when she'd told him she was going to Florida for two weeks. She just hoped he wouldn't drive someone else home while she was gone. Or start seeing Miriam again.

Joanna pushed her thoughts aside as she boarded the bus.

She and Mandy sat next to each other, with Elaine and Daniel across the aisle. They'd barely left the city limits before Elaine started gossiping. "Did you hear about Paul's Laura?" she asked. People were often identified by their father's name—Joanna had been Nehemiah's Joanna most of her life, even though there hadn't been another Joanna in the district she grew up in. Elaine added, "Laura's the youngest in that family."

"A few years older than I am?" Mandy asked.

"Jah. She's marrying a man from New Holland." Elaine lowered her voice. "It's quite rushed, if you know what I mean."

"Mammi!" Mandy glanced around. Joanna hoped no one was listening. Daniel was already snoring, so he hadn't heard. Joanna dug her book out of her bag and opened it.

As the hours passed she would read some and then watch the landscape for a while. First the snow-covered fields of Pennsylvania. Then the hills of Maryland and Virginia and the forests of North and South Carolina. At each stop,

Joanna took off a layer. Her coat. Her fleece. Her boots. Her sweater. By the time the bus crossed from Georgia into Florida, she wore only her cape dress, apron, and tennis shoes. She dozed as the bus traveled west across Florida. When she awoke, they'd reached Sarasota.

Palm trees swayed in the morning breeze and Englischers wore shorts and T-shirts. A few minutes later she spotted an Amish couple wearing sandals. Then an older Amishman driving a golf cart. Joanna stared, guessing he was from a district with different rules than she was used to.

The bus turned into a parking lot and stopped.

"We're here." Elaine stood. Mandy and Joanna did too. Daniel waited until they started toward the front of the bus and then followed. As they stepped onto the asphalt, Joanna took in a welcome breath of warm air. Once she had her roller bag, she turned toward the street, where a small group of people had gathered.

"Joanna?"

She squinted into the sunshine.

"It's me." Adam Slaybaugh stood fifteen feet in front of her." He wore a short-sleeved shirt and his pants were rolled up a few turns.

"Adam!" Elaine grabbed Mandy's arm and hurried toward him. "We were hoping we would see you."

Daniel stopped beside Joanna. "Who is that?"

"Becky and Ike's grandson."

Daniel hooked his thumbs through his suspenders. "He needs a haircut."

Joanna laughed. He did. Maybe life in Florida hadn't changed Adam that much.

"Elaine and I both thought he would have returned to

Lancaster County by now. Ike and Becky need him close—perhaps you girls can convince him to move back."

Joanna doubted that.

Mammi Lu, Becky, and Elaine were all in a quilting bee together, although Joanna didn't know how Becky had time to quilt. But, no doubt, she participated more for the gossip—or rather, fellowship—than for making quilts. She imagined the women all talked about their grandchildren and wanted as many of them as possible to live close by.

Daniel spoke quietly. "What's Elaine up to?"

Joanna whispered, "I don't know."

Elaine was speaking loudly, although Joanna couldn't make out exactly what she was saying, and gesturing wildly with her free hand. Daniel dropped his voice even lower. "Mandy and Caleb are getting married in March."

Joanna nodded. Their wedding hadn't been formally published yet—it would be when they returned home—but that was all she'd heard about from Mandy for the last couple of months.

Mandy turned and motioned to Joanna.

"Go," Daniel said. "Rescue the girl."

Joanna left her suitcase by Daniel and stepped forward. "Hallo, Adam," she said. "How are you?"

"*Gut*!" His grin was as warm as the Florida sun. "What a surprise!" His bright blue eyes were definitely on her, not Mandy. It appeared he'd forgiven her for being brusque with him in May. He asked, "How long are you here for?"

"Two weeks," Elaine answered before Joanna could. "Maybe you could show Mandy, and Joanna of course, around."

Adam kept his eyes on Joanna. "I'd love to. There's a singing in the park tonight. Want to come?"

Joanna, caught mid-yawn, put her hand over her mouth. As she took it down, she smiled at his audacity, and then said, "I think we'll be too tired—"

As Elaine said, "Denki, Adam. What time?"

"Six o'clock. There's a potluck at five but don't worry about bringing anything. You'll have another chance next week."

Elaine said, "We'll see you then!"

Joanna turned back toward Daniel. The Amishman driving the golf cart had stopped beside him. As the man loaded their bags onto the back of the cart, Daniel asked, "Is it okay if I drive?"

The man gave him a curt nod and climbed into the passenger seat. Elaine struggled onto the back seat as she called out, "Walk behind us," to Mandy and Joanna. Then she rattled off the address in case they couldn't keep up.

Joanna nudged Mandy and pointed at Daniel driving the golf cart out of the parking lot. "What is going on?" she squeaked. Daniel Troyer would never be allowed to drive a golf cart back home.

Mandy laughed. "Have you ever heard the saying 'What happens in Pinecraft stays in Pinecraft'?"

Joanna hadn't, but it made her laugh. Daniel, as a bishop, wouldn't break the *Ordnung*. The rules in Pinecraft seemed to be as opposite the ones back home as the winter weather was.

The cabin had two bedrooms, and the owner had stocked the fridge with groceries Elaine had ordered. Once they'd unpacked, Mandy and Joanna decided to walk around while Daniel and Elaine took a nap.

Mandy had come to Pinecraft with her grandparents and

Miriam a few years ago, so she led the way to the ice cream shop. "Lots of the Youngie hang out there," she said. "Maybe we'll see Adam."

"Shouldn't he be at work?"

"It seems like people have weird schedules here," Mandy said. "Lots of things are different than back home." That was for sure.

Adam wasn't at the ice cream shop and neither were any other Youngie. Families with little kids were, though. And older people. Lots of older people.

Joanna thought of Jacob back in Lancaster County, and her heart constricted. She hoped he was thinking of her—not Miriam—too.

The potluck was for the entire community, and Elaine managed to make a chicken, broccoli, and cheese casserole from the groceries that had been delivered. But when it came time to go, she claimed to be too tired. Then she said to both girls, "I expect a full report in the morning over breakfast about everyone you see." Joanna was pretty sure Elaine meant a full measure of gossip.

Daniel decided to stay with Elaine.

As Joanna carried the picnic basket and Mandy walked beside her, someone called out her name. She turned. Adam rode a bike toward them, grinning from ear to ear. He'd called out her name—not Mandy's. Joanna couldn't help but return his smile. There was something about Adam Slaybaugh that brought a jolt of joy to her heart.

When he reached them, he jumped from the bike and took the basket.

"You can't carry the basket and ride the bike too." Joanna reached to steady the bike.

"Nee, I can." But when he tried, his knees bumped against the basket, which hit the handlebars. He laughed and stood.

"When did you learn to ride a bike?" Joanna asked.

"As a boy. Our district didn't forbid them."

"I'll push the bike." Joanna reached for the handlebar.

"Can you ride?" Adam asked. Before she could answer, he added, "Give it a try."

She shook her head.

"Come on," he said. "Mandy and I won't tell anyone." He grinned again, as if challenging her. "Besides, you're in Pinecraft."

Joanna actually had ridden a bike before. Her older brother Leon had one while on his *Rumspringa*, and he had taught her how. She swung her leg over the bar, positioned her right foot on the pedal, and pushed down with her left. The bike wobbled, and she shifted her weight as she grasped the handlebar a little tighter. A few more pushes on the pedals and the bike stabilized.

"Look at you!" Adam jogged alongside her.

Joanna glanced over her shoulder at Mandy, whose eyebrows were arched. Joanna slowed the bike and called over her shoulder, "Want a turn?"

"Nee." Mandy's voice was firm.

Joanna slowed more and hopped off the bike. Steadying it with one hand, she reached for the basket with the other. "I should walk with Mandy."

As she reached for the basket, Adam said, "Only if you go canoeing with me later."

She smirked. "Only?"

His face reddened. "There's a creek by the park. My friend has a house on the creek and a canoe docked nearby."

Joanna glanced back at Mandy, who was only a few steps behind, and then said to Adam, "We'll see." Canoeing with Adam did sound like fun. But why? She was interested in Jacob, not Adam. Jah, she had wanted to be Adam's friend that night in the van, but he'd rejected that idea. Had he changed his mind?

Mandy caught up with Joanna. Adam continued to chatter away until they reached the park. He pointed to the grassy area on the other side of the volleyball court, where a group of barefoot women played. All of them were dressed in blue and purple dresses and some wore heart-shaped Lancaster County Kappa.

Fifteen minutes later, Mandy yawned several times while they ate, and then didn't want to get pie. "I'm going to go back to the cottage."

Joanna took both of their paper plates and stood. "I'll go with you."

"You can stay," Mandy said.

Another girl, about their age, stood and said to Mandy, "I'm walking back too. We can go together."

The girls came off the volleyball court and one of them called out to Adam, "I'm ready to get that ice cream cone you promised."

He glanced from Joanna to the girl and back to Joanna.

Was ice cream Adam's predictable move when it came to asking someone on a date? "Who is that?" Joanna asked. The girl looked familiar.

Adam's voice was deep and low. "Ruthie."

Joanna took a step backward as her stomach lurched.

Ruthie from Spartansburg. Adam's girlfriend who he'd broken up with at Emily's wedding. Had Ruthie followed him to Pinecraft?

She exhaled. Why the reaction? She reminded herself again that she was interested in Jacob—not Adam. Ruthie didn't matter. Nor did any other girl Adam dated. She got the idea he'd gone out with a lot more people than she had.

"Go get your ice cream," she said to Adam. "I need to go back to the cottage with Mandy anyway."

~

The next day, Daniel hired a driver to take the four of them to the beach. Joanna had been to the Maryland shore one time as a child with Mammi Lu and Dawdi Marcus, and she'd seen photos of tropical beaches in books, but the sugary white sand of Siesta Beach exceeded her expectations. Groups of palm trees swayed in the breeze. The gentle waves of the Gulf of Mexico rolled in, one after another. The salty air filled her senses.

Elaine and Daniel brought chairs to sit on, and Joanna and Mandy kicked off their flip flops and ran across the warm sand. Joanna turned toward the east, her face pointed at the morning sun. She closed her eyes for a moment. Sea gulls squawked in the distance. A child yelled. The warmth of the sun bathed her face.

"What's wrong?" Mandy asked.

"Nothing." Joanna opened her eyes. She lifted the hem of her dress above her knees and started toward the waves. She'd never felt so alive. So joyful. So carefree.

Mandy followed.

After wading for an hour, they turned back toward Mandy's grandparents. Adam sat on the sand next to Elaine. Both were laughing.

"Ugh," Mandy said. "She's probably gossiping with him—about me. For some reason Mammi thinks Adam would be a better match for me than Caleb."

"Why?"

"Honestly?"

Joanna nodded.

"Because of his grandparents' business. You work for them—you know how successful they are, moneywise."

Joanna hadn't thought much about Ike and Becky's finances. They didn't flaunt their wealth, and they always had her on a strict budget when it came to supplies. Neither Becky nor Ike ever talked about their profits, not that anyone in the district did. It went against the Amish way.

But besides all that, they were very generous with all kinds of people. Becky was always sending the team to help Amish and Englisch neighbors alike, whether it was patching a roof, fixing a school porch, or repairing a fence for an older couple.

Mandy crossed her arms over her chest. "Mammi thinks I'd have more security if I married Adam."

Joanna recoiled at Elaine's meddling. Mammi Lu would never do such a thing. Besides, Mandy and Caleb *were* getting married. The time to meddle, if there was such a time, had passed. And Caleb was perfect for Mandy. "Does Adam know what your grandmother is thinking?"

Mandy wrinkled her nose. "I hope not."

"Is there anything I can do to help?"

Mandy shook her head but then smiled. "You could keep Adam occupied while we're here. As a friend of course, but maybe Mammi Elaine will think he's interested in you."

It was Joanna's turn to wrinkle her nose. "But what if word gets back to Jacob? I don't want to risk my relationship with him."

"The only person who would say something would be my Mammi, and I don't think anyone would believe her anyway."

4

Adam stood on the white sand, watching Joanna run through the waves. When she turned toward him, he waved. She shaded her eyes with her hand and then grinned. She wore a lavender dress that was wet at the hem, and the ties of her heart-shaped Kapp bounced on her shoulders as she started toward him. Her hair appeared lighter in the sunlight. Her dark blue eyes, which reminded him of the kaleidoscope Mammi Becky had given him when he was a child, glimmered over her rosy cheeks. She radiated happiness, something he hadn't seen in her previously. Not that she'd seemed unhappy before—she'd just seemed serious and overly aware of everything going on around her. But now she appeared to be truly enjoying herself. She was even prettier than she'd been the day before.

As the girls approached, Adam asked, "Do you two want to go see the house I'm working on? It's only a half mile from here."

Joanna squinted. "How did you know we were here?"

He grinned. "I have my sources."

"You girls should go with Adam." Elaine smiled coyly. "Make hay while the sun shines." She laughed.

Mandy rolled her eyes.

Elaine said, "Come back in an hour or so and tell us all about it. Then we'll have our lunch before we leave."

Joanna playfully put a hand on her hip. "Why would we want to go look at the house you're working on?" Being sassy looked good on her.

Adam grinned again. He said, "Well . . ." drawing out the word, "I don't know if Mandy would want to, but I assume you would. I heard you're still working for my grandparents."

"Who told you I'm still working for your grandparents?"

He hesitated and then said, "Ruthie."

Joanna had both hands on her hips now. "How would she know?"

"She has a cousin who lives near Strasburg."

"Oh." Joanna wrinkled her nose. "Your Mammi Becky didn't tell you?"

"Nee." She hadn't mentioned Joanna once in any of her letters. Adam had assumed she wasn't working for his grandparents anymore.

"So do you want to go?"

Joanna nodded as Mandy shook her head.

"Go along," Elaine said, motioning to Mandy. "The walk will do you good."

Adam took off toward the parking lot. Joanna, in two strides, caught up with him, while Mandy trailed behind a few steps.

Wanting to choose a subject both might be interested in, Adam asked, "What have you been reading lately?"

Joanna glanced at Mandy, who answered, "Nothing right now. I've been busy."

"How about you?" Adam asked Joanna as she slowed her pace, apparently so Mandy would catch up with her.

Joanna patted the bag hanging from her shoulder. "*Sense and Sensibility*."

"What is it about?"

"Two sisters who are very different from each other. One's self-controlled while the other is impulsive."

Adam's face grew warmer, and he hoped it wasn't red. "Do you think I'll like this one if I liked *Little Women*?"

Joanna slowed a little more and Mandy caught up. Then she asked, "What did you like about it?"

"I enjoyed reading about the sisters and how they all interacted. And their friendship with Laurie."

Joanna gave him a side-eye glance.

His face grew hot as he remembered he'd told her women and men couldn't just be friends. He quickly added, "Of course, once he's grown he falls in love with Amy."

Joanna stared at him for a long moment, making him feel restless, and then said, "Then I think you would like *Sense and Sensibility*. I'm almost done. I'll leave you my copy."

Even though it was only a half mile, Adam was hot and sticky by the time they reached the three-story house that sat across the road and above the beach. Mandy appeared to be even more overheated than he was. Her face was bright red. But Joanna was fine, probably because she'd pulled a bottle of water out of her bag and sipped it the entire way. Joanna passed the bottle to Mandy, but she declined to take it.

Adam punched the code into the keypad on the brick post next to the wrought iron security gate. Mandy walked through first, followed by Joanna. All three stopped in the driveway and took in the property.

Adam adored the house; it was his favorite of those he'd worked on so far. It had a large wraparound porch, massive palm trees on each side, and a courtyard with a swimming pool in the back.

"I'm the only one working today," Adam said.

"But you're not working." Joanna gave him another sassy smile.

He liked this Joanna, but he still rolled his eyes, hoping to encourage her playfulness. "I'm on my lunch break."

She tipped her head. "A rather long one."

He shrugged, hoping it wasn't obvious how much he was enjoying being with her.

Joanna asked, "What kind of work are you doing?"

"Clean up." Adam pointed to the front door and started toward it. "I'll give you a tour."

Joanna linked her arm through Mandy's, and they followed Adam across the driveway and up the steps to the porch. Adam punched in another code as he explained the house had four bedrooms and three bathrooms and was over four thousand square feet. "The front faces the Gulf and the back is on a canal."

He led the way through the brick entryway and up the stairs to the large living area, which had windows that looked over both the ocean and the canal. Drop cloths covered the floor, and ladders and paint buckets were scattered around the room. He opened the sliding glass door onto the deck overlooking the back and motioned for Mandy to go through first. Then he followed Joanna.

She pointed to a sailboat headed toward the Gulf. "That

looks like so much fun." One of the people on the boat, a young woman wearing a sundress, waved. Joanna waved back with enthusiasm, while Mandy barely lifted her hand.

Adam continued the tour, going through the bedrooms on the main floor and then the massive kitchen with a huge stove, two refrigerators, and two dishwashers.

"What a great house to raise a family in," Joanna said.

Mandy shook her head. "It's way too fancy."

"Jah," Joanna said. "But it's spacious and in such a beautiful setting."

Adam laughed. "I think it's more of a party house than a kids' house."

"Every house should be a kids' house." Joanna gave him an impish smile. "I always like to imagine the family who will buy a property," she said. "And what kind of home they'll make out of it." She stepped to the window above the sink that looked over the deck and the canal. "Imagine working in this kitchen while your *Kinder* played on the deck."

"Nee," Mandy said. "What kind of life would this be for kids? No fields to run in? No animals to care for?"

Mandy had a point, but Adam appreciated Joanna thinking about children regardless of the setting. He always thought of the family who would occupy a house he worked on too. That's what it was all about—creating a home. Joanna got that.

After he took them to the lower level, with another view of the canal, they walked outside into the courtyard and the pool area and then around the side of the house, where the driveway led to a three-car garage.

Joanna pointed to the dumpster. "So that's your tool of the trade?"

"Jah." He grinned. "Teamwork requires a variety of roles and implements."

She nodded. "I'm just joking. I'm the team member who cleans the toilets in the rentals back home."

Adam's heart skipped a beat. If only he'd stayed in Lancaster County to work with Joanna. He'd been impulsive to leave the way he had because she'd hurt his feelings, and in the dark of night no less.

"Could we sit for a few minutes?" Mandy asked. "In fact, could I stay here? Joanna, would you ask Mammi and Dawdi to have the driver swing by and pick me up?"

With alarm in her voice, Joanna asked, "Are you all right?"

"Jah. Just overheated."

Joanna held up her water bottle. "I'll fill this for you." Then she said to Mandy. "You're probably dehydrated. We were on the beach for a quite a while, not to mention the walk." Joanna turned to Adam. "We should go get Daniel and Elaine."

"All right." He opened the door back into the house as he said to Mandy, "You should sip the water and wait on the front porch. There's more shade. I'll give your grandparents the address."

Adam set a fast pace on the way back to the beach, and Joanna met it stride for stride. "I hope Mandy's okay."

"You're probably right about her being dehydrated," Adam answered, even though he felt anxious about her too. "We see it here all the time, especially the first day or two. People have traveled for an entire day and then aren't used to the warmer weather. It's a bad combination."

"Do you think I should have stayed with her?"

Adam shook his head, although he wasn't certain. "She has water and shade. She should be okay. I'll come right back—she won't be alone for long. You can direct Elaine and Daniel's driver to the house if needed."

Joanna nodded and then said, "Denki for the tour. No surprise, but I've never seen anything like that house. It's beautiful." They talked about it for a few minutes and then Joanna asked teasingly, "Where do you live? In a house like that?"

He laughed. "I rent half a room in Pinecraft, in a two-bedroom cottage with three other guys."

"How did you get to the beach?"

"I rode the bus, with my bike."

"With your bike?"

"Jah. There's a rack on the bus."

Comically, Joanna glanced around at the multimillion-dollar houses on both sides and then up and down the road. "Where's your bike now?"

"I locked it up by the restroom at the beach. It won't take me long to get back to Mandy."

Was Joanna increasing the pace? Adam adjusted his to keep up with her. "Want to go canoeing tonight on the creek?" he asked.

"What about Ruthie?" Joanna was marching now.

Adam quickly said, "She's just a friend."

Joanna increased her pace even more. Her voice grew louder. "You said men and women couldn't be friends, except now, apparently, they can be?"

He started to jog to keep up. "Well, sure, if neither wants more of a relationship."

"Ruthie doesn't want to court you?"

His face grew even warmer. Ruthie did want to.

"Sounds like a double standard to me." Joanna certainly didn't hold back.

Adam was getting more and more out of breath. "She's just a friend, I promise. Want to go canoeing?"

Joanna ignored his request but turned her head toward him. "Can *I* just be your friend?"

He shot her a wry smile. "What do you think?"

When she didn't answer, he asked, "How about that canoe ride?"

She looked straight ahead again. "Not if we can't be friends. Besides I'm courting someone back home."

Adam's breath hitched. "Jacob?"

"Jah."

"For how long?" Adam heard the unmistakable quaver in his own voice.

Joanna tilted her head as she said, "A while."

Adam felt a pang of jealousy. It sounded as if Joanna had started going out with him right after they first met. Right after she'd told Adam she wouldn't court him without being his friend first.

Adam turned sideways in the street and sidestepped as he asked, "Is Jacob your friend?"

"Jah."

"How long have you two known each other?"

"Eight months."

Still sidestepping, he asked, "So the same amount of time as me?"

"No. I've known you for five days in Pennsylvania, and now two days here. Eight months versus seven days."

He laughed and then stumbled. As he caught himself and faced forward again he asked, "Are you always so literal?"

She increased her speed even more. "Jah. Literal—and serious."

He laughed again. "I take it you're the in-control sister as opposed to the impulsive one in the book you're reading. It seems you always have a plan."

She grinned. "You're a fast learner."

He couldn't help but smile at her response, although he wished she'd known him—instead of Jacob—for eight months. But he wouldn't say that.

Sirens wailed, growing louder. Both an ambulance and a fire truck came toward them, and they quickly stepped to the edge of the road.

"Oh no." Joanna put her hands over her ears. "What if it's Mandy?"

"We're almost to the beach," Adam said as the emergency vehicles passed by. "I'll get my bike and ride back to the house." Joanna began to run. She was faster than Adam would have thought possible. He took off after her. "There's a phone booth by the restrooms," he called out. "Get Daniel to call for their ride." He rattled off the address.

When they reached the restrooms, Joanna waved and veered off toward the beach.

Adam reached Mandy a few minutes later. She was fine. The ambulance and fire truck were parked a block down the road. Adam felt embarrassed that he'd reacted with fear to the sirens. Thinking it through, he was surprised Joanna had reacted the same way. She seemed so calm and collected, as if she'd be good in an emergency. But the sirens had scared her too.

Joanna reached the house before Daniel and Elaine. Adam was shocked to see her, until he realized she'd run back. "Are you all right, Mandy?" she asked, gasping for air, as she reached the porch.

"I'm fine. Just embarrassed," Mandy said from the corner. "I'm not used to the heat."

When Daniel and Elaine arrived, Joanna, her voice low, asked Adam, "Does the canoe come with life jackets?"

"Jah." Adam tilted his head toward her.

"Oh *gut*. I changed my mind."

5

Joanna arrived at the park at three forty-five and sat on the grass among a patch of daisies. First she people watched. Several older Amish and Mennonite men played bocce ball while a group of Mennonite women, some older, played volleyball. The ringleader reminded her of Becky.

Joanna picked daisies and then began connecting them. After a couple of minutes she felt eyes on her and raised her head. Adam. He was about ten feet away.

She stood and slipped the daisy chain around her wrist—it wasn't big enough for her neck—and said, "I was thinking maybe you'd changed your mind." But she didn't really mean it. She didn't think Adam was the kind of man who would stand someone up.

"Did Mandy come?" Adam asked.

"Was she invited?" Joanna was surprised at how sassy she sounded. There was something about Adam that brought that out of her.

Adam shrugged. "I thought Elaine might make her come with you."

"Nee. She was napping when I left. So were Daniel and Elaine."

As they walked, Adam commented on her daisy chain. "Nice bracelet."

"Denki." She held up her wrist. "Not sure my bishop back home would approve, but I'm pretty sure my bishop here won't care."

Adam laughed and then said, "The creek is called Philippi. It's a tidal creek that flows out to the Gulf. The tide is coming in right now, which means it's higher." After his explanation about the creek, he grew quiet. Much quieter than usual, which seemed odd.

"I've only been canoeing a couple of times," Joanna said, filling the silence. "My oldest brother had one." Leon was three years older than she was and had been the best big brother she could ask for. "He used to take it out on the Susquehanna River, and I went with him a few times."

"Then you can show me how to canoe," Adam said. "I usually go in one of my friend's kayaks, but he doesn't have a double one."

When they reached the creek, Joanna stopped. The water was high on a bank lined with oak trees draped in Spanish moss. A breeze made the leaves and the moss and all the other foliage sway back and forth. Birds flitted about. And tropical flowers bloomed on both sides of the creek.

Adam motioned to a dock. "We're almost there."

She skipped for a few steps, her eyes still on the enchanting scene before them.

When they reached the boathouse, he grabbed two lifejackets and handed one to Joanna. She promptly put it on and buckled it, while Adam simply slipped his on.

"Buckle it," she said.

"I'm a pretty good swimmer."

She wrinkled her nose. "You still need to buckle it." She was a good swimmer too, thanks to Leon.

He swept his hands up and dramatically clicked the latch into place. Then he grabbed two oars and motioned to the canoe. "You should get in first."

She followed his instructions.

"You made that look easy." Adam handed her an oar.

Then he untied the rope, threw it in the back, and climbed into the canoe while holding his oar, sending the craft rocking. Before he sat down, Joanna pushed away from the dock, ready to be on the water.

Adam laughed. "Are you trying to tip me out?"

"I'd never do that." She shot him a smile. "At least not at the beginning of a trip."

The creek was wide and high from the winter rains, and the trees leaned over the water. It was all so beautiful. She was happy, very happy, she'd agreed to go canoeing with Adam.

He steered out to the middle. Adam increased his strokes and Joanna did too. She told him about Leon. "He always looked out for me. He loves to hike and fish and canoe. He's the one who had a bike for a while."

"Does he live in Lancaster County? Or Maine?"

"Maine. He married when he was twenty. I like his wife—Katie. They have a little one now." Joanna paused a moment and then said, "Katie is a big help to my Mamm."

"Do you your miss your family?"

Joanna looked back at Adam. "Honestly?"

"Jah." He had an *of course* expression on his face.

"Not really." She knew it sounded bad. Perhaps ungrateful,

maybe even childish. She thought of Elinor in *Sense and Sensibility*, who was always so composed, so mature. "I think about them, but I'm much happier living with Mammi Lu and Dawdi Marcus for now." She wouldn't bother to explain that her father had wanted her to move to Maine. Once Becky hired her, he was content for a few months that she had a job. But then he grew restless and started up about it again. Just recently, Jacob's uncle, Enoch Byer, had written to Dat and told him what a good match she and Jacob were, so he'd stopped asking her to move for now.

"What about Leon?" Adam asked. "Do you miss him?"

"Jah, but he's busy with his own farm and now his little family." She stared straight ahead and shrugged. "We've grown up. It wouldn't be the same if I lived in Maine."

"What about the rest of your brothers?"

She turned her head again, just a little. "What do you mean?" Was he asking if she missed them?

"What are they like?"

She laughed. "A pack of wolves."

"Pardon?"

"Boys," she said, louder. "They're a big bunch of boys. Two sets of twins. The older set is fifteen months older than I am. Then one more brother and last, another set of twins. There was never a dull moment." Her father was the wildest of them all. "What about your family?" she asked. "I remember seeing your mother and stepfather, and your two little brothers." She paused for a moment. "Your family is half the size of mine. Are your brothers wild too?"

He laughed a little. "My next youngest one is a smart aleck. The very youngest is sweet, though. At least he was last time I saw him."

After a while Joanna noticed the light was waning. Because it was so warm, the lowering sun threw her off. Dusk would fall soon and the sun would set by six o'clock. "We should head back. Elaine will start wondering where I am."

When they reached the dock, as Adam stood to step onto the planks, he lost his balance. Joanna reached out to him. Trying to catch himself, he instead lurched backward.

"Adam!" Joanna called out as he fell out of the canoe and into the creek. As he hit the water, the canoe flipped. Joanna tried to lunge out into the creek, but the canoe pulled her under, submerging her. She quickly surfaced underneath the capsized canoe. Leon had told her what to do—keep calm and swim out from under it.

She took a breath, dove under the water, and swam out toward the middle of the creek. When she surfaced Adam swam toward her, his hat in one hand. He gasped, "Are you all right?"

"I'm fine." She began laughing as she treaded water. "At least the water is warm."

"Jah." He smiled a little. "Are you sure you're all right?"

"Absolutely," she said. "We'd better get the canoe righted." She swam toward the dock. "I'll get out. Push it toward me. I'll grab it and then we can flip it together. Watch for my oar—I think it's still under the canoe."

Joanna managed to climb onto the dock. As she stood, her dress clung to her legs. Thankfully both her sandals were still strapped to her feet. Her plan worked and a minute later Adam put the oars in the boat house while she tied the canoe to the dock cleat.

As Adam took his life jacket off, Joanna noted the shirts in Pinecraft seemed thinner than the ones back home. She looked away from his pecs and biceps and glanced down with alarm at her dripping wet dress. She quickly took off her life jacket, handed it to Adam, and then folded her arms over her chest.

"I'm not feeling very modest right now." She cringed and said, "I don't think the bishop would approve of this back home or here. Sorry."

"Not your fault." Adam gave her a sympathetic smile. "I'm the one who flipped the canoe."

"It's not your fault either. You didn't do it on purpose. I'm just trying to figure out what to do. I can only imagine what Elaine will think of me if I show up at the cottage looking like this."

"Come to my place," Adam said.

She giggled. "That's probably worse than me going back to the cottage dripping wet."

"No one will know," he said. "I promise. My roommates are all at work. It's only a few blocks from here. I have a dryer."

~

By the time they reached Adam's cottage, the sun was setting. As he unlocked the door, he said, "I have a pair of sweatpants you can wear. And a sweatshirt."

"Are they clean?"

"Of course. I wouldn't do that to you." He grinned and then pointed to her wrist. "Your bracelet."

She held it up.

"I'll put it on the windowsill," Adam said.

She slipped it off and handed it to him.

Adam stepped into the kitchen with it and then returned.

"Wait here." He motioned to the small table with two chairs. "I'll put on dry clothes and then set things up for you." As he walked toward his room, he slipped his suspenders off his shoulders.

It didn't take long for him to change and gather what Joanna needed. She rinsed her wet clothes, wrung them out, hung her Kapp up on the shower curtain rod, and then changed into his sweat suit.

As her clothes dried, Adam made ham and Swiss cheese sandwiches. While the two ate their supper on his patio, Joanna thanked him for his help. He'd known exactly what to do.

He leaned toward her as he said, "You're welcome."

She tilted her head. What had she missed about Adam Slaybaugh the first time she'd met him? Jah, they'd only known each other seven days, but it felt like much longer. He was so easy to be with. "When do you plan to come back to Lancaster County?"

"To stay or to visit?"

"Either." She took another bite of sandwich.

"I'm not sure. I'm committed to my work here for a while. . . ." His voice trailed off.

When he didn't say anything more, she concentrated on eating. Maybe he didn't want to come back. Maybe he planned to stay in Florida indefinitely. She thought she'd felt chemistry, as Mandy would say, between them earlier in the day as they hurried back to the beach. And then as they walked to the creek. And on the canoe. And especially after he capsized the canoe. But she must have been wrong. She finished her sandwich as the dryer buzzed.

"Perfect timing." Joanna popped up to retrieve her clothes,

taking her plate into the kitchen first. After she changed back into her dress and apron and put her wet Kapp over her wet hair, she looked in the mirror. Her apron was wrinkled and her Kapp looked ridiculous. But at least her dress wasn't clinging to her body. She just needed to get to the cottage, take a shower, put on her nightgown, and climb into bed and read for a while.

As she stepped out of the bathroom, Adam stood at the open front door talking to . . .

Ruthie.

They must have seen each other at the same time because Ruthie squealed, "Adam. What is *she* doing here?"

Mortified, Joanna froze. Ruthie put her hands on her hips. Joanna took a step forward. And then another. She found her voice, "I was just leaving." She couldn't tell what was going on between Ruthie and Adam, but it seemed to be more than he had let on. Worse than that, though, who knew what Ruthie might say about Joanna being in Adam's cottage. If Elaine found out, Joanna doubted she'd keep it quiet. What if the gossip reached Jacob?

She quickly added, "Adam just let me use his bathroom—that's all."

Ruthie took a step into the house.

"Excuse me." Joanna sidestepped around Adam and then Ruthie.

"Wait," Adam said as she marched out the door.

Joanna waved. "I need to get going. Denki!"

"What's going on?" Ruthie's voice was loud and hurt.

"Joanna!" Adam hurried after her.

She turned and quietly said, "Please don't make this worse than it looks."

He stopped. She waved again, this time at Ruthie. "Have a good evening!"

Why did she feel guilty? She'd done nothing wrong. Except maybe go out with someone who was courting someone else. Was Adam trying to play her? She held up her wrist. She'd forgotten her daisy chain. Oh well. She wasn't going back. It was a soggy mess anyway.

She looked for Adam at the beach and the park over the next week but didn't see him. Obviously he was avoiding her. It didn't matter. She'd go home to Jacob; Adam would stay in Pinecraft with Ruthie.

When she finished *Sense and Sensibility* the next to the last day of the vacation, she thought of Adam. She wondered if he still found her more on the side of sense than sensibility. Usually, she saw herself as practical and in control. But a few times on the trip, she'd found herself moved by emotions, both on the beach and then canoeing on the creek with Adam. And in his cottage, until Ruthie arrived. She sighed at the memory. There was something about Adam that she found appealing, but that didn't mean he was the right man for her.

However, she had said she'd loan him the book, and she'd keep her word. She guessed they knew him at the ice cream shop. She wrapped the book in brown paper, wrote *Adam Slaybaugh* on the front, and dropped it off on her way to the park to make one last daisy chain, this one big enough to go around her neck.

6

Adam didn't see Joanna again during her time in Pinecraft even though he looked for her every day at both the beach and the park. He saw Elaine once and Daniel a couple of times. He didn't have enough courage to ask where Joanna was. He knew how much Elaine gossiped.

The truth was, Adam found Joanna as appealing—more so, even—as he had eight months ago. She was more confident. More talkative. And more fun. The one day, well, most of the day, that he'd spent with her while she was in Pinecraft had been his favorite day since Emily and Noah's wedding.

Over and over, he kept thinking about their canoe trip on the creek and their plunge into the water. And their time in his cottage. Why had Ruthie shown up? It didn't matter. Joanna was courting Jacob Byer. They'd probably be married by the next time he visited Lancaster County.

A couple of weeks later when he went into the ice cream shop, the server grinned and said, "You're Adam Slaybaugh, right?"

"Jah," he answered.

"I have something for you." He reached under the counter and pulled out a brown package. Adam quickly opened it. *Sense and Sensibility.* There was no note, not even a short one. But obviously, Joanna had left it. "Denki," he said to the server, tucking it under his arm.

As he finished the novel, he felt gutted by the happily-ever-after ending. No other girl he knew compared to Joanna. He was tempted to write a thank-you note to her but decided not to. The less he thought about Joanna Grebel the better.

7

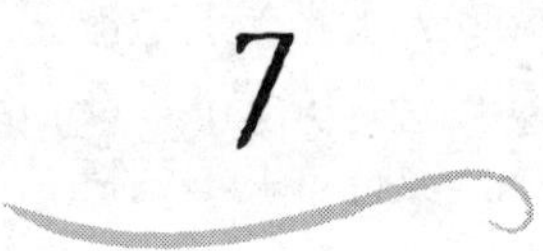

Ten months later when a knock fell at the back door, Joanna expected Ike. Instead, she found Adam standing on the porch with a box of food and snow falling behind him.

"Happy Thanksgiving," he said.

Joanna's heart skipped a beat. She was shocked—and unprepared—to see Adam. As she reached for the box her hand brushed against his.

He pulled the box back. "May I come in?"

She took a step backward. "Of course." Dawdi Marcus had passed away a month earlier and Mammi Lu was deeply grieving. So was Joanna, for her grandfather mostly, but also because Jacob had broken up with her with no explanation six weeks ago.

Becky had invited Mammi Lu and Joanna to Thanksgiving dinner, but Mammi didn't feel up to it. So Becky said she'd send dinner over for them.

"I'm sorry for your loss."

"Denki."

Joanna led the way into the kitchen and Adam followed.

Mammi Lu turned toward them from the sink and smiled. "Adam. How are you?"

"*Gut*." He shifted the box under one arm and brushed his bangs from his forehead with his free hand. "Sad for you and Joanna. Marcus was a good man."

"Jah, he was." Mammi lifted her apron and dabbed at her eyes. "How long are you home for?"

"I'll take the bus back next week." He put the box on the counter beside the peanut-butter-and-chocolate pie Mammi had made.

"Can you stay and eat with us?" Mammi Lu asked.

Before Joanna could intervene, sure he needed to get back to his grandparents and house full of relatives, Adam said, "I'd like that."

"What about your family?" Joanna asked.

"There's like a hundred people over there. All these second and third cousins I can't keep straight. They won't miss me." He grinned at Lu. "I'll go back in time for pie, or maybe I'll have a piece here and another one there."

There was no doubt Adam brought a little cheer to Mammi Lu. And to Joanna too. He carried the conversation, telling stories about Pinecraft and his work. After they finished eating their pie, Joanna sent Mammi Lu to the living room to rest. She assumed Adam would follow or go home, but he stayed in the kitchen and helped Joanna clear the table.

Once the leftovers were put away, Joanna said, "I'll wash up Becky's dishes and send them back with you."

Adam reached for a towel. "I'll dry."

As Joanna put the first serving bowl in the rack, she asked, "How's Ruthie?"

Adam paused. "Who?" He appeared to be stalling.

"Ruthie." Joanna hoped she didn't appear as exasperated as she felt. "Your girlfriend from Spartansburg. You were spending time with her in Pinecraft."

"I'd *see* her sometimes in Pinecraft. We went for ice cream together *once*, before you came down. She went home soon after you did. Ruthie and I definitely weren't meant for each other."

"So you two *were* dating when I was in Pinecraft?"

"Nee," he answered. "We weren't."

Joanna wasn't sure whether to believe him or not. Ruthie, standing at the front door of Adam's cottage that night after he capsized the canoe, certainly looked as if she were in possession of him.

He placed the bowl in the box. "Denki for loaning me *Sense and Sensibility*." He took out a book-shaped parcel and put it on the table. "I enjoyed it. I could kind of sympathize with them needing a home, but not knowing how it would work out and being dependent on others."

Joanna hesitated a moment before asking, "Do you need a home?"

Adam laughed. "Jah, eventually. That half room I rent keeps getting smaller and smaller."

"What about Spartansburg?"

He shook his head a little. Joanna didn't press him. She wanted to ask if he was courting anyone now, but didn't want him to ask if she was. She'd have to admit she wasn't, that Jacob had broken up with her.

Adam said, "You should bring Lu down to Pinecraft. It would do her good."

Joanna turned toward him, thinking of running on the

beach with Mandy. How she'd love to wade in the water with her grandmother. "That would be lovely." But she doubted Mammi Lu would want to go.

Adam said in a quiet voice yet teasing voice, "We could take her on a canoe ride."

Joanna's mouth dropped open. "I thought that was our secret."

He smiled. "I haven't told anyone."

She lowered her voice. "I haven't either, including Mammi Lu." Why hadn't she? She could have skipped that they capsized. Maybe she hadn't said anything because she didn't want to get her grandmother's hopes up that perhaps, just possibly, Joanna could be interested in Adam.

"I heard you and Jacob broke up."

"Ouch." She swallowed the lump in her throat, along with her pride, and plunged her hands back into the water.

"Sorry." Adam's voice was kind. "Taking some time to figure things out? Or is it for good?"

Did he think she'd broken up with Jacob? Not sure how to answer, she shrugged and said, "We'll see."

Adam put one of the bowls in the box. "So what are you reading now?"

"*Jane Eyre*."

"Who wrote it?"

"Charlotte Brontë."

"Oh. I thought maybe it was another one by Jane Austen."

"Nee." Joanna put a serving platter in the rinse water.

"Do you like the story?"

"Jah." Joanna put the platter in the drying rack. "I read it several years ago and then started it again last week."

"Then you must really like it to be reading it again."

"Jah. I find it fascinating." She wouldn't tell him she'd had a nightmare the night before about the *Feiyah* at Thornfield Hall. The first time she'd read it was before her family's home had caught fire.

~

Joanna expected to see Adam at church on Sunday, but he wasn't there. Perhaps he'd already left for Florida. Or maybe he'd gone to see his family in Spartansburg. Miriam was at church but gave Joanna the cold shoulder. Later she and Jacob talked in the corner of the Byer shed where the service was held. Before Joanna could ask, Mandy assured her there was nothing going on between Miriam and Jacob. "She's courting someone in Berks County," Mandy said. Miriam had gotten a job there as a mother's helper. "She's the one who broke up with Jacob. She doesn't want him back."

Joanna didn't tell Mandy that Jacob had told her *he'd* broken up with Miriam. One of them wasn't being honest.

She thought about Adam several times over the next month. Thanksgiving dinner was the first time she hadn't been aware of Mammi Lu's deep loss since Dawdi had passed away. She hadn't been grieving the end of her relationship with Jacob as much either since then.

Adam had been interested in her when they first met, but she'd rebuffed him, thinking she wasn't ready for a relationship. Would he be interested in her again? She wished she and Mammi Lu could go to Pinecraft on vacation. It would do them both good. Ike and Becky would look after their home, and Joanna would do everything she could to make sure it was safe before they left. She suggested the idea of going to Florida to her grandmother, who replied, "I'm not ready to go anywhere yet."

Joanna understood.

Instead of planning a vacation, Joanna focused on the Lord and others. She spent time reading her Bible and journaling and helping Mandy paint the interior of the farmhouse she and Caleb had recently moved into. She talked with Daniel about taking the class to join the church in the spring.

In February her Dat's parents, Mammi Rhoda and Dawdi Hiram, moved across the county and retired near Strasburg in the cottage Mammi Rhoda's parents had left her. Joanna had never been as close with them as she was with Mammi Lu and Dawdi Marcus, even though they'd lived across the road from where she grew up.

Mammi Rhoda joined the quilting group that Becky, Elaine, and Mammi Lu belonged to. All three of the other women seemed to be going out of their way to make Mammi Rhoda feel welcome, which Joanna appreciated. Mammi Rhoda wasn't exactly warm—yet it seemed her old friends accepted her as she was.

Regardless of Mammi Rhoda's demeanor, Joanna tried to do little things for her paternal grandparents, such as take a plate of cookies or a pie by their cottage every other week or so. Mammi Rhoda seemed minimally appreciative and Dawdi Hiram barely responded. He was nothing like Joanna's father, who was energetic and outgoing and also loud and controlling.

Joanna hadn't told her parents that she and Jacob were no longer courting, but Mammi Rhoda did once she put it together. Immediately her Dat started writing her letters, first suggesting she move to Maine and then demanding it. She wrote back but didn't address the issue at hand.

In April Jacob waited outside of the warehouse one evening after work. He hopped down from his buggy and smiled as if they'd last talked about something important that morning instead of six months ago. "Want a ride home?"

Joanna hesitated.

"Come on." He motioned to the buggy. "You can get in on my side."

She drew in a deep breath. What was he up to?

He took a step toward her and lowered his voice. "We need to talk."

She had wanted to talk. She had wanted to know why he'd broken up with her. Was he courting someone else now?

He extended his hand. "Are you willing to talk?"

"Jah." But she stepped away from him and to the other side of the buggy. She climbed up on her own.

They talked, a little. Jacob said he regretted breaking up with her. She said he'd hurt her, but she couldn't manage to explain how deeply. Jacob said he'd needed time to think about things and jah, he had taken someone out.

"Miriam?" According to Mandy, Miriam had broken up with the man she'd been courting in Berks County, although she was still living there and working for a family with ten children.

"It's a big decision to stay with one person for the rest of your life," Jacob said without directly answering her question, but she surmised that he had. "But I'd like it to be you."

"I need to think about it," Joanna said, miffed that he'd apparently gone out with Miriam again. For all of Jacob's talk about being friends when they first met, it hadn't worked that way. She'd decided it wasn't as important as she once thought, and they'd gone straight to courting. She wanted to backtrack and become friends, but when she told Jacob that, he said, "But we were more than friends. That's what I want again."

She hadn't planned to play hard to get, but perhaps that's how it seemed to Jacob. She ignored him and took the class to join the church. She focused on her relationship with God and, after she finished the class, was baptized.

In June, Mandy told her that Miriam had broken up with a second boyfriend in Berks County. "I wish she'd settle down and get married and move back home," Mandy said. "She drives me crazy, but I miss her." Joanna didn't ask if Mandy knew anything about Miriam dating Jacob again.

At the end of July, Jacob's mother passed away and he went back to Ohio for her service. Joanna's heart hurt for Jacob, and she put a sympathy card in his box at work. She'd never met his mother and Jacob hadn't spoken about her much, so it wasn't as if Joanna felt she knew her—but she mourned her for Jacob's sake.

When he returned, Jacob didn't want to talk about his mother, but he did continue to ask Joanna out every few weeks. Finally, a year after he broke up with her, she accepted a ride home from church and then rides to singings. Jah, she was guarded with him at first, but slowly she started trusting him again. And the letters from her Dat, written by her mother, stopped. She hadn't told them she and Jacob were courting again, but someone had. Enoch Byer or Mammi Rhoda—or probably both.

Mammi Lu was cold when Jacob came to the door for Joanna. One time she said to Joanna, "You haven't dated anyone else. How can you know if he's the right one?" Mammi Lu hesitated a moment and then asked, "Have you kissed anyone besides Jacob?"

Joanna's face grew hot, and she wondered what things were like back in Mammi Lu's day, all the way back in the 1970s. If anything, wouldn't things have been even stricter than they were now? "How many boys did you kiss?" Joanna couldn't help but ask. She was genuinely curious.

"More than just your Dawdi, I can assure you," Mammi Lu answered with a little humph.

Joanna laughed. "Tell me more."

Mammi chuckled. "I've already told you enough for you to get the idea."

Once again, Joanna felt seen by the community when she was with Jacob. Surely he would bring up marriage soon. Jacob would take over his uncle's farm, but Joanna would still be close enough to Mammi Lu to see her regularly and help when needed. No doubt she'd only grow closer to Mandy, considering Jacob and Caleb were friends. Soon they'd all have children close to the same age. Jacob would be a respected member of the community, and so would she. She would finally truly belong.

She was aware that she and Jacob didn't seem as close as Mandy and Caleb, but surely that would come with time. On the other hand, she was sure they were already closer than her parents.

Just when she trusted him again, he grew distant. In May, three years after she'd first met Jacob, she asked if something was bothering him on the way home from a singing. He slowed the horse and said, without looking at her, "I'm mulling some things over is all." She assumed whatever it was had to do with his uncle's farm or a work problem. She didn't press him.

But then in the second week of July, as he gave Joanna a ride home from work, he stared straight ahead again and said, "I need to tell you something."

She rubbed the sweat on the back of her neck as she waved goodbye to Becky. It had been unbearably hot and humid for the last week. "All right." She guessed it was about work. He sometimes found fault with a decision she'd made; usually he claimed she was too meticulous. She sighed, too tired to care.

"Joanna?"

"Jah?"

"This is serious." His gaze darkened. "You need to listen to me."

"I am." She turned toward him.

He turned his head and stared at the road. "I'm breaking up with you. This time for good."

8

Becky positioned her thimble onto her finger, her mind wandering as Rhoda talked about the good deal she'd gotten on the fabric for her new curtains, and pushed the needle into the quilt top.

A deep voice came from the doorway. "Mammi?"

She jerked her head as her needle plunged into her thumb. "Ouch!" She hadn't forgotten Adam had arrived in the middle of the night, yet his voice surprised her.

"*Ach du lieva*!" Lu said. *Oh my goodness*. "Adam!"

He grabbed a paper napkin from the snack table and handed it to Becky as he grinned at Lu.

"Denki." Becky wrapped it around her thumb and held it away from the quilt and her new dress. "Say hello to the ladies."

He turned toward Lu and Rhoda.

Lu grinned from across the quilting frame, her reading glasses perched on her nose.

He said, "Lu, it's so nice to see you."

Everyone loved Adam.

"This is Rhoda." Becky motioned to her right. "She's Joanna's paternal grandmother."

Adam smiled at Rhoda. "I'm pleased to meet you."

Rhoda gave him a curt nod, which was her style.

"How long are you in town for?" Lu's voice overflowed with warmth, which was her style.

Adam shrugged. "I'm not positive, but perhaps permanently."

Becky certainly hoped he'd stay for good this time. "He came in late last night." Becky turned toward Adam. "Did you decide to work today after all?"

"Jah." He ran his hand through his thick hair. "Am I too late?"

"Probably not. Hurry over to the warehouse."

"Will do." He waved at the other ladies. "It's *gut* to see all of you."

They all smiled and Lu said, "*Gott segen dich.*" That was Lu's style also—to say God's blessing over someone who was leaving. She added, "Stop by and see us sometime soon."

Us. Becky knew Lu meant Joanna.

Adam glanced over his shoulder on his way to the front door. "I'll take you up on that!"

Becky doubted Rhoda knew Jacob had broken up with Joanna—again—yesterday. Becky could tell by Lu's demeanor that she did. Of course she knew. Lu and Joanna were as close as any grandmother and granddaughter she'd ever known.

Sometimes there seemed to be tension coming from Rhoda concerning Joanna. Rhoda had never been close with the girl, and yet Rhoda had assumed that when she moved to

Strasburg Township Joanna would visit and confide in her. Joanna did visit—but she didn't confide in Rhoda. No one needed to tell Becky. It was obvious.

And Becky didn't blame Joanna. Rhoda had always been brisk, even when they were all girls, but she'd grown even more so to the point she could be harsh. And oftentimes judgmental. However, she didn't gossip the way Elaine did, at least not in front of Becky.

As soon as the door clicked Becky sighed. "It's wonderful *gut* to have Adam back. He quit his job in Florida—I'm hoping he stays here."

"At least we don't have to worry about Joanna." Rhoda glanced at Lu. "Don't you think she and Jacob will marry before winter?"

Lu pursed her lips.

Becky's neck tightened. When she'd seen the two of them leaving work the day before in Jacob's buggy, Joanna had a pained expression on her face. She'd confirmed Becky's suspicions with her five thirty a.m. phone message saying she wouldn't be in to work until noon.

"What is it?" Rhoda glanced from Lu to Becky and back to Lu.

Rhoda put the square she was stitching in her lap and leaned forward. "Don't tell me Jacob broke up with her again."

Lu met Rhoda's gaze and said, "Jacob broke up with Joanna again."

Rhoda groaned. "They were perfect together."

Becky knew they weren't, but she wouldn't say so in front of Joanna's grandmothers. Well, at least not in front of Rhoda. She wouldn't hesitate to share her opinion with just Lu.

Rhoda clucked her tongue. "That's a pity. Joanna's stood beside him for so long." Rhoda had a way of insinuating she knew more about a situation than she actually did. She'd always been that way. She directed her attention toward Lu. "I think they'll get back together, don't you?"

Lu shrugged. Becky knew her friend was doing her best not to share too much information. If she did, it was bound to get back to Joanna.

Rhoda clutched the square in her lap. "Why did he break up with her?"

Lu shrugged again.

Rhoda wrinkled her nose.

Becky panicked for a moment. She needed to distract Rhoda from asking any more questions. Joanna didn't talk about her private life, and she would be mortified to find out she was the topic of choice at the quilting circle—well, three-quarters circle. Usually, with Elaine, there were four of them. She guessed that made it a quilting "square." Elaine had left a message on Becky's machine this morning too, saying she wasn't feeling well.

They all needed to be able to share about their families, as much or as little as they wanted, without being afraid Elaine would gossip about everyone. Becky quickly came up with a plan. "We all have grandchildren at or near the marrying age, right?"

Rhoda and Lu both said, "Jah."

Rhoda shifted in her chair toward Lu. "I still don't understand why Jacob—"

Becky interrupted. "What if we start a letter with prayer requests for our grandchildren who are marrying age? And for other requests in our families too. Whatever's on our minds."

"Why a letter," Rhoda asked, "when we meet in person?"

"A letter—a circle letter—will remind us to pray, at home." Becky lowered her voice for emphasis. "It will keep us from gossiping here."

Rhoda's face reddened.

Did Lu just suppress a smile?

Becky hadn't meant to direct her comment at Rhoda, not when it was Elaine she was worried about. She was the one who gossiped about anything and everything, including her three lifelong friends. "Write whatever requests you want in the circle letter. We'll pray for our families. I'll send out the first letter in a day or two and include instructions."

Lu agreed immediately, as expected. Rhoda hesitated and then said, "I guess so." Becky had known both women, along with Elaine, since she was a girl. Each had the same personality they'd had by the time they were Youngie—so many things had changed, but the essence of all of them, Becky included, had stayed the same.

Two hours later, Lu started to clear the snack table as Becky watched Rhoda walk down the front steps. Hiram sat in their buggy, waiting for her, at the end of the walk.

Lu picked up Becky's sleek white coffee cups as Becky carried the white serving trays of peanut butter bars and raspberries into the kitchen. Lu followed.

As Lu put the mugs in the sink, she asked, "How did you know Jacob broke up with Joanna?"

Becky hesitated and then asked, "Was it that obvious that I knew?"

"Jah."

Becky winced. "I saw them in the buggy together. Joanna's

expression was like an open book. And she called in this morning."

A horn honked.

Becky glanced at the clock over the kitchen doorway. "Ike wants me to go with him to see a new property."

"I'll finish cleaning up."

"Wunderbar! Denki." Becky followed Lu into the hallway. "Let's put the frame up first." Ike had installed a pulley system to raise the frame, with the quilt on it, up to the ceiling. As she pulled on the rope, Becky said, "I'll send the letter to you first. You pray for Adam—I'm hoping he'll find the right girl, settle down here, and take over the business in a few years. And I'll pray for Joanna."

Lu gave her a wave of confirmation as she tied the rope in her corner of the living room.

Becky thanked the Lord every day for a friend like Lu. She was kind. And loyal. Back when Becky decided she didn't want to have one child after another like her mother had, Lu never questioned her decision. And when others gossiped, passing on what Elaine had told them, that Becky wanted only one child, Lu shut them down in her quiet way.

Lu, even as she grieved losing Marcus, had remained an attentive friend. Becky knew she wasn't supposed to worry, but since Marcus died, she had been waking up in the middle of the night numb at the thought of losing Ike. She would find his hand and squeeze it. Once he returned the gesture, she'd be able to fall back asleep, reassured he was all right.

"Denki, Lu!" Becky called out as she grabbed her bag.

"Gott segen eich!" Becky's heart swelled at the sound of Lu's blessing as she opened the back door with one hand and stepped into the midday July heat. She searched her leather bag with the other, touching her notebook. She dug deeper.

Her hand grasped her pen, and she squeezed it. Hopefully she'd have a few minutes of peace to start the circle letter today.

She hurried down the steps, waving at Nick. Would she share her own personal request in the circle letter? She'd have to think about it. For the first time in years, the business's finances were tight. She'd given too much money away in the last couple of months. As the oldest of eleven children, each of whom she'd mothered at one point or another during her growing up years, Becky felt a responsibility to help when she could. And Ike had always been supportive of her generosity, quoting from the verse in Luke, "For unto whomsoever much is given, of him shall be much required."

She'd told Ike a couple of weeks ago that she'd stretched their money too thin, but he still wanted to buy the Federalist-style house on Pequea Creek. They'd both admired the property for years, and when it came on the market two weeks ago, they jumped in with an offer, which was accepted.

Her hope was to get the business in good shape over the next few years and then turn it over to Adam so Ike could retire. Jah, Marcus's death had been a shock. She didn't want Ike to have to keep up the long hours he'd been working his entire life.

As she reached the van, she decided she wouldn't reveal all of that to the girls, not even to Lu. Everything would work out, just as Ike always assured her. She'd keep their business concerns to herself.

9

Joanna's sandpapery eyelids blinked back more tears as she scootered along the highway to work just before noon. Her chest felt tight, and each time she pushed off with her right foot, she felt as if she might fall over in a heap.

It was hot and a trickle of sweat ran down the back of her leg. Then another. She tried to increase her speed but felt as if she were moving in slow motion.

Mammi had tried to warn her after Jacob wanted to get back together a year ago. At first, Joanna listened, but gradually she'd been won over by Jacob proving he'd had a change of heart. Or so she'd thought.

How did the saying go? *Fool me once, shame on you. Fool me twice, shame on me.* She groaned. At twenty-two with no prospect of a husband, she'd be officially an *aldi Maydel* soon. It felt as if the floor had just fallen out from under her. Her Dat would probably come to Lancaster County and force her to move to Maine.

When she reached the warehouse, she unlocked the door

and stepped into the warm cavern. It smelled of wood and linseed oil, and diesel for the generators that powered the tools. After she stashed her bag in her drawer in the office, she headed to the props section. She needed to stage the farmhouse to get it ready to sell. She raised the overhead door and began carrying items to the loading area—a floor lamp, a table lamp, and two living room chairs. She pushed a couch and the dining room table through the door. She packed four place settings, a centerpiece, and towels for the kitchen and two bathrooms into a crate. Finally she picked out artwork for the first floor.

Soon Nick arrived at the warehouse in the larger panel van Ike and Becky had purchased when they started staging houses. Together they loaded the furniture and other items. A half hour later, Joanna sat in the front of the van as Nick turned onto Maple Road. The farmhouse they'd been renovating for the last five months came into view above a creek at the end of the lane. It was time to put her troubles aside and get to work even though she'd soon see Jacob face-to-face.

As Nick pulled around the curve of the driveway, one figure—Jacob—stepped over the ridge of the roof to the other side, and another man climbed a ladder. Ike must have found someone else to work on the project.

Nick shot a glance her way. "You all right?"

Joanna swallowed the lump in her throat and nodded. But she wasn't.

Nick gave her a sympathetic smile. How did he know? Did everyone? Joanna's heart beat faster. Perhaps she should have taken the whole day off. Maybe by Monday she wouldn't feel as vulnerable. Or shattered.

She focused on the house. They'd gone over Becky's imposed deadline by a couple of weeks. The kitchen counters were delivered a week late. The foundation needed more work than Ike realized. The roof was taking longer than anticipated.

Nick pulled up by the side door of the house. "I'll get one of the guys to help me unload the big items."

"Denki," Joanna said. "I'll do the rest."

Joanna had chosen the flooring, light fixtures, switch plates, kitchen cabinets, vanities for the two bathrooms, sinks, counters, tile, paint colors. Everything. It was the first house she'd been completely in charge of, working from a budget Becky had established.

Joanna's goal for the house was to keep it simple—after all, an Amish contractor had renovated it—but make it attractive. She was pleased with the results.

As Joanna carried the floor lamp into the house, Nick came out the door with Tim, one of the workers. Tim, who wore coveralls, gave her a sympathetic smile too. She ducked her head.

Over the next half hour, they unloaded the van and positioned the dining room table and chairs and the living room furniture. She'd decided to leave the bedrooms and the family room unfurnished.

Tim went back to painting the trim in the upstairs hall, and Nick said he needed to pick up Becky and Ike. "Then I'm going to take Becky shopping."

Joanna gave him a wave. "Have fun."

"Oh, I will. I'll know all the gossip when we're done, no doubt."

Joanna's face grew warm as he spoke. Hopefully, none of

the gossip would be about her. "No doubt," Joanna echoed, surprised at how flat her voice sounded. She wasn't doing all right. Not at all.

~

As Joanna hung dish towels in the kitchen, a bolt of lightning flashed across the kitchen window. Yesterday, she would have flown out the kitchen door and called to Jacob to get off the roof. Today? Surely he'd figure it out himself. The crash of thunder came fast and furious. The electrical storm was only a few miles away.

Rain began to fall in torrents, battering the dining room window. Drops raced down the glass faster than tears.

Joanna sighed and marched through the kitchen toward the door as it flew open. A man rushed in, bringing the scent of the rain with him. He collided with Joanna, knocking her off balance. She staggered. As he grabbed her shoulders, he said, "Sorry." Then he let go. "Joanna?"

"Adam?" It was definitely Adam. Longish dark hair soaked from the rain. Faded blue work shirt, also soaked. She quickly raised her eyes back to his face. Blue eyes. No hat.

"So we meet again." He grinned down at her, his eyes sparkling.

"What are you doing here?"

"Working for my Dawdi and Mammi."

"Since when?"

As he let go of her shoulders, he answered, "This morning."

"Are you planning to stay?"

"I'm not—"

Another crash of thunder interrupted them. When it ended, Joanna couldn't stop herself from asking, "Is Jacob coming in?" No matter how hurt she was, she couldn't *not* care about his safety.

"I told him to. He didn't answer. He's not very talkative, is he?"

Joanna shrugged.

"He said he didn't remember me." Adam raised his eyebrows as he spoke. "I definitely remember him."

Joanna didn't want to think of her conversations with Adam over the years, first about being—or not being—friends, and then about how she'd been willing to court Jacob but not him.

But she *was* thinking about those conversations, until Jacob pushed his way through the half-closed door into the kitchen. "I hope this doesn't last long." He glanced at the empty pot on the counter and then at Joanna. "Is there coffee, Jo?"

"Feel free to make some." Joanna turned toward the dining room. She needed to put the runner on the table.

Jacob followed her. "You don't need to be rude."

"I'm not being rude. You can make coffee."

Jacob crossed his arms. Joanna pulled the quilted runner from the plastic bin. The best thing, right now, was to stay quiet. The less she said, the better. "Is there someone else?" The words flew out of her mouth. She grimaced. So much for being quiet.

"Nee." Jacob took a step toward the kitchen. "Why would you even ask?"

"You've been acting weird for weeks now."

Another crash of thunder made Joanna jump.

"Wow!" Tim's voice came from the staircase. "This is crazy."

Adam, who had stayed in the kitchen, asked, "Need some help upstairs?" Joanna wondered what Adam had overheard.

"Sure," Tim answered. Their voices faded away, followed by the thud of feet on the stairs.

And another crash of thunder.

"Would you just make the coffee? I'm tired."

"Oh." Joanna's voice burned with sarcasm. "Were you up all night?"

He jerked his head toward the kitchen. "The coffee."

Joanna flung the runner down the middle of the table. "I already told you—make it yourself."

Jacob took a step toward her. "Don't act like this."

She picked up the runner and stretched it between her hands, like a shield. She could use a cup of coffee too, but not enough to make one for Jacob.

Finally he turned back toward the kitchen. She spread the runner down the middle of the table. There was a clatter, and a couple of minutes later the kettle whistled on the stove. When possible, Becky stocked their worksites with coffee and lunch supplies.

Joanna continued setting the table.

There was another crash of thunder, farther away. The storm had moved west. When she turned toward the kitchen again, Jacob stood in the doorway with a mug in his hands, watching. Joanna's face grew warm again. She stepped back to the table and continued working. When she glanced at the door again he was gone. A minute later, he was yelling, "Adam. The storm's over. Let's go."

"I'll be right there."

"Hurry!"

Joanna pulled the cutlery box from the crate. Once she had the table set, she stood back and assessed how it looked.

"That looks great." Adam stood in the doorway.

Joanna agreed and asked, "What made you decide to leave Florida?"

He shrugged. "I needed to come home."

Jacob yelled, "Adam!"

Joanna rolled her eyes.

"Is he always like this?"

Joanna shook her head.

"You go out with this guy?"

She shrugged as tears stung her eyes.

"Sorry." Adam's expression was full of concern.

She waved him off. "I'm fine." A few seconds later the back door closed. It seemed Becky had told everyone except Adam that Jacob had broken up with her.

Joanna worked as quickly as she could, listening to the footsteps on the roof and hoping Nick would return soon and take her back to the warehouse. She moved to the living room and plugged in the floor lamp. Next she took the artwork, watercolors of Lancaster County landscapes by a local Amishwoman, from the second crate and began positioning them around the room.

The front door opened. She stepped toward the entryway, expecting Nick. It was Caleb.

"Hallo," she said. "Did you go look at the property with Ike?"

Caleb shook his head. "Mandy had an appointment."

"Oh."

Caleb shrugged. She wouldn't press him for any more information, but she hoped Mandy was all right. They'd been married for two years now and didn't have any children and, as far as Joanna knew, Mandy wasn't expecting. She knew how Mandy longed to be a mother. Perhaps that was the reason for the appointment. Mandy was fortunate to have a husband like Caleb—Joanna knew he would do anything he could to support Mandy.

"Are you working on the roof? Or helping Tim?"

"The roof," Caleb answered. "Is Adam up there?"

Joanna nodded.

Caleb smiled a little. "Were you happy to see him?"

Joanna tilted her head. "I was surprised to see him." And puzzled that Becky hadn't told her he was moving back to Lancaster County.

His expression grew serious. "I'm sorry about Jacob. Forget about him. He's not worth it."

Tears stung Joanna's eyes again, and she blinked a few times. "I need to get back to work. Be safe up there—it might be slick from the rain."

10

Adam stood on the edge of the roof, facing west. The farmhouse was on a knoll and the countryside spread out before him, the afternoon sun shining over acres and acres of lush green farmland. A hawk soared over the next property. He wasn't sure if he felt at home in Lancaster County because it was where he'd been born or because it was so beautiful.

He slid a little, but the tie-off rope caught him. He hadn't done a lot of roofing before—just enough so he could muddle through. He made his way back to the stack of shingles. As he slid a second time, Jacob came toward him. Adam, glancing upward, asked, "So are you and Joanna courting?"

Jacob grunted.

"Sorry." Adam spoke louder. "Could you repeat that?"

Jacob didn't respond.

Adam tried another approach. "Have you been working for Ike and Becky since you were first hired?"

Jacob gave him a puzzled look. "Why do you call your grandparents by their first names?"

Adam shrugged. "I thought maybe it would get your attention."

Jacob frowned. "Jah, I've been working for them since then."

The same amount of time Joanna had.

A head popped into view at the top of the ladder.

Adam let out a sigh of relief.

"It's like a sauna up here," Caleb said.

"Jah." Adam wiped his forehead with the back of his hand. "Feels like Florida."

Jacob nodded toward Caleb and then barked at Adam, "We need to get back to work."

Adam strengthened his grip on his hammer and then pounded away on the roof, moving across his section, mindful of his feet.

An hour later, when Caleb called for a water break, Adam headed down the ladder and joined Jacob next to the cooler. Jacob was at least six feet three, four inches taller than Adam, and broad shouldered. He was bigger than Adam remembered. He'd probably bulked up working in construction too.

Jacob tossed his paper cup in the brown bag and headed back to the ladder.

Caleb stepped up to the cooler, grabbed a cup, and as he pushed the button said, "Jacob broke up with Joanna yesterday."

"I wondered if that was the case. She was teary earlier." That would explain their argument.

Adam had prayed for several months about whether he should accept his grandparents' offer to go back to Lancaster County and work in the family business. He was aware he'd let them down before—and he didn't want to do it again. He waited until he was sure. Was it significant that he'd arrived in Lancaster County the day Jacob broke up with Joanna—after he'd stayed away for three years because of Joanna's lack of interest in him?

"It's been one thing after another with their relationship," Caleb said. "This is the second time he's broken up with her."

A pang of sadness for Joanna shot through Adam. He wasn't sure when he saw her the Thanksgiving before last who had broken up with who.

"He used to be an okay guy. Mandy and I liked him—we thought he and Joanna were a good match, better than him and Miriam."

"Miriam? Mandy's twin?"

"Jah. He went out with her before Joanna. Not for long, though." Caleb took another drink of water.

Adam felt ill. So Joanna and Jacob hadn't started courting right after he met both of them, the way it had appeared. He'd agreed to go to Pinecraft with his Spartansburg friends because Joanna had shown interest in Jacob instead of him. But then Jacob chose to court Miriam. What if Adam had stuck around instead of fleeing?

Caleb dragged his hand across his mouth, pulling a few beads of water into his beard. "But Jacob changed in the last few months. I mean, obviously, he broke up with Joanna before, but when they got back together he treated her well for a while. Until he didn't. Mandy wished he'd never started courting Joanna again. She's afraid he's only made things worse—Joanna dealt pretty well with the first breakup, but Mandy's afraid she won't a second time."

Adam rubbed the back of his neck. Jacob was a fool.

An hour later, the panel van turned into the driveway of the farmhouse. Adam couldn't see the driver get out nor hear his door close over the pounding of the hammers, but a few minutes later the panel van backed out of the driveway. Joanna was in the passenger seat. She glanced toward him and made eye contact. Adam raised his hand to wave, but she turned her head away. He realized he'd raised his hammer. He put it down.

By the time Caleb called it a day, Adam felt as if he'd sweated away ten pounds. Nick gave them a ride back to the warehouse—he'd returned in the passenger van they'd taken to Spartansburg three years ago. Jacob sat up front, Caleb and Adam sat on the first bench seat, and Tim sat behind them.

When they reached the warehouse, Adam went inside. There were shelves of paint and supplies. Shingles and hammers. Ladders and shovels and rakes. Off in the corner of the warehouse was a collection of furniture that all appeared to be quite Englisch. Dawdi wasn't staging his houses for Amish buyers.

Neither of his grandparents were at the warehouse, so Adam headed down the lane to their house. The back door was open, and he smelled chicken on the grill. On the back porch, he wriggled out of his boots and then stood still for a minute. There was nowhere in the world that brought him as much comfort as his grandparents' home. He padded into the kitchen.

Mammi stood at the stove and turned toward him. "Adam, there you are. How was your day?"

"*Gut*. How was yours?"

"Wunderbar." She cocked a lid on a pot and turned down

the heat. "Dawdi and I have a new project in the works. A big house near the Pequea Creek covered bridge. Do you remember it? It's three stories—Federalist-style."

"Jah," Adam said. "I think I know that one—it looks haunted, right?"

"Nee." Mammi laughed. "Just old. The owner died and his son is selling. It needs a lot of work."

"Where's Dawdi?"

"Doing chores." She sniffed dramatically and then laughed. "You need to go clean up."

He sniffed too. She was right.

She headed toward the door with a big fork. "I'm going to turn the meat. We'll be ready to eat in fifteen minutes."

Adam had always loved his grandparents' place. The property consisted of the house, the warehouse with the apartment above it that were fifty yards from the house, a barn, and stables, all on fifteen acres. They had a few horses and always a handful of steers they sold for beef. Dawdi Ike said it was good to have a couple of sources of income. Besides renovating houses, Dawdi also used to have a roofing crew he led. But since Mammi wouldn't let him get on a roof anymore, that side of the business wasn't thriving.

Adam hoped Dawdi didn't want him to lead a roofing crew. It was his least favorite job when it came to construction work, although he still preferred it to farming. But he knew how essential a good roof was to protect the rest of the house.

Twenty minutes later Adam sat at the oak table in the kitchen with his grandparents. After Dawdi Ike led them in a prayer, Adam said, "I saw Joanna Grebel at the worksite today."

Mammi Becky paused a moment and then said, "You knew she worked for us."

"Three years ago. I didn't know she still did."

"Joanna is a big asset to our company." Dawdi passed the chicken to Adam. "I can't know for sure, but I'm guessing we make five percent more on the houses she stages than we would otherwise."

Adam took in the figure. That would add up over a year. "Caleb told me Jacob—what's his last name?"

Mammi, with a clip to her voice, said, "Byer."

Adam continued, "Just broke up with her."

Mammi passed him the potatoes and muttered, "Thankfully."

Adam raised his head. "Why do you say that?"

Mammi jerked her head up. "Did I say that out loud?"

"Jah."

Dawdi laughed.

"Pretend I didn't." Mammi smiled. "I never thought they were a good match. Jacob is a fool, thankfully."

Mammi passed the chicken to Dawdi. "I've been thinking about the trip to Spartansburg way back, the one when Joanna and Lu and Marcus all rode with us. Whose wedding did we go to?"

"Noah's." Adam's face grew warm. Had his grandmother overheard his conversation with Joanna in the backseat of the van on the way home?

"That's right. Noah and Emily's wedding."

Adam had been so sure Joanna would court him. It was *Liewi* at first sight for him, and he'd never felt that way again.

Nor before Joanna. But Joanna didn't want to court, and no wonder. She didn't know him from—well, from Adam. She'd wanted to be friends, but he'd insisted it was impossible.

Then, when they spent that day together in Florida he'd thought maybe she did have feelings for him. Romantic feelings. But Ruthie showed up, and Joanna abruptly left.

"Adam?" Mammi's voice was full of concern.

"Sorry."

"What were you thinking about?"

"Nothing."

She put her hand on his forearm. "We're glad you're home. We've missed you."

It wasn't really home—but it felt as if it was. It was the closest thing he had to a home.

Mammi's gaze met his. "Are you going to stay?"

He shrugged. "I'm not sure." He'd planned to, but having Joanna working for his grandparents complicated things.

Dawdi cleared his throat. "I hope you will. In fact, I hope you'll take over the business in a few years, so we can retire."

That complicated things even more.

11

Usually on a Friday evening Joanna would be on a buggy ride with Jacob or the two of them would be sitting on Mammi Lu's porch drinking lemonade. But tonight she skipped dinner with Mammi Lu and headed out to weed the flower garden instead, hoping to keep her mind off Jacob. And off herself.

Joanna thought of Mandy and wondered how she was doing. No doubt Caleb—or maybe Elaine—had told her friend Jacob had broken up with her. It would be best if she left a message for Mandy anyway.

She leaned her hoe against the fence by the sweet William and headed to the phone shanty at the end of the driveway. After she dialed, she sat down on the bench. When no one answered, she left a message, "Hi, Mandy. It's me. I just wanted to let you know that Jacob and I broke up—I mean he broke up with me. In case you hadn't heard." She wanted to ask Mandy to pray for her, but they didn't really ask for that sort of thing, even though she did pray for Mandy and hoped her friend prayed for her too. "Also, I've been thinking about you and hope you're doing well."

After she said goodbye and hung up the phone, Joanna slumped against the wall of the shanty. She wanted friendships with other women like Mammi Lu had with her friends, and Mandy was the closest she had to that. Her hope was, as they grew older, they'd grow closer.

She stood, squared her shoulders, and returned to the garden to tend the bachelor's buttons and zinnias.

Two hours later Mammi Lu stood at the gate. "Joanna," she called. "Come sit. I have a sandwich." She held up a glass. "And lemonade."

Joanna strode to the fence, leaned the hoe beside the gate, and took the glass from her grandmother. The sound of horses' hooves caught her attention and Joanna's head jerked toward the road.

Mammi Lu asked, "Are you expecting someone?"

Joanna tightened her grip on the cold glass. "Nee."

The buggy grew closer. Joanna squinted through the poplar trees, trying to make out the driver in the dim light. Ike Slaybaugh waved and called out, "Hallo!"

Then Becky poked her head around Ike and waved too.

"Where do you think they're coming from?" Mammi Lu asked.

"They're probably just out for a ride." Joanna and Jacob often saw Becky and Ike riding in their buggy on Friday nights. It seemed they preferred that to sitting on their porch. Joanna thought it odd an old couple would be acting like Youngie, but Becky and Ike often surprised her. They didn't always act their age.

"God bless 'em." Mammi's voice was a whisper, but

Joanna heard each word. She didn't think her grandmother was jealous, not exactly.

The sun dipped lower in the sky. It would be dark soon.

Mammi led the way up the steps to the porch. As they settled into the two rocking chairs, Mammi picked up her knitting and asked, "Did you see Jacob today?"

"Jah." Joanna didn't want to talk about him.

"Was Adam working on the house too?"

"Jah, that was a surprise." Joanna put the lemonade down on the table between the two chairs, beside the plate with the sandwich. "How did you know he's back?"

"I saw him at Becky's this morning." Mammi put her knitting down. "Do you ever wish you'd given Adam a chance?"

"What are you talking about?"

"That night coming home from the wedding. When Adam said he wanted to court you."

Joanna's face flushed.

"I'll admit I was eavesdropping. Not on purpose. But I couldn't help but hear your conversation. Do you remember?"

"I do. But in my own defense I was only nineteen," Joanna said. "I'd never gone out with someone I did know—let alone someone I didn't." She and Jacob went out for ice cream a couple of days after they met but didn't start courting until months later. "Besides, I thought Mandy might be interested in him." She picked up the glass of lemonade and held it to her cheek. "Do you think I should have been less cautious with Adam?"

"Nee," Mammi said. "I just wondered if you regretted not courting him."

Joanna shook her head. "I wanted to be his friend, but he wasn't willing to be mine. Why would I court someone who didn't want to be my friend? What kind of relationship would that be?"

"You have a point," Mammi said.

~

After she washed the dishes, Joanna told her grandmother good night, put on her head lamp, and headed back out to the garden.

Once she latched the gate behind her, she stepped next to the rows of plate-sized dahlias. Her Dat wasn't a fan of flower gardens, saying they were a waste of space and effort and too fanciful. He believed all labor should go toward producing food or earning money.

Dat moved through life like a rambunctious bear, driven this way and that by his latest whim. On the other hand, Joanna's mother barely moved at all. Looking back, Joanna guessed her mother had been depressed, besides being overwhelmed with seven children in eleven years, including two sets of twins.

The farm Joanna had grown up on had been in her father's family for nearly two hundred years, and Mammi Rhoda and Dawdi Hiram lived across the road that dissected the farm in two. But Joanna had always been a little afraid of her father's parents, especially her grandmother.

They lived in the bigger house, just the two of them, while Joanna and her family crowded into the smaller one. As her brothers grew into men who were over six feet tall like their father, the house became more and more crowded. The fact the land couldn't support more than two families was the reason Joanna's Dat had decided to visit Maine and look for land to buy. He hoped to farm with as many of his sons as possible.

It was from the porch across the road that Dawdi Hiram first saw the smoke on the frosty February morning they planned to travel to Maine. Joanna, the only girl in the family, was cooking breakfast while her Dat and her brothers did the chores. Dawdi began ringing the fire bell on his porch and at first her brothers ran across the road thinking the big house was on fire, but Dawdi redirected them.

The roof of the smaller house—their house—was on fire. Joanna's littlest brothers, the young twins, were still asleep and their mother ran to wake them and shoo them out the front door. Then Mamm ran to the phone shed to call 9-1-1 while Dat and Joanna's oldest brothers grabbed ladders and the garden hose and started up on the roof. Another brother began to toss the luggage and hampers stacked by the front door onto the porch, directing the little boys to haul them on down the stairs and out into the yard. As sparks began to fall, they dragged the suitcases and hampers of food to the driveway.

Mamm came back from the phone shanty and told Joanna to go back in the house with her. "We still need to eat."

There were no flames in the house, but smoke hung along the ceiling and in the stairwell. Joanna grabbed a potholder and the frying pan filled with scrambled eggs and Mamm grabbed the pan of sausage. As they walked out of the house, Mamm called for the younger boys, who were wearing pajamas, winter coats, and boots, to follow her across the road to her in-laws' house.

As they climbed the porch steps, Mammi Rhoda called out from the door. "Joanna, did your cooking set the house on fire?"

Mortified, Joanna turned around. Her father and three of her brothers were on the roof now. Dawdi Hiram shouted directions from the ground. She hadn't done anything different two hours earlier when she stoked the fire than she had any other morning.

Mammi Rhoda laughed at her own joke, but Joanna didn't think it was funny. She knew she hadn't started the fire—most likely Dat hadn't cleaned the chimney when Mamm reminded him it needed to be done.

Five minutes later Dawdi commanded Dat and the boys off the roof and to come eat their breakfast. Twenty minutes after that the fire trucks finally arrived to find the roof engulfed in flames.

The vans arrived to take them to Maine and the drivers grew impatient. Dat asked them several times to wait. "I'll pay you just the same," he said.

Finally Dat, Dawdi, and the fire chief conferred. Then Dat and the boys cleaned up and changed their clothes at Mammi and Dawdi's house, and the boys loaded the luggage into the vans. "All the more reason for us to find a new place," Dat said.

"I don't want to go," Joanna said. "Can you drop me off at Mammi Lu's?" She made the mistake of asking in front of Mammi Rhoda.

Her grandmother's lips tightened. Then she said, "You can stay here. I'm going to get a head start on my spring cleaning—you can help."

Joanna turned toward her mother, hoping she'd say Joanna could go to Mammi Lu's.

"You need to come with us," Mamm said. Joanna followed her to the van.

Joanna thought of how cold it had been that day, compared with the heat in the garden now. She swiped her hand across her forehead. Then she gathered up the weeds she'd pulled, stepped through the gate, and dumped them in the waiting wheelbarrow. She pushed it to the compost pile. Another buggy was on the road, a lantern hanging from a pole by the driver's side. On any other Friday night, she would have expected it to be Jacob. Could it be him? The buggy kept going. Joanna returned to her weeding and to her memories of the day her childhood home burned. Life hadn't been the same since. But it wouldn't have even if the house hadn't burned.

Dat made an offer on two farms in Maine while they were there—one for him and one for Leon. Joanna slept the entire trip to Maine in the backseat of the van, only getting out to use the restroom. What if the fire had started after they'd all gone to bed instead of in the morning? The thought of what *might* have happened was worse than what *had*. The house had no fire alarms, even though she'd begged Dat to install them several years before.

Joanna had never trusted her father's judgment. He sent Leon into the silo alone at age ten. More than once he'd taken Joanna up a ladder and then lifted her onto a barn rafter to rescue a kitten. And he put the younger twins on top of wagons of hay for the trip from the far field to the barn starting when they were three.

She begged her parents to drop her off at Mammi Lu and Dawdi Marcus's on the way home. For the first time in her life, Joanna got her own way, mostly because Leon had backed her up. "Dat, she needs a break," he'd said. "We can manage. Besides, Mammi Lu and Dawdi Marcus could use some help." For some reason, for once, Dat complied.

Joanna never returned to the house, which ended up being razed, nor to the farm. She never had any desire to.

Mammi Lu often said, "Nothing ever stays the same." Joanna was beginning to see her point.

~

Staying up late and weeding didn't help Joanna sleep. Instead she tossed and turned and finally went out on the porch while it was still dark, staying there until the sunrise spread over the barn and oak tree. She blinked a few times and then shuffled into the house to shower and dress. Then she lit the propane stovetop and made a pot of coffee. After she had a cup, she cut a bucket of flowers from the garden—zinnias and bachelor's buttons, roses and sweet William, black-eyed Susans and dahlias—and quickly made bouquets, just as she did each morning, tying each with a strand of twine. She put the bouquets in a bucket and carried it out to the flower shed on the road, placing the large sign that read *1 bouquet, $10* where it was easy to read. There was a tin can with a slot in the top nailed to the counter of the shed for people to put the money in. Every once in a while someone took flowers without paying, but almost without fail they did pay, usually more than the sign requested.

She also cut lavender to dry in the kitchen for Mammi Lu to make sachets and soap from in the fall. After a couple of bites, she scraped her oatmeal into the compost, washed her dishes, and then checked the messages in the phone shanty. Mandy had returned Joanna's call last night. "I'm not just saying this to make you feel better—Jacob doesn't deserve you. It's his loss, not yours." Mandy's voice grew a little shaky. "I'm doing all right. Denki for letting me know about Jacob."

That was one of the things Joanna liked about Mandy. Surely she'd already known about the breakup, but she hadn't mentioned that. Instead she focused on what Joanna had told her. She was a good friend.

Fifteen minutes later, Joanna rode her scooter the half mile to the warehouse. She usually worked a half day on Saturdays, unless a project needed to be finished. Since she'd taken the morning off the day before, which she now regretted, she needed to work a full day.

As she gathered her supplies in the warehouse, Jacob ignored her. When they loaded their gear in the passenger van, he didn't help. When they climbed inside, Jacob sat up front and Joanna climbed in through the side door.

"Wait!"

Joanna leaned her head out the door. Adam ran toward them. As he reached the van, Ike called out Jacob's name from the door to the office. And then, "I need you on the other job. We'll take my buggy."

They were a day away from completing a small remodeling job in a house nearby.

Adam jumped into the front seat and shot a smile back at Joanna. Then he gave Nick a hearty "Hallo!"

Joanna leaned back in her seat. She was relieved Jacob would be working somewhere else, but she wasn't looking forward to spending the day with Adam either. She hoped he wouldn't ask her about Jacob.

Tim and Caleb both had the day off, so it would just be Adam and her. Perhaps if it had just been her and Jacob they could have talked things through, although Ike and Becky never scheduled her and Jacob to work alone.

Adam was chatting away about the weather with Nick. "I can't complain—it's so much cooler than Florida." He pointed at the farmhouse as Nick turned up the driveaway.

"I think Dawdi will get above the asking price. It's gorgeous." He glanced back at Joanna. "The team did an amazing job."

For a moment, Joanna felt better. Adam's positivity was contagious. But then she sank into the seat. Jah, she was good at her work. Why couldn't she be good at other areas of her life too?

When they reached the house, Adam and Nick unloaded the crates from the back while Joanna headed straight upstairs to finish the painting. She could hear Adam on the roof and was thankful Ike insisted all of his roofers tie off.

At lunchtime, Joanna put the lid on the bucket of paint and headed down to the kitchen. As she made a half sandwich, she heard a clatter outside. Adam was tied off on the roof. He couldn't have fallen—at least not too far.

Still, she rushed to the door, flung it open, and hurried down the steps.

"I'm all right."

She glanced toward the voice. Adam sat at the bottom of the ladder, rubbing his left ankle.

"What happened?"

"I fell."

"You weren't tied off?"

"Not to come down the ladder."

Joanna realized a little late how ridiculous her question was. "Are you sure you're all right?"

"Jah." He kept rubbing his ankle.

"How can I help?"

"Could you bring me my backpack? It's in the kitchen."

"Sure." If Ike was going to put the house on the market Monday, the roof had to be completed today. She was nearly finished with the painting, so at least she could cross that off the list.

When she returned, Adam took the backpack from her and opened it, taking out a brace. Then he took off his boot, slipped the brace on his ankle, and laced it up.

Joanna said, "It looks like you've injured your ankle before."

He put his boot on. "A couple of times. Playing basketball."

She imagined him at the park in Pinecraft, up against a few Englischers.

"I'm fine." He stood and hopped to the ladder.

"You don't look fine."

He winced as his left foot landed on a rung. After that she couldn't see his face.

Joanna went back into the house and ate a few bites of her sandwich. She still didn't have an appetite.

After she finished the painting, she cleaned up and stepped back outside, listening to Adam on the roof. He was definitely determined and a hard worker. She couldn't deny that. And having Adam around made her think of her past interactions with him and, in turn, brought her a measure of comfort. Which surprised her.

12

Adam worked carefully—but far too slowly, he feared—to finish the roof by five when Nick said he'd stop by to take them back to the warehouse.

He'd been happy not to have to work with Jacob, but now he wished Dawdi Ike had sent him along. Adam feared being a disappointment to his grandfather, as he'd often been to his stepfather. He'd assured Dawdi Ike at breakfast that Jacob said it would take only a half day to finish the roof. That was probably why Dawdi had sent Adam on the job by himself. Why had Adam believed Jacob? He seemed full of himself, besides being rude to Joanna.

Cleary, Jacob didn't deserve her.

Adam concentrated on his work, shuffling along. A few times he had to hop on his right foot going down the slope of the roof. He carefully nailed the shingles, one after another. His stepfather had always shamed him when he "injured himself."

After what seemed like a long time, Joanna called out to

him. She stood at the top of the ladder, her head sticking over the roofline, and extended a cup of water to him.

"It's getting hotter," she said. "You need to hydrate."

The chore of navigating the space to her didn't seem worth the water.

"I can come to you," she said.

"Nee." He took a step toward her. "It's not safe." He shuffled as quickly as he could.

Joanna watched him with concern. "Be careful."

As he reached her, he said, "It was stupid of me to twist my ankle."

She tilted her head. "Did you fall on purpose?"

"Of course not."

"Then why would you call yourself stupid?"

She had a point. Without answering her, he took the cup. The sound of a vehicle caught his attention, and he turned his head. The panel van headed toward the house. He had a better view and told Joanna. "Nick's back."

"After I clean up, I'll be done," she said.

"I'm not even close." Adam drank half the water and then said, "Nick's early." He drained the glass as his Dawdi climbed out of the front seat. Then Jacob climbed out of the side of the van.

Adam groaned.

"What's wrong?"

"Reinforcements."

"Isn't that a good thing?"

"Jah . . ." It was.

Joanna took the cup and disappeared. Adam turned around and shuffled back to the roofline. A few minutes later, Dawdi Ike and Jacob climbed up the ladder.

"What are you doing?" Adam asked when his grandfather stepped onto the roof.

"I'm going to help."

"Nee." Mammi Becky wouldn't want him to. Adam didn't want him to either.

Dawdi Ike said, "It's the last time I'll roof. I promise."

Adam gave in. A couple of minutes later Dawdi Ike asked Adam what he did to his ankle. "You're limping."

"I turned it is all."

Dawdi had a look of compassion on his face. "It appears to be painful."

It was. Adam paused a moment before he said, "I'm okay."

~

After a half hour, Joanna popped her head up over the edge of the roof again. "Ike!" she called out. "What are you doing up here?"

"Working," Dawdi Ike grumbled. "Don't tell Becky."

"I absolutely will." Joanna was serious. "You need to get down."

"This is my last roofing job. I promise."

Joanna shook her head. "You said that last time. Give me your cell phone—I'm going to leave a message for her."

Dawdi Ike shook his head. "I promise I won't do this again."

Joanna pursed her lips and then sighed heavily. "How about some sandwiches? And coffee? Would a snack help?"

"Jah and jah and jah," Dawdi answered.

Joanna brought the coffee up first, one mug at a time, followed by three ham sandwiches on one plate. She came back fifteen minutes later. Jacob handed her the empty plate and cups and somehow she carried everything down the ladder. As the three of them returned to work, Joanna began cleaning up the grounds. Adam caught glimpses of her carrying old shingles and debris that had fallen on the lawn to the dumpster in the driveway.

Adam, Jacob, and Dawdi continued to hammer the shingles as the sun began to lower in the sky, shooting streaks of pink and orange across the horizon.

"We can do this," Dawdi said. "We'll be done by sunset."

Just as the sun dipped out of view and twilight cast over the rooftop, Adam pounded the last nail in his section. As he started over to help his grandfather, Dawdi stood with his hand on his back. "Done."

They both shuffled over to Jacob's area and gave him a hand. A few minutes later, the roof was complete. Dawdi took a couple of headlamps out of the equipment bag and gave one to Adam and the other to Jacob. "You two clean up," he said, breathing heavily. "I'm going to go down." Adam watched his grandfather slowly make his way across the roof.

Adam and Jacob worked quietly, packing up the tools, collecting the extra shingles, and gathering up wayward nails. Finally, they carried everything down. As Adam limped toward the van carrying the bag of tools, Joanna stepped to his side and grabbed half of it. Embarrassed, he said, "I've got it."

She didn't let go. She didn't say anything. She just kept walking beside him.

~

Mandy and Caleb hosted church the next morning, for the first time according to Mammi Becky. Adam limped into their shed behind Jacob and ended up sitting beside him. He glanced over at the women's side but didn't see Joanna. The single women must have been in a row behind him. Adam's ankle began to throb during the singing. He needed to elevate it. After four songs he faked a cough and then excused himself past the others in the row and managed to make his way out the back of the already sweltering shed.

There was a bench under the willow tree in the middle of the lawn, and Adam made his way toward it. He sat on it lengthwise, elevating his left foot and leaving his right one on the ground. Caleb and Mandy had a nice place. He guessed her grandparents helped them finance it.

He smiled a little, thinking about Mandy being interested in him way back when. He was the one who had suggested they get ice cream with Caleb. Adam was proud of his one venture into matchmaking.

After the service ended, the men converted the benches into tables and the women carried food from the house to the shed. Adam ate quickly, hoping to leave as soon as possible. He'd brought the buggy and second horse Dawdi had said he could use until Adam had a chance to buy his own. He saw Joanna a couple of times—carrying food, serving coffee, picking up dirty bowls—but he didn't have a chance to speak with her.

When he limped out to the pasture to retrieve his horse, he caught a glimpse of Jacob at the edge of Caleb's property, deep in conversation with a young woman Adam didn't recognize. She appeared a lot younger, seventeen or eighteen, and had blond hair. Adam hardly knew any of the Youngie in the district and had never seen the girl before, not that he remembered. The ones he had known years ago were married now. Some had children.

As he drove home, he wondered if he should stay in Lancaster County after all. He could go back to Spartansburg. But to do what? His next brother, Victor, was seventeen now and farming. Adam's stepfather didn't need more help, nor would he want it. He could always go back to Florida, but that had never been a long-term plan. It had been fun for the first year, tolerable the second, and then dreary—even in the sunshine—the last. It wasn't home.

He spent the afternoon on the porch with his ankle propped on a stool, staring off across the pasture toward Lu's farm. Toward Joanna's home.

When Dawdi Ike and Mammi Becky returned, they headed straight into the house for their once-a-week nap. Dawdi probably really needed it after the workout he had the day before finishing the roof. Adam hadn't planned to go to the Youngie singing that evening, but it was at Caleb and Mandy's. Perhaps he should. He needed either to make some friends—unmarried—in Lancaster County or move on.

Mammi was working in the kitchen when he went inside to wash up before he left for the singing.

She turned toward him and gasped, her hand going to her chest.

He smiled. "Did I startle you?" He used to love doing that as a child. She always overreacted.

She shook her head and spoke softly. "You look so much like your father."

They seldom spoke of his Dat. Adam was just a couple of years younger than his father had been when he'd died. Perhaps Adam resembled him more than he used to.

"I need to talk with you." Mammi sounded so serious. Had Adam done something wrong?

He leaned against the counter, taking his weight off his ankle. "What's the matter?"

"I'm not saying you should tattle on your grandfather, but if he engages in dangerous behavior, it wouldn't be wrong for you to include that information in a conversation with me." Her eyes sparked as she spoke.

"All right," he said.

"His well-being is essential to all of us, for many reasons. He thinks he's in perfect health, but he's not."

"Oh?"

"He has high blood pressure and high cholesterol. He should be exercising—but not on a roof."

Adam winced. Dawdi was thin and muscular and appeared to be in good shape. "He promised it was the last time."

"He's promised that before." She picked up an oven mitt. "I can't run this business on my own. And I don't think you're ready to."

"I'm not," he said.

"So let's keep your Dawdi Ike alive for as long as we can." She turned toward the stove. "For more than the business. I don't want to live without him."

Adam didn't respond. His grandmother had never been typical. She was a go-getter. And up-front. But he wasn't used to even her talking about what *she* wanted. Most Amish people talked about wanting what God wanted. Although, no doubt, God didn't want Dawdi Ike up on a roof anymore either.

"I'm going to the singing," Adam said.

Mammi Becky swung back around to face him, a smile

spreading across her face. "I'm so glad to hear that. We want you to be happy here."

"Denki," Adam said.

"Would you do me a favor?"

"Of course," Adam answered without thinking.

"See if Joanna wants a ride." Mammi turned back toward the stove. "She needs a friend right now."

~

The last thing Adam wanted to do was show up at Lu's and ask Joanna if she wanted a ride to the singing, but he'd promised Mammi Becky he would. He couldn't break a promise, especially not to his Mammi.

Joanna wore a faded blue dress and stood in Lu's flower garden, between rows of delphiniums and foxgloves. She wasn't working, not technically. After all it was the Lord's Day. Perhaps she was planning her work for the next day.

As he pulled his horse to a stop, he asked, "Want a ride to the singing?"

She wrinkled her nose, which made her eyes dance a little. "Nee."

Relief washed through Adam.

"Joanna!"

Adam turned toward the house. Lu stood on the back porch. "I forgot to tell you. Elaine told me Mandy needs your help tonight."

Joanna exhaled, slowly, and said, "Give me a few minutes."

"Gladly," Adam lied. Once they showed up at the singing together, people would start gossiping about them. And if Jacob was there, especially if he was with the young woman from earlier in the day, there would be tension.

Adam's ankle began to ache as he turned the horse and buggy around in front of Lu's back porch to wait. Joanna clearly wasn't interested in him after all these years. She wasn't the type to have a rebound relationship—and he didn't want her to. If she was ever going to be interested in him, he wanted it to be on his own merit. Not on the lack of Jacob's.

Ten minutes later, Adam watched in the rearview mirror as Joanna walked toward him, her stride brisk. She'd changed into a mint green dress and a freshly pressed apron and Kapp. As she climbed up into the buggy, she said, "Thank you for thinking of me."

"You're welcome." He'd never, not in a million years, tell her that Mammi Becky had suggested he stop by. In fact, he regretted not thinking of it himself. Joanna did need friends now more than ever. They chatted about how hot it was and whether the clouds on the horizon would bring a thunderstorm before the day was done. Joanna appeared to be fine.

When they arrived at the singing, Adam let Joanna off by the house, where a group of women had gathered, and continued on to the pasture to unhitch the horse. Several men stood in a circle at the gate. Caleb opened it for Adam and then jogged alongside him. Adam glanced back at the group. Jacob wasn't among them.

After he unhitched and hobbled the horse and scooted the buggy alongside the fence, Adam walked with Caleb back to the front yard, where the benches were set up for an outdoor singing. Several of the Youngie played volleyball in the side yard, including Jacob and the woman he'd been talking to after church.

Adam searched for Joanna but couldn't find her. He guessed she was in the house with Mandy and headed to the kitchen.

"What are you doing in here?" Mandy asked after he stepped through the door.

"Hallo to you too." He grinned.

Mandy rewarded him with a sweet smile, while Joanna kept her back to him. It appeared they'd been having a private conversation, which he'd interrupted.

"I wondered if I could help with anything?"

"Jah." Mandy pointed to a couple of pitchers of water. "You can take those out and put them on the picnic table."

As he lifted the pitchers, Mandy said to Joanna, "Anyway, I really appreciated your phone call. I feel a little more hopeful now." Adam stepped quickly to the door as Mandy said, "Speaking of phone calls, Miriam called yesterday. She's thinking about moving—"

Adam continued down the back steps, pondering why he'd ventured into the kitchen in the first place. *Joanna.* He'd wanted to be where she was, even if he hadn't been wanted. He needed to be more guarded.

Fifteen minutes later, Caleb called everyone to the front yard, where the benches sat. The young woman walked with two other girls ahead of Jacob. Joanna and Mandy didn't come out of the house until the singing had already begun. When they did, Joanna had her head down. Halfway through the singing, the young woman who had been with Jacob stood and walked up the aisle and away from the gathering.

"Where's Veronica going?" one of the girls asked.

"Shh," someone replied.

A short time later, Jacob stood and headed down to the pasture. Not long after, he came up the driveway in his buggy.

Adam stood and headed toward the house. Sure enough, Veronica was standing by the lane. Jacob stopped, climbed down from his side of the buggy, and hurried over to open her door.

Adam turned toward the group. Joanna stood at the back, watching the buggy. Until her gaze fell to Adam. Then she quickly looked away.

13

Lu unpinned the first sheet and started to put it in the wicker basket when Joanna yelled, "I'll do that!"

Squinting into the sun, Lu turned. Joanna jogged toward her. Her granddaughter insisted on folding the laundry as it came off the line instead of waiting to do it in the house. She was happy to have Joanna do whatever she preferred.

As Joanna reached her, she held up several envelopes. "You have a letter from my Mamm. And one from Becky." Joanna cocked her head. "Why would Becky write to you when she lives a half mile away?"

Lu pursed her lips. "Who knows why Becky does what she does." She reached for the envelopes with her free hand, hoping Joanna wouldn't ask any more questions.

She didn't. Instead she touched one of the daisies on the wilting chain Lu had made a few hours ago and wore around her neck. "I remember making these with you when I was little."

Lu lifted her gaze and met Joanna's. "I remember that too. And making hollyhock dolls."

Joanna's eyes glimmered.

"My favorite days were when you visited." Lu lifted the chain of daisies over her Kapp and handed them to Joanna. "Your turn."

Joanna grinned and pulled it over her head. "I won't tell anyone."

Lu groaned. "Are you remembering that time Elaine scolded me?"

Joanna nodded. "Mandy and Miriam were here. Elaine said you were being fanciful."

"Jah. If Elaine—or anyone else—stops by, take the chain off."

Joanna pressed her hand against her daisy necklace. "Not until the last one has completely wilted." She took the bedsheet from Lu with her other hand. "Go sit."

Lu obeyed her granddaughter. What would she do without Joanna? Losing Marcus had shattered her heart. Joanna was the glue that held her together. And now Joanna's heart was broken too.

Lu sat in her rocker on the back porch and opened her daughter's letter. She was the second of Lu and Marcus's four children and the only girl. Two of her sons had chosen not to join the church and now lived in Indiana, near each other, and the third had moved to a northern New York Amish community where his wife was from.

After trying to read Suzanna's small cursive, Lu reached for her reading glasses on the table next to her chair. Suzanna wrote they were all working fifteen-hour days to make the most of the long hours of light in Maine.

It takes a lot to prepare for winter here.

Besides the vegetable garden, they were growing flowers for the first time. Lu read the line again—her son-in-law Nehemiah had never allowed Suzanna or Joanna to grow flowers, saying doing so was both fanciful and frivolous. Suzanna wrote,

I've been selling bouquets at the farmers' market—I can't believe how much Englischers will pay for a bunch, which is the only reason Nehemiah agreed to me growing the flowers in the first place.

Lu gripped the page a little tighter.

That's all for now. Write to me with your news. I need an update from Joanna too, hopefully that she and Jacob will decide to join us here. No doubt Enoch Byer wouldn't be in favor of Jacob leaving, but the money Enoch could get for his farm when he's ready to retire might lessen that worry.

Suzanna and Enoch had been in school together and Nehemiah had become acquainted with him, which was part of the reason Nehemiah felt so positive about Jacob.

Lu finished the letter, folded it, and slipped it back into the envelope.

"What did Mamm have to say?" Joanna, with the basket against her hip, had reached the porch.

"She's been selling flowers at the farmers' market."

"Really?" Joanna hurried up the steps. "Dat is allowing that?"

Lu nodded.

"Ach. So flowers sell well in Maine too?"

"Apparently," Lu said.

Joanna shifted the basket to her other side. "Is that all she wrote about?"

Lu held up the letter. "You can read it."

"I will, later." Joanna went into the house, and Lu opened Becky's letter. It was short, just three lines. She asked for prayer for Adam that God would provide friends for him in Lancaster County and a wife. She asked that, if it was God's will, Adam would stay in Lancaster County and be willing to take over the family business in the future so Ike could retire. Although Becky didn't talk about it much, Lu knew she was concerned about Ike's health. Lu would pray about that too. At the end Becky wrote,

Lu, include your own request and mail the letter to Rhoda. Then, Rhoda, mail your letter and the previous letters back to me.

Lu put the letter on the table adjacent to her chair and found the pen under her notebook and Bible. She wrote a short paragraph asking for prayer for someone she dearly loved who was grieving a loss. She wasn't going to specifically name Joanna, even though everyone would know, nor ask that the Lord would bring someone new into Joanna's life. She wasn't ready for that. And she certainly didn't want the Lord to bring Jacob back.

~

Lu opened her eyes. Had she dozed? She leaned forward. The sun hadn't moved much. If she had fallen asleep it hadn't been for long. She turned her attention to the garden. Joanna was weeding. Her flowers had never been so big, all thanks to her granddaughter's care.

She walked down to the garden and as she approached asked Joanna if she'd seen Jacob at work.

"Nee. *But* I would like to talk with him."

"About?" Lu asked.

Joanna stood up straight. "He took Veronica home from the singing last night. They left halfway through."

"Veronica?" Lu stepped into the garden and began weeding too.

"Troyer. You know. She's Daniel and Elaine's granddaughter. Mandy and Miriam's little cousin, who isn't so little anymore."

"Oh. Jonathon's daughter, right?" Lu fully registered what Joanna had said, but still she asked, "Jacob took her home?"

"Jah."

That sounded odd.

"She was there with a couple of her friends, who are from our district." Joanna swiped the back of her gloved hand along her chin. "It was a relief when he left. I was just surprised she went with him." Joanna glanced up at her grandmother. "What do you think is going on?"

Lu gave her granddaughter a sympathetic look. "Only time will tell. Try not to dwell on it."

"Veronica is only seventeen."

"Maybe he was just doing her family a favor by taking her home. They'd probably made plans ahead of time."

Joanna straightened her back. "Did you and Dawdi ever break up?"

"Once." Lu stood too. "He was so sure I was the right

one—but I was the only girl he'd ever taken out. I broke up with him and said he couldn't know for sure until he dated someone else. I said I wouldn't go out with him again until he took out at least three other girls."

Joanna grinned. "What happened?"

"He took three girls out." Lu couldn't help but smile. "All at once."

Joanna laughed. "Quiet Dawdi Marcus did that?"

"Jah. He took them to the creamery. He asked Ike to take me at the same time, so I'd see that he'd taken three girls on a date—Ike convinced me to go by saying Becky would be there."

Joanna looked the happiest she had in weeks. "Becky was one of the girls there with Dawdi Marcus?"

"Exactly. She was one of his dates." Tears sprang into Lu's eyes.

"I'm sorry," Joanna said.

"Nee. It's a good memory." Lu blinked quickly. "I'm glad you asked."

"Who were the other girls?"

"Rhoda and Elaine." Lu laughed even as she cried. "Can you imagine all of us forty-eight years ago?"

Joanna began to laugh too. "Nee. I can't. What happened next?"

"Becky rode home with Ike, and your Dawdi gave me and Elaine and Rhoda rides home. He dropped them off first."

Joanna had a twinkle in her eye.

"We were married a year later." Lu sighed. "How could I resist?" Marcus was no Jacob, that was for sure. He was a good man.

A half hour later, Lu and Joanna were both sitting on the porch. "Lu! Joanna!" Becky came sashaying toward them in a fresh dress and apron. She wore a black bonnet over her white Kapp. Becky always looked her best.

Lu called out, "You missed me telling Joanna about the time Marcus took you, Rhoda, and Elaine to the creamery on a date."

Becky slapped her thigh as she reached the porch. "No matter how old I get, I'll never forget that. And then it still took you a year to marry him."

"A year isn't long." Lu smiled. "Unless you are the standard."

Becky put her hand to the side of her mouth and whispered to Joanna as she sat, "I had to ask Ike to marry me. He was taking his own sweet time."

Joanna didn't have to feign being surprised. She really was. "Wow."

"He was scared I'd say no if he proposed. I don't know why. I was as crazy about him as he was about me—we married three months later."

Lu knew they were still crazy about each other.

"Joanna," Becky said, "I need you to go with Ike and me tomorrow to see the Federalist-style house I was telling you about." Lu could tell by the tone of Becky's voice that she was pleased about the property.

Joanna straightened. "All right." Lu would be forever grateful to Becky for giving Joanna her job. She'd grown so much more confident working for the Slaybaughs. Joanna added, "I've always wanted to see the inside of that house."

"It's gorgeous," Becky said. "Well, it will be gorgeous. Currently it's a mess, but it's all cosmetic. The structure is sound."

Joanna's eyes lit up.

"Adam will go with us too," Becky said. "We're going to put the two of you in charge of the project."

Joanna's volume dropped as she said, "All right." Lu assumed Joanna felt a little overwhelmed to be in charge of such a big house. Hopefully she hadn't caught on that Becky wanted to play matchmaker between her and Adam.

The next morning, Joanna arrived at work before Becky. She made the coffee, cleaned up the counter someone had dirtied the day before after she left, and then busied herself tidying the staging area, covering several pieces of furniture with sheets and then putting couch pillows in plastic bags.

She replayed Sunday night. Adam had seemed extra kind and attentive on the way home, but he hadn't mentioned Jacob or Vernonica. Joanna hadn't either. Nor did she have a chance, with so many people around, to ask Mandy about Jacob and Veronica before the evening ended.

Mandy had opened up about her doctor's visit while they were alone in the kitchen, saying she had a couple of previous visits and they were trying natural measures. She didn't go into detail, and Joanna wouldn't expect her to, but she seemed hopeful. And Mandy had reiterated that Jacob didn't deserve her. Joanna paused, holding a wayward pillow against her chest. Did Mandy know something she didn't?

The warehouse door opened and a stream of light bounced across the concrete floor, followed by a shadow.

"Guder Mariye." It was Adam. "I smell coffee." The steps stopped. "Joanna, are you in here?"

She stepped out to where she could see Adam, still holding the pillow. "Jah. I'm here." She tossed the pillow to the couch. She'd deal with it later.

He grinned. "Denki for the coffee."

"You're welcome."

He kept walking toward the kitchen area, still limping a little, and took two white mugs out of the cupboard. "Do you take sugar? Cream?"

She pointed to her travel mug. "I already have some." Adam put one mug back as Joanna said, "I have an extra travel mug." She opened the far cupboard, pulled it out, and handed it to him.

Adam said, "Denki." And then as he poured his coffee he asked, "How are you doing this morning?"

Before she could answer, the door opened further and Ike stepped inside. He squinted into the dimness of the warehouse. "Adam? Are you in here?"

"Jah. I'm here."

"Have you seen Joanna?"

"I'm here," she called out.

"Nick just pulled up. We need to go."

Adam took a couple of sips and then headed toward the door with his travel mug in his hand.

Becky was sitting on the front bench seat of the van. "Adam, sit in the back." She patted the seat beside her. "Sit here, Joanna." Both did, of course, as Becky ordered.

Ike climbed into the front seat as Jacob yelled from across the yard, "Wait! I have another question."

"I'll be right back." Ike jumped to the ground.

Jacob stood by the wagon, holding a tool in his hand. Joanna couldn't tell what it was, but he appeared frustrated.

Becky turned toward Adam. "Your coffee smells good."

"Want some?"

"Jah."

Joanna kept watching Jacob as Becky took a drink from Adam's mug and then said, "Wonderful *gut*." She offered the cup to Joanna. "How about you?"

"Nee." Joanna glanced out the window again and back at Becky. "I have my travel cup." She patted her bag.

Becky handed the coffee back to Adam and then rustled in her bag.

"Joanna?"

She turned her head, embarrassed. Of course Becky was talking to her.

Becky said, "The Realtor will be there, since we haven't signed the papers yet. I have some notes we need to go over about the house before we arrive."

Adam leaned toward them. Joanna could smell his coffee along with a woody scent, probably from his soap.

Becky held a notebook in her hand. "The house was built in 1837. It's six thousand square feet, so it's by far the largest house we've done. We had an initial inspection before we made the offer. We have a few electrical updates, which we'll use our regular electrician for. We're hoping we can do the rest. Today, we want to talk about design ideas."

Ike climbed back into the van and Joanna forced herself to look straight ahead, instead of at Jacob. Becky kept talking as Nick pulled onto the highway. It was a short ride. When they reached the house, Nick turned the van down the driveway and crossed a narrow bridge over Pequea

Creek. The Realtor waited on the portico at the front of the house.

Once Nick parked the van, Joanna opened the door and jumped down. She'd admired the home from the time she was a young girl visiting Mammi Lu and Dawdi Marcus with her family. She would tag along with her brothers when they went exploring, and one time they played in the creek by the covered bridge fifty yards down the road.

The house was three stories with a brick facade and a pine tree on each side. It was definitely fancier than the places they usually renovated. It would be a great distraction from thinking about Jacob.

"Let's start with the first floor," the Realtor said as she unlocked the door. The hardwood floors in the foyer were worn and scratched but salvageable. The walls were lathe and plaster. Ahead was an open staircase with a cherrywood banister.

The Realtor opened pocket doors into the living room. It was large and had a cavernous fireplace with a wide hearth. Maple trim framed the room along with a coffered ceiling. Floor-to-ceiling windows covered the north wall of the living room. With each step through the house, Joanna felt lighter and more positive.

The kitchen needed to be gutted—that meant choosing new cabinets, an island, and all new appliances. She pulled a yellow legal pad from her bag and began jotting down notes. All of the bathrooms needed new tile, showers, vanities, and mirrors. The light fixtures all needed to be replaced.

By the time they reached the backyard, Joanna had pages

of notes. But she ignored them as they stepped onto the veranda. It needed to be cleaned up and some of the brickwork repaired, but it was a lovely area lined with benches and then roses growing in beds on three sides. A carriage house sat off to the right, and off to the left was an old red barn.

The Realtor's phone rang, and she stepped back toward the house.

As they walked toward the barn, Adam asked, "What kind of shape is it in?"

"It needs some repairs," Ike said.

Adam took his hat off and ran his hand through his hair as he walked. "The roof doesn't look like it's in very good shape."

"We can fix it."

Adam's limp became more noticeable. Joanna stifled a laugh. She wasn't sure if he was joking or remembering the last roof. As they walked into the barn a swallow flew up through a hole in the roof and out the top.

Adam pointed upward. "That's not a good sign."

Ike winced. "We came in the late afternoon last time. The light wasn't as bright."

Becky turned around slowly. "This may cost more than we anticipated." It wasn't like Becky and Ike to miss a deteriorating roof.

"We could raze it," Ike said. "The place has a carriage house. Does it really need a barn?"

"Jah," Joanna and Adam said in unison. Joanna studied Ike for a minute. Was he serious? Of course a massive house in Lancaster County on nine acres needed a barn.

After a long pause, Ike said, "I guess you're right."

Becky stepped to his side. "Are you sure you're feeling all right?"

"Jah." Ike sighed and rubbed the back of his neck. "It's going to be a lot, I know. It's the most we've taken on so far."

Becky patted his shoulder. "It'll probably be the most we ever take on—but how could we pass on a property we've admired our entire married life?"

As they waited on the front porch for Nick, Becky asked Joanna what she thought of the house.

"I love it," Joanna answered. "I need to do some research, but I think we can come up with renovations that show off the character of the house in a way that will appeal to a modern buyer."

"It might take us a while to sell it once we're done," Becky said. Did Joanna detect a measure of stress in her voice? "We'll need just the right buyer."

Nick turned onto the driveway.

"Where are you going next?" Adam asked his grandparents.

"We have another house to look at." Ike pulled his pocket watch from the fanny pack he wore. "In fifteen minutes. We're late."

"How about if Nick drops Joanna and me off at the café on the highway? We can talk through ideas," Adam said. "And you can pick us up there."

"Wunderbar." Becky turned toward Joanna. "If that's all right with you?"

"Jah." She gave Adam a sideways glance.

He mouthed, *Sorry. I should have asked you first.*

It's fine, she mouthed back.

Becky beamed. Ike took his wife's hand, something most other Amish husbands would never do in public, and started toward the van. Joanna and Adam followed along behind them.

After they ordered, Joanna flipped to a fresh page in her notebook.

"What other ideas do you have?" she asked.

Adam put down his water glass. "The banister is amazing but needs work. Did you notice the cracks?"

Joanna nodded. "Can't they be filled?"

"I think so. And I can refinish it." Adam shrugged. "We'll see what Dawdi decides."

Joanna gave him a sly smile. "You mean Becky."

Adam laughed. "They definitely work together."

The waitress dropped off their coffee. After she left, as Joanna wrapped her hand around her cup, she asked, "What else?"

Adam dumped sugar into his coffee. "I think we should knock down the pantry wall to enlarge the kitchen."

Joanna wasn't sure about that, but she added it to the list. She liked Adam's idea. He definitely had a vivid imagination, something Becky said was essential for the work they did.

"What are you reading now?"

Joanna laughed. "That was an abrupt subject change."

He grinned. "You're always reading something."

She shrugged. "A gardening book."

"No novels?"

She shook her head.

He leaned back in his chair. "That's sad."

It was, but she wasn't going to agree with him. She'd stopped reading novels during the second time Jacob had courted her.

He asked, "Are you sure you're not reading an actual story?"

The waitress dropped off the cinnamon roll Adam had ordered. He asked, "May we please have another fork?"

"I don't want any," Joanna said.

He smiled. "Just in case."

Her mouth watered. She actually did.

Once the waitress dropped off the fork, Adam slid the plate over to Joanna. "You first."

She took a bite. It was delicious. She took another bite, a big one, and slid the plate across the table to Adam.

He poked his fork into the cinnamon roll. "I loved *Jane Eyre*."

An involuntary smile spread across Joanna's face. "Reader, I loved it too."

Adam laughed. "That was funny."

She smiled, glad he remembered Jane's line—"Reader, I married him"—in the book. She turned serious. "I'm glad you liked it." It was a long book. "Why did you read it?"

"Because you were reading it at Thanksgiving, when I saw you."

Her heart lurched a little. Adam made her feel warm from being seen and cold from being exposed. All at the same time. She used to think Jacob listened to her, saw her, but now she wondered if he ever had. She thought of the glimmer in his eye when he'd tilt his head, lean toward her, and flash his charming smile. Maybe he hadn't ever really heard her. Maybe he only pretended to.

Adam slid the plate back across the table. "Do you remember that night in the van, on the way back from Noah and Emily's wedding?"

"Jah." Joanna cut off another piece of the cinnamon roll. "I remember you said that men and women couldn't be friends. You said the same thing—well, that we couldn't be friends—in Pinecraft. Do you still believe that?"

He hesitated for a long moment and then said, "I remember saying that both times, and jah, generally, I still think that's true."

She slid the plate back toward him again and took a drink of coffee, a long one. She'd lost her appetite.

15

At the end of the day, Becky, Ike, Adam, and Joanna sat around the office in the warehouse after everyone else had gone home. "We're not going to make an offer on the second house we saw today. That would stretch us much too thin." Ike glanced at Becky and she nodded.

Joanna had overheard her bosses talking about cash flow problems recently. She was glad they were being cautious, not only with money but also with labor resources.

"We'll start on the remodeling project at the Garden Lane house tomorrow. Jacob, Caleb, and Tim moved supplies over today. A dumpster was scheduled to be delivered this afternoon." Ike held a pen tightly in his hand as he glanced from Joanna to Adam. "What other ideas did you come up with for the Pequea Creek house?" As Ike talked, his flip phone, which was approved by Daniel to be used only for the business, rang in his fanny pack. He pulled it out, accepted the call, and said, "Hallo."

There was a pause and then he said, "Jah, we can sign the papers in the morning." There was another pause and Ike said, "It's always a pleasure to work with you too."

He ended the call with a smile. "Glad that's taken care of." He slipped the phone back into his fanny pack and made eye contact with Adam. "Back to your thoughts."

Adam and Joanna presented their list, ending with tearing down the pantry wall to make the kitchen bigger.

Ike didn't respond, but Becky said, "We'll need to put more thought into that." She leaned forward. "Ike, are you feeling all right?"

He stood. "Just a little buggy." It was a joke that the team often laughed at when one of them was feeling off, but no one laughed now. "I think we should talk about this in the morning."

Joanna was beginning to worry about Ike too. She turned to Becky and asked, "Is there anything you want me to do before I leave?"

Becky shook her head as she walked around the desk to Ike. Adam stepped toward the office door. Joanna stayed seated.

Ike sat back down.

Becky's voice was pitched higher than usual. "What's wrong?"

Ike slumped back in his chair, dropped the pen in his hand, and clutched his chest. He tried to stand but fell, pushing the chair backward.

Becky gasped. Joanna was at Ike's side in a split second and steadied the chair. "Tell me how you're feeling."

"Dizzy," he said. "And like I might be sick." He clutched his arm again.

"Where's your pain?"

"My arm. And my chest."

"I'm going to get your phone."

He nodded.

She unzipped the fanny pack and fumbled his flip phone out of it.

Becky was on Ike's other side now. Joanna stepped away. Adam took her place. She pressed the SOS button. It took what seemed like forever for a dispatcher to come on the line. Joanna quickly told her what happened and gave the address of the warehouse.

Becky caressed Ike's face. "Can you hear me?" she kept saying over and over.

"Hurry," Joanna said to the dispatcher. "Please hurry."

The dispatcher replied, "If you can go out to the road and direct the ambulance, that would be helpful."

"All right." Joanna ended the call, sure she should take the phone in case the dispatcher needed to call her back. She lowered her voice and said, "Adam, do you know CPR?"

"Jah."

"Good, just in case." She held up the phone. "I'm taking this—so I'll have it if the dispatcher calls back."

Adam gave her a nod.

"Stay calm," Joanna said. "Everything is going to be all right." As she hurried out the door, she thought of Dawdi Marcus. He'd had a seizure in the middle of the night. Mammi woke her, and Joanna ran out to the phone shanty in her nightgown and robe to call 9-1-1. After she made the call, she ran out to the road too, just as she was doing now.

She'd taken a CPR class through the Red Cross after Dawdi Marcus had passed away. Perhaps Adam had taken first aid through his job in Florida. Construction sites could be dangerous.

She waited another eternity—seven minutes according to Ike's phone—for the ambulance to arrive. She heard the siren first and stepped into the road and began waving her arms as it crested the hill right before the turn to the warehouse. The ambulance slowed and the driver's window lowered.

Joanna pointed toward the warehouse. "He's in there. The door is open."

The driver gave her a nod, turned, and sped up. Joanna ran behind the ambulance. When she reached the warehouse, two men were carrying equipment inside.

After they loaded Ike into the ambulance, Joanna pulled his phone from her pocket and said to Becky, "I'll call Nick and ask him to take you to the hospital."

"Denki." Becky's voice was flat, even as she begged to be allowed to ride in the ambulance with Ike. The paramedics said she couldn't, and Joanna hoped that wasn't a bad sign.

Joanna left a message for Nick. A minute later he texted he was on his way. As they waited, Mammi Lu came up the lane. A strand of her gray hair hung loose against her cheek, and she wore a work dress. "I heard sirens," she called out. "Is everyone all right?"

"Lu." Becky staggered toward her friend. "It's Ike."

Mammi Lu stretched out her arms for her friend.

"It's his heart," Becky said. "Just like Reuben."

Joanna sat next to Adam in the ER waiting room of Lancaster General Hospital, aware of how frightened he must be but at a loss for what to say.

So instead she concentrated on her grandmother and Becky. Mammi Lu held her friend's hand—which Joanna understood. She felt compelled to take Adam's hand in hers, but of course she wouldn't. It would be inappropriate for her to do such a thing. She wasn't a sixty-seven-year-old grandmother.

Mammi Lu had always been soft. Not plump, just soft. Her lap was soft when she held Joanna as a child. Her face was soft when she put her cheek against Joanna's now. Her breath, her words, her voice. All of her was soft, in a comforting way.

Becky, on the other hand, was always moving. She never walked—she marched. Even when she sat behind her desk, she moved. She was energetic and unpredictable. Everybody loved Becky. And everyone loved Mammi Lu too. Joanna had never loved either of them more than she did as she watched them now.

After a while a doctor approached, saying, "I'm looking for Becky Slaybaugh."

"Right here," Mammi Lu answered, patting Becky's knee.

The doctor offered her hand. "I'm Dr. Flander." Becky took it. Then the doctor sat next to Becky and said, "You married a fighter."

Becky choked back tears. "Is he all right?"

"Yes," the doctor said. "He's most likely going to need surgery—we'll run tests as soon as we can."

"Can I see him?" Becky asked.

"A nurse will come get you soon. I'll have a cardiologist speak with you about what to expect over the next few days."

Adam hiccupped. Or was that a sob? Joanna whispered, "Are you all right?"

He stood. "I need to get a drink of water."

"I'll go with you." Joanna stood and stepped toward her grandmother. "We're going to go get something to drink."

"Go to the cafeteria." Mammi patted her side. "I guess I didn't bring my purse."

"I have money." Joanna had grabbed her bag before she locked the warehouse.

"Bring Becky and me something to drink too," Mammi Lu said. "And a snack."

Adam had already reached the hallway. Joanna hurried to catch up. By the time she did, he'd stopped at a water fountain.

When he stood, Joanna said, "Let's go to the cafeteria. Mammi wants me to bring back something for her and Becky."

Adam swiped the back of his hand across his eyes and then over his mouth.

Not once had Joanna seen Jacob become emotional, not even after his mother died. She led the way, one she knew from the times Dawdi Marcus was hospitalized, and Adam followed. She parked him at a table and then gathered bottles of juice, premade sandwiches, and an order of fries to share with Adam.

He stared straight ahead when she reached the table. He seemed startled when she sat down. She opened one of the bottles of juice and handed it to him, brushing his arm as she did. "Are you okay?"

He took the bottle and nodded.

She knew how he felt. She'd lived it with Dawdi Marcus.

And she had the same feelings now about Ike—not only was he her boss, but he was also her surrogate grandfather.

Adam had lost his father as a boy and had just witnessed Ike collapse. She was worried about him. But she didn't tell him that. Instead, she asked, "Where did you learn to do CPR?"

"I took a class in Florida."

"Why?"

"I saw Dawdi do CPR when I was little. I always figured it was something I should know how to do."

Joanna held a fry in midair. "Who did your grandfather do CPR on?"

"My Dat."

~

After they returned to the waiting room with the juice and sandwiches for their grandmothers, Becky asked Joanna to leave a message on Daniel and Elaine's phone. "And on Caleb and Mandy's phone too. They're apt to check before Daniel does, although who knows how many times a day Elaine checks. Someone needs to do our chores and yours too in case we're here for a while."

Joanna stepped out the front door and did as she was told. She hesitated a minute when she'd finished, and then made one more call, to her Dawdi Hiram and Mammi Rhoda. She left them a message asking them to pray.

It wasn't long until Becky and Adam were called back to see Ike. "The doctor will be down soon," the nurse said.

Ike's cell phone rang. Joanna recognized Caleb and Mandy's number and stood, stepping away from Mammi Lu and the other people. She answered it quickly.

It was Mandy. "I got your message. Is Ike okay?"

"I think he's going to be." Joanna headed outside to talk in privacy. "Becky and Adam went back to see him and speak with the doctor."

"What a shock. Caleb's hitching up our buggy. We'll stop by Dawdi Daniel and Mammi Elaine's and let them know what's going on and then head over to do the chores at the Slaybaughs' place and yours too."

"Denki." Joanna knew she could depend on Mandy and Caleb.

"Do you want Dawdi Daniel to go to the hospital?"

"Nee," Joanna answered. "It's getting late. Becky or I will call in the morning."

Mandy chuckled. "Don't get used to Ike's cell phone."

It felt good to joke a little. "It's just a flip phone, so, you know, a smartphone would definitely be a different matter."

Once she returned to the waiting room, Joanna sat back down by Mammi Lu. Neither spoke for several minutes. Finally Joanna asked, "Who's Reuben?"

Mammi Lu bristled. "Who mentioned Reuben?"

"Becky did, to you. After the ambulance came."

Mammi Lu sighed. "That's right. Reuben was Adam's Dat."

"I wondered." Joanna hesitated for a minute. "When did he die?"

"Twenty-one years ago."

"When Adam was three?"

"Jah. Adam was with him when it happened. Reuben, Elizabeth, and Adam lived in the apartment above the warehouse. Reuben went to do the chores and took Adam with him—he collapsed in the barn." Mammi Lu folded her hands. "Elizabeth finally went to check on them. She found Adam beside his Dat, stroking his forehead. She screamed for Ike and Becky."

"Was Reuben dead?"

Mammi shook her head. "Ike did CPR on Reuben until the ambulance arrived, but they couldn't save him. It was too late."

Joanna knew Adam's father had died when he was young, but she assumed it had been in an accident. "What did he die from?"

"It was something to do with his heart." Mammi Lu sighed. "It was such a hard time."

Joanna thought how awful it must have been for Becky to watch Ike collapse after losing her son that way. One time Mandy said her grandmother believed Becky never wanted more than one child, which meant she probably used birth control. "Can you believe it?" Mandy had asked Joanna, her eyes wide. "The bishop before my Dawdi even talked with her about it, but she denied she only wanted one child. My Mammi figured that Becky had grown so tired of taking care of her younger siblings that she thought one child was enough. And then that only child died."

Joanna asked Mandy how Becky and Ike's son had died, but she didn't know. "No one talks about what happened. Not even my grandmother." Joanna knew if Elaine didn't talk about something it was definitely a taboo topic. She became convicted of talking about Becky—of listening to gossip about her—and quickly changed the subject. She thought about all of that now as she watched Mammi Lu rub her temples.

"Becky asked for an autopsy after Reuben passed," Mammi Lu said quietly.

Joanna wasn't surprised to hear that. Many Amish parents would have attributed a sudden death like that to God's will and not sought an explanation. But not Becky.

16

Adam sat at his grandmother's desk the next morning, looking at the schedule. He needed to call the Realtor to figure out when his grandparents could sign the papers. And he needed to add up all the employees' hours for the last two weeks so Mammi could write the checks and have them ready on Monday.

Nick was taking Mammi to the hospital, which meant Jacob, Caleb, and Tim would need to take the wagon to the remodeling job, which was two miles away. Adam doubted Jacob would be happy about that.

Adam reached down and rubbed his ankle, which still ached. He felt as unqualified to run his grandparents' business as he had to finish the roof on the farmhouse by himself. What made it even worse was Joanna would see him fail with the business, far worse than he had on the roof. Thinking of Joanna, the apartment above the warehouse needed to be cleaned for a four o'clock check-in. Did she know that?

The apartment. He'd lived there with his parents but he didn't remember those days. The only memory he had of his father was when Dawdi Ike performed CPR on him until Mammi Becky swept Adam out of the barn to the phone shanty and then to the swing set.

"Adam." Caleb stood in the doorway. "Guder Mariye. How are you?"

"I'm fine."

"What's the latest news on Ike?"

"He definitely had a heart attack. They're running more tests." Adam gripped the pen in his hand.

Caleb stepped closer. "Did you sleep last night?"

"A little."

"Adam?" It was Joanna's voice. She stepped to the doorway, behind Caleb. "Any word about Ike?"

"A nurse left a message. He had a rough night, but she said he's holding his own. Nick's taking Mammi back to the hospital now."

"Should you have gone with her?"

Adam shook his head and held up a piece of paper. "She gave me a list of things to see to."

A phone began to ring—a cell phone.

Joanna's face reddened as she pulled Ike's phone from her pocket. She held it up as she took three steps toward the desk. "I meant to give this to you last night." She handed the ringing phone to him.

Adam, his heart racing, took it and accepted the call. "Hallo."

"Adam? Is that you?"

Relief filled him. "Jah, Dawdi. It's me. How are you?"

"Fine. Do me a favor. Go with the crew on the remodel this morning. Jacob and Caleb haven't been doing their best work." Adam forced himself not to look at Caleb, hoping

Dawdi's voice wasn't carrying across the room. "I'll do that," Adam replied. "Now, you do me a favor. Don't think about work, at all. Put your energy into healing. We need you."

Dawdi chuckled. "Everyone's replaceable."

Adam felt ill. Jah, when it came to a job, most people were. But when it came to a person, no one was. His father certainly hadn't been. "Please take care of yourself." Adam couldn't control the fear in his voice. "I'll phone *you* if I can't figure something out."

He ended the call. He wouldn't contact his Dawdi no matter what.

Caleb slipped away.

Adam asked Joanna, "Could you hear what Dawdi said?"

She shook her head.

"It wasn't anything, really. He wants me to check on the remodel."

"Okay." Joanna stepped into the middle of the office. "I'm going to clean the apartment, and then I'll take the buggy to the other rental. Guests are checking in there tomorrow."

"How far is it?"

"A mile. Not far."

"All right." Adam stood. "You take the cell phone. I'll be at the remodel or here. I'll call you if I have any questions."

As Joanna took the phone, their hands brushed. Adam felt a jolt of electricity up his arm. He cleared his throat.

Joanna met his eyes. "Jah?"

"Denki for your help yesterday," he managed to say. "I don't know what we would have done without you. You called 9-1-1. You knew exactly what to do. You came to the hospital. You were a good friend to us."

Her eyebrows shot up. "*Were?* Past tense?"

"*Are*." He smiled at his mistake. "Definitely present tense."

She started to say something more but stopped. He'd deserve it if it was about *him* not committing to being a friend to her—and yet he was thanking *her* for being a friend to him.

She gave him a little wave and said, "I'm going to get to work."

After Joanna left, Adam sat at the desk with his head in his hands. He'd told Joanna he still didn't believe men and women could be friends. But that wasn't true. He hadn't known what he was talking about when he first told her that, but he'd had plenty of friends who were women in Pinecraft. Women he had no desire to court.

The difference was he still wanted to court Joanna. Their story could be like Dawdi Ike and Mammi Becky's—love at first sight—if only Joanna had fallen for him like he had for her. Because he'd never changed his mind about her.

But he couldn't tell her that. She was going through enough without him harassing her. He'd only make her apprehensive about being around him, and he didn't think he could run the business without her.

After Nick dropped Adam and Mammi off at the house the night before, Mammi sat him down at the table and said if they were going to keep the team working, they needed to sell the farmhouse as soon as possible and then quickly move on the Pequea Creek property. She said their costs were higher on the farmhouse than expected so their profit would be lower. "It's going to be up to you, Adam. We may need you to take over the business sooner than we thought. Now is your chance to shine."

When they arrived at the Garden Lane property, they unloaded the supplies in the driveway of the one-story house. After they finished, Caleb showed Adam around. The house was built in the 1980s and had an open floor plan. The tour ended in the kitchen, which they would immediately start gutting.

"What's the deadline to be finished?"

Caleb cracked his knuckles as he said, "Three weeks."

"When are the kitchen cabinets going to be delivered?"

"They were supposed to arrive yesterday—I thought they'd be in the garage—but they're not here."

Adam asked, "Did anyone call to find out why they weren't?"

"I'm not sure."

Adam leaned backward a little. "Did anyone tell Dawdi?"

Caleb's shoulders lifted. "Ask Jacob."

Jacob and Tim were both in the side yard. Adam stood with his thumbs linked through his suspenders, something he'd seen his grandfather do a thousand times. "What's the status on the cabinets?"

Jacob shrugged. "You should call and find out."

"What's the number?"

"It's in the file, back at the office."

Adam let go of the suspenders with a snap. "Why is the file in the office?"

"I thought you'd grab it." Jacob rubbed the back of his neck. "You can call when you get back to the warehouse."

Adam said he'd take the wagon back to the warehouse. "I'll either come get you at quitting time or send Nick."

As he urged the horse to go faster on the highway, he worried about the cabinets. And his grandfather. And his grandmother. And Joanna. He sat up taller. He needed to take charge of what he could and leave the rest to Gott.

Still, the day progressed with one frustration after another. He stood in the phone shed after making the call, thinking he should have kept Dawdi's phone. No one answered at the cabinet shop, so he left a message. Now he'd have to come back and check the messages.

As Adam reached the warehouse, Joanna came down the outside staircase with a basket of laundry in her arms.

Adam said, "I guess I should take the phone after all. I don't think I'll get any work done without it."

She balanced the basket on her hip and took it from her apron pocket.

He asked, "Will you be all right at the other property without a phone?"

"I'll be fine." She handed it to him and said, "I've never worked with the phone before. How are things going at the remodel?"

He explained the cabinets hadn't arrived.

"I'll call." She put her hand out for the phone.

Adam handed it back.

Joanna put the basket down, punched in the password, pushed a few more keys, and put the phone to her ear. A few seconds later she said, "No, it's Joanna." She explained Ike was in the hospital. "We're carrying on without him but need to know why the cabinets weren't delivered yesterday."

She nodded her head a couple of times as she listened.

"All right. So we can expect them by this afternoon?"

Another pause.

"What time?"

After another pause, she said, "Thank you for making

the delivery a priority." After another pause, she said, "Ike's grandson Adam is in charge and will have Ike's phone. If anything comes up, please call him ASAP."

After she said thank you again and ended the call, she handed the phone to Adam.

"Impressive."

She gave him a smile—all sweetness and no sass. "I'm glad to help. Seriously, let me know when problems come up. I'll probably at least have an idea of what to do."

"I appreciate that." He really did.

She continued on to the laundry area in the back corner of the warehouse. He wished there was a way he could help her without making her think he wanted to court her. True, he'd court her in a minute if it was what she wanted. But it wasn't. His attention wasn't what she needed now. If only he hadn't been so stupid about asking her to court back when she didn't even know him.

Surely there was something he could do to encourage her now.

~

The next morning, Dawdi called the cell phone at seven. Adam, who was filling the trough for the steers, accepted the call as he tried to calm his racing heart. He asked, "Is everything okay?"

"Of course," Dawdi said. "I was just thinking you and Joanna should go back out to the Pequea Creek house today. Measure everything."

Adam turned off the faucet. "Don't you already have the measurements?"

"Nee, only what the Realtor gave me. Chart everything

out on paper. See how it will look with the pantry wall torn down—and without it torn down. Talk through the changes to the bathrooms. Make a list of everything you know we'll need. Joanna can pull out the file on the farmhouse and you can see how we do it. The Realtor is bringing the papers up to the hospital this morning—we need to get moving on it as soon as possible. Call and ask her to unlock the house before she heads this way."

"All right."

"Call me if you have any questions, but don't tell your grandmother I called you. She's upset with me."

"What about?"

"Calling you about work."

Adam expected him to say more, but he didn't. "Are you still on the line?"

"Jah. Your grandmother doesn't know this yet—I'll tell her when she gets here this morning. But the test results came back, and I'm going to need bypass surgery. Probably on Monday."

Adam's own heart lurched. Why? He wasn't surprised. Of course his grandfather needed surgery.

The volume of Dawdi's voice decreased. "I don't want to think about the bills."

"Don't," Adam said.

"I don't even know if I should have the surgery. I'm getting old."

"Of course you should have it—you're only sixty-eight. You could have a good twenty or even thirty years left."

"Did I ever tell you my father died at forty-nine?"

Adam hesitated and then said, "No. That's all the more reason for you to have the surgery."

Dawdi didn't respond.

"Mammi needs you." Adam tried to hide the fear in his voice. "I need you."

When Dawdi didn't answer, Adam cleared his throat. "Would you ask Mammi to call me when she reaches the hospital?"

"What for?" Dawdi's voice was low.

Adam walked toward the house. "I just need to talk with her is all." He wasn't sure what he should do. Tell Mammi that Dawdi thought the surgery might not be worth it? Go to the hospital instead of back to the Pequea Creek house?

Adam got ahold of the Realtor and then he and Joanna scootered to the house. As they measured and graphed the floor plan on paper, Joanna took the lead on recording everything. She was good at math, quickly calculating square feet for the flooring and the counter lengths and cupboard dimensions. As they measured the last bedroom on the third floor, the cell phone rang. Adam quickly fumbled it out of the fanny pack. "Hallo?" He said it a little too loudly as he accidentally let go of the tape measure.

Joanna stepped back and gave him a thumbs up.

"Adam. It's Mammi. Your Dawdi just remembered you wanted me to call."

"Jah. How is he? Did he tell you about the surgery?"

"He said it's an option."

Adam lowered his voice. "It's not an option. He needs it."

She sounded tired. "He said it's not a guarantee."

"It's his best choice," Adam said. "I knew a Mennonite man in Florida who had bypass surgery in his early seventies. He was ninety-two when I met him."

"Really?"

"Jah." Adam stepped to the window that looked directly out on the barn roof. He felt as ragged as it looked. "Don't let Dawdi make this decision on his own. Talk to the doctor with him."

"All right," Mammi said. "Denki."

"Call me back after you talk to the doctor." He should have gone to the hospital.

"I've got this," Mammi said. She lowered her voice. "Dawdi has been worried about money—more than usual. But the church mutual fund will help. It won't be all up to us."

"We'll figure it out." Adam gazed down at the backyard. It was more overgrown than he'd realized.

"We can talk more this evening," Mammi said. "I'd like it if you came back and saw your Dawdi on Saturday, before any surgery. I'll be at the house with a few women who are going to come to clean and make meals for next week."

"All right," he said. "I'll do that."

Saturday morning before going to see Dawdi, Adam went into the office to finish up the file for the Pequea Creek house.

"Need any help?" Joanna stood in the doorway with a cup of coffee in her hand.

Adam shook his head.

She lifted the cup. "This is for you."

"Denki." He stood and walked around the desk. "I appreciate your kindness." She met him halfway.

"How are *you* doing?" Adam asked as he took the coffee.

"All right."

She and Jacob hadn't worked together this week—Adam

had made sure of it—but he still wondered if she was comfortable seeing him in the warehouse in the morning and at the end of the day. As he retreated to the desk, he said, "I have a question for you. Please be honest."

She nodded.

"Do you think we should incorporate the pantry space into the kitchen? Or leave it as it is?"

She sat in the chair across the desk. "I've been reading about kitchens lately. I don't think there's any reason for a separate pantry. A pantry cabinet can hold as much as a whole room used to. A larger, open kitchen would have more appeal."

"Denki," Adam said. "I'll present the idea to Dawdi and Mammi and see what they think." He picked up his pen again. "Are you working today?"

Joanna stood. "No. Mammi Lu and I are going to your grandparents' house to give it a good cleaning and make meals. My Mammi Rhoda and Elaine will be there too, and maybe a couple of other women." She touched the magazine tucked under her arm. "I left this here yesterday and wanted to pick it up."

"You made coffee even though you're not working?"

"Jah. I thought you could use some."

His heart warmed to match the cup in his hand. She'd done something just for him. "Mammi said Lu, Elaine, and Rhoda were coming over to the house, but I didn't realize you were too."

"I am." Joanna grinned. "Someone needs to supervise the four of them."

Adam laughed. "That's true. They seem to be a handful."

Joanna held up four fingers. "Not quite. They need one more member."

Adam laughed. "That could be you."

Joanna shook her head. "I can't keep up with them, honestly. You should hear some of their stories about when they were our age—well, even younger than us."

That was an amusing thought, even without any actual stories. Thinking of Mammi Becky and her friends as young women made Adam think of Jacob breaking up with Joanna again. This time he asked, "How are you *really* doing?"

Joanna wrinkled her nose. "Compared to Ike? To Becky? To you?"

"Nee," he answered. "Compared to no one. How are *you*?"

"Oh, you know. Hanging in there." She shrugged. "See you soon."

As she turned to leave, Adam wondered again how he could encourage her. Once he finished his work, he had ten minutes before Nick would arrive to take him to the hospital.

Adam riffled through the drawers in Dawdi's desk until he found a lined piece of paper and an envelope. Joanna was a words person. She loved to read and take notes and write out everything. He'd write her a short letter to encourage her, in the cursive handwriting he'd learned in school, not the scratchy printing he used every day.

He wrote,

Dear Joanna,

As you go through this difficult time, I hope you'll know others are watching over you. Remember, the one who loves and cares for you the most is leading you. I hope you will find encouragement in His guidance and also in the following verse:

For I the L*ORD thy God will hold thy right hand, saying unto thee, Fear not; I will help thee. Isaiah 41:13*

He debated for a minute how to sign it. *Your friend, Adam*? Or should it be anonymous? If he signed his name, would she think he was interested in her? Harassing her? Even stalking her? Most likely he would scare her off even more than he already had.

The Lord didn't want Adam to make it about himself; the Lord valued good deeds done in secret. He decided an anonymous signature would make the letter about Joanna.

Adam signed the note *Someone Who Cares*, folded the piece of paper, and slipped it into the envelope. Then he wrote Joanna's name across the front of the envelope and put it on the counter by the coffeepot so she would see it Monday morning.

With the file under his arm he headed out the door, locking it behind him, and waited for Nick. He would do everything in his power to make his grandparents' business profitable. And he'd do all he could, at the same time, to encourage Joanna.

17

Becky stood in the first-floor hallway of her house, fighting tears. Elaine and her granddaughter Veronica were in the kitchen making casseroles to freeze, while Rhoda made her specialty—beef stew.

Upstairs, Joanna, Lu, and Mandy were doing a thorough cleaning, which they would do on the first floor too. Joanna had told Becky to get her laundry ready to be washed so she wouldn't have to worry about it Monday morning.

Monday. The day Ike would have open heart surgery.

She moved toward the staircase. She needed to grab Adam's laundry too. When she reached his room, the door was closed. Joanna poked her head out of the sewing room. "I didn't think we should clean Adam's room without his permission."

"I did before he arrived—it's fine." Becky doubted Adam needed anyone to clean his room anyway. He'd lived on his own long enough to know how to take care of himself. "I'll go ahead and strip his sheets and grab his clothes, though," she said. She might not have time to do the laundry the week after next either. She expected Ike would be home then, and she'd be busy caring for him.

"All right." Joanna stepped back into the sewing room. "Yell when you have all the laundry together, and I'll get it started."

Becky opened the door to Reuben's room. No, it was *Adam's* room. Would she ever stop thinking of it as Reuben's? The bed was perfectly made down to the hospital corners. His dirty clothes were in the collapsible mesh hamper he'd brought with him. There was a Bible on his bedside table, an English translation, and another book underneath it. She stepped closer. *Jane Eyre*. It was her copy.

She smiled. She remembered Adam borrowing it and taking it back to Florida with him.

Lu had said *Jane Eyre* was one of Joanna's favorite books. Becky had assumed that was why Adam had asked to borrow it, but she hadn't asked. He was so much like his father. And his grandfather. Not that Ike would have read *Jane Eyre* or any other book Becky liked, but he certainly cared enough about her to be interested in her world. Reuben had been the same.

A hollowness settled in Becky's chest.

Sometimes when she saw Ike and Adam together, the long-term, dull ache she felt over losing Reuben turned back into the soul-wrenching one. It had been two decades and yet sometimes the pain was as intense as the day it happened.

Reuben was the missing link. They'd lost him, and they'd nearly lost their relationship with Adam too when Elizabeth remarried. It had taken a lot of finagling to stay in his life.

She pulled back the quilt on Adam's bed, a Star of Bethlehem pattern in shades of blue, and pulled the hospital corners apart and the sheets off. Next she tackled the pillowcases. She stuffed everything into the hamper, grabbed the used towels out of the upstairs bathroom, and carried everything down the stairs. Once she'd added Ike's and her things, she yelled up the stairs to Joanna that the laundry was all collected. "I'll leave it at the top of the basement stairs."

"All right," Joanna answered. "I'll get it started in a minute."

At noon everyone stopped for lunch except for Joanna. She was outside hanging the wash and insisted they start without her. The day had turned hotter than expected—the sheets and clothes would dry in no time. And the towels soon after. Lu had brought chicken salad and homemade buns. Becky led them in a silent prayer and then, as they started to eat, Rhoda said, "I got the letter, Lu. Why would you ask for an anonymous request when we all know who you were referring to?"

"What are you talking about?" Elaine asked. "What letter?"

Becky shot Rhoda an exasperated look. Thank goodness Joanna wasn't in the house. Becky said, as sweetly as she could, "It's something we discussed at the quilting day you missed." She raised her eyebrows. Becky hadn't wanted Elaine to know about the circle letter at all, but she especially didn't want Mandy and Veronica to know. "We'll fill you in at the next meeting."

Elaine picked up her sandwich. "What's wrong with right now?"

Lu stood. "Oh, I didn't grab the chips!" She stepped to her basket that sat underneath the worktable. "Rhoda, would you mind reaching one of Becky's serving bowls? They're—"

"I know where they are." Rhoda was the tallest of all of them.

Becky turned her attention toward Veronica. "Where are you working now?"

"As a mother's helper for the Byers."

Becky cocked her head. "Which Byer family?"

"The Paul Byers. They have five little ones."

Becky had heard Paul's wife hadn't bounced back after her last pregnancy. She'd had five in seven years.

"Didn't they build a house on Enoch Byer's farm?" That was where Jacob lived.

Veronica's face turned pink. "Jah. A couple of years ago, on the other side of the property."

~

Midway through the afternoon as Becky made coffee to go with the snickerdoodles Lu had brought for their afternoon snack, she heard a buggy roll over the gravel. She stepped to the back door.

"Who is it?" Elaine called out, pulling her cornbread from the oven.

Becky squinted. Was that Mandy? No, she was in the living room dusting. Becky stepped onto the back porch. "Miriam!"

As Miriam waved, steps fell behind Becky. And then Elaine was at her side. "What is *she* doing here?"

Becky said, "I didn't know she was back from Berks County."

"Jah." Elaine didn't sound pleased. "She is."

Becky hoped having Miriam show up wouldn't make things awkward for Joanna, but maybe that was all water under the bridge, especially now.

"Dawdi Daniel told me about the frolic!" Miriam grinned as

she tied the horse—Daniel's—to the hitching post. "Mammi, why wasn't I invited?" Miriam asked in a playful tone. She'd always had a lot of spunk.

Becky studied her. The strip of blond hair in front of her Kapp appeared lighter than before. It was definitely lighter than Mandy's. Perhaps Miriam spent a lot of time outside. She sashayed a little as she walked toward them. She and Mandy were identical twins, but Miriam had always sparkled a bit more than Mandy.

"You're just in time for a snack," Becky said.

"Oh good!" Miriam was coming up the steps now and smiled at Elaine. "Hi, Mammi. I told Dawdi I'd give you and Mandy and Veronica a ride home."

Becky kept an eye on both Elaine and Joanna as they all sat around the table. Elaine seemed uptight, but Joanna appeared to be fine. Lu asked Miriam where she was staying.

"With Mandy." Miriam grinned at her twin. "A least for now."

Joanna shot Mandy a glance, but she just shrugged. It seemed Joanna hadn't known Miriam was staying with Mandy, or maybe even that she was back in Lancaster County.

"Since when?" Apparently Veronica didn't know either.

"Two days ago." Now Miriam was grinning at Veronica. "When did you get so big? You weren't even wearing a Kapp last time I saw you."

Veronica's face grew red. "That's not true."

Becky felt a pang of sympathy for Veronica.

"Dawdi filled me in on Ike," Miriam said, quickly changing the subject as she directed her attention to Becky. "And he said Adam moved back. Does he plan to stay?"

"I hope so," Becky answered. "He's running the business right now."

Elaine gripped her mug with both hands. "Speaking of, I heard Tim was out in his buggy last night with a young lady."

"Who?" Mandy asked.

Veronica squealed a little. "I know!" She glanced around the circle of women. "She's my friend. Wendy Yoder."

"The tiny one with the dark hair? Who's from your district?" Mandy asked.

"Jah," Veronica said. "She's smitten with Tim."

Elaine grinned.

Becky didn't understand Elaine's interest in who might be courting who. It wasn't anyone's business besides the couple's and their family's.

A few minutes later, Joanna stood and said, "Let's get back to work. I'm going to go pull the laundry off the line."

Mandy stood too. "I'll help."

A few minutes later, Becky stepped onto the back porch. Mandy and Joanna seemed to be deep in conversation as they folded the clothes.

The women went home just after five, leaving the house spotless, the beds made, the laundry put away, eight casseroles in the freezer in the shed, Rhoda's stew in the refrigerator, and a pan of lasagna baking in the oven. Becky stood on the front porch and watched Lu and Joanna, the last to leave, walk down the road toward their house.

Loneliness flowed through her like a cold draft in an old house. Becky had stopped by to see Lu nearly every day since Marcus passed away because she was concerned for her best friend. But also because, in some twisted way that she could see now, she felt if she did all she could to help

Lu it wouldn't happen to her. She wouldn't lose Ike like Lu had lost Marcus.

Losing Ike was her worst fear. She'd felt that way since the day she met him and even more so after they married, but it was losing Reuben that intensified the feeling even more. Jah, she had ten younger siblings, nearly a hundred nieces and nephews, and she had no idea how many great nieces and nephews, but Ike was her whole world now. Nee, she *wasn't* supposed to be so dependent on a person. And jah, she *was* dependent on God. She clasped her hands together and then said a prayer that she'd depend on God even more.

Selfishly she'd always hoped she would pass away first. Jah, Ike would miss her, but he wouldn't be lost without her. He'd go on with his life. He'd work too many hours. He wouldn't retire. He'd probably start roofing again. But he wouldn't be without purpose.

She guessed everyone thought the opposite—that Ike would be lost without her, but she wouldn't do okay if she lost him. Not at all.

Joanna and Lu both waved as Nick turned the van toward the house. Adam sat up front. Both Nick and Adam had serious expressions on their faces. Had something happened?

Becky started down the stairs. The cold draft inside became an icy wind. She stumbled a little on the bottom step and then caught herself. Nick stopped the van. His face didn't look as serious as he rolled down his window. "Hallo, Becky. What time do you want to go up to the hospital tomorrow?"

She sighed in relief. "What time works for you?"

"Either before or after church, if that's all right."

"Of course." Sometimes she forgot Englischers had church every week. Becky remembered Nick's church service started at nine thirty and ended at noon. Of course, he'd need to eat afterward. Her heart lurched.

"Before is fine." Nick smiled.

"I'll be ready by eight. I'll plan to stay until midafternoon."

"You can call me when you're ready to come home."

Adam gave Nick a wave and said, "Denki." What would they do without Nick?

Becky waved goodbye to Nick as Adam started up the steps with a file under his arm. He held the door for her, and she stepped into the house first.

Adam followed. "It smells good."

"The ladies left a lasagna baking in the oven." Becky quickly changed the subject. "How was your Dawdi doing when you left?"

"*Gut*. Tired, but he seemed in good spirits." He held up the file. "We went over the Pequea Creek house details. I think he'll have less worries now." Adam led the way through the living room and into the hall. He glanced back at Becky. "He's missing you."

"Did you tell him I'd be back tomorrow?"

"I did." Adam smiled. "That made him happy."

When they reached the kitchen, Adam breathed deeply. "Who made the lasagna?

"Elaine and Veronica." Becky put her hand on the small of her back. She felt extra tired. "Did you know Miriam is back?"

Adam had a puzzled expression on his face. "Mandy's twin?"

"Jah. She came to the frolic."

"How is she?"

"*Gut*, it seems. Much the same."

Adam took a drink of water. "How long until dinner?"

"It's ready now. We can eat as soon as I get everything on the table."

"What can I do to help?"

Jah, Adam was so much like his father and grandfather. If only the right girl would come along. If only that girl was Joanna.

~

After Becky put the food away and Adam finished the dishes, he asked, "Want to go on a walk?" He hung the dish towel on the peg by the sink to dry.

Becky didn't tire very often, however she'd felt weary ever since Ike's heart attack. But she'd probably sleep better if she walked first. She ran her fingers under her eyes. "That's a *gut* idea."

When they reached the road, Adam asked if she wanted to turn right or left.

"Right," she answered. "Let's stop by Lu's. Maybe she and Joanna are out on their porch." More likely, Joanna would be gardening. The girl could not sit still.

As they strolled along, Adam linked his arm through Becky's. Sunset was a couple of hours away and the evening was still hot and muggy without a breeze. When they turned up Lu's lane, Adam called out, "Hallo!"

Joanna's head popped up out of the vegetable section of the garden. She waved. Lu stood on the porch and called out, "Becky, what are you doing? I thought you'd be resting."

"Adam and I are out for a walk. We thought we'd stop by."

"Come sit for a while," Lu said. "I have more snicker-doodles."

Joanna brushed her hands on her apron. "I'll get them, Mammi."

"Nee. Becky and I can. Maybe Adam can help you finish picking the beans."

"Jah, I'd be happy to," he said.

Once they reached the gate, Becky let go of Adam's arm.

"When are you going to see Ike tomorrow?" Lu asked as Becky walked toward her.

"Early."

"Adam," Lu called out. "Joanna and I are going to stop by Daniel and Elaine's in the morning, but we'll be home by noon. Please join us for dinner."

"All right."

Becky turned her head and watched her grandson unlatch the gate and step into the garden. He smiled at Joanna and then asked, "Which row should I start on?"

She pointed to the far one and handed him a bucket. "Denki."

He nodded and began picking.

Becky stepped onto the porch with a smile on her face. Just because Lu asked Adam to Sunday dinner didn't mean she thought Adam and Joanna were a good match. Lu was quieter about these things and not prone to matchmaking, but Becky hoped she thought the two would make a good pair. Becky was praying for it—and she hoped her best friend was too.

18

Rhoda sat at the kitchen table of the cottage she and Hiram had retired to, wishing she was back on the family land with Nehemiah and his family. She had good memories from the farm, but there was so much she'd do over if she could, such as helping her daughter-in-law, Suzanna, more. And she would have encouraged more upgrades to Nehemiah and Suzanna's house too. And a chimney inspection now and then.

She often blamed the end of that time on the fire, but Nehemiah had always been restless. He'd been itching to move, yet Rhoda believed they were safe from his dreaming until he visited a friend who had moved to Maine.

Rhoda pulled the box of stationery she'd purchased at the discount store closer and took off the lid. Here she was living in the township she'd grown up in, without a single offspring still in Lancaster County except for her one granddaughter, Joanna, whom she'd never been particularly close to.

Rhoda had assumed that once she moved back to Strasburg, the two of them would become close. She should have known better. Not once when Joanna lived across the road had Rhoda thought of spending time with just her. Now people talked about "nurturing the young" and "developing relationships," but when Rhoda was growing up there was no such talk. Not once had she thought of who Joanna would be as an adult and what kind of relationship Rhoda wanted to have with her.

Joanna hadn't been an easy child to be around. She was quiet. A bit of a loner. She always had her nose in a book. It wasn't that she was shy or timid. Joanna was as capable as any of her brothers, and more than most. She was always ready to acquire a new skill and focus on a task. Always learning. Always working for the family.

She could prepare an entire supper by the time she was eight. By the time she was nine she could harness a horse to a buggy and run errands for Suzanna. For Rhoda too. She was doing the laundry by the time she was ten. She was tall and lean, like Rhoda, and strong. And she had been from a young age.

But to be honest, Rhoda had always found Joanna a little boring. Rhoda was much more interested in the antics of the two sets of twins. They couldn't walk across the yard without racing each other or wrestling or playing leapfrog. Rhoda smiled at the memory.

She'd always been so proud—so pleased—with all of those strapping grandsons that reminded her so much of her own sons that she'd hardly noticed her granddaughter. She regretted that now.

The cuckoo clock struck nine. Rhoda yawned. Her father had left the cottage to her in his will. She'd rented it out for years but finally decided to move to Strasburg Township after they grew too lonely with Nehemiah and his family gone and farming the land they had left became too taxing for Hiram.

Rhoda took out her favorite pen from her stationery box. She wouldn't write to Becky. She'd write to Elaine. Why shouldn't the bishop's wife be included? And she wouldn't follow Lu's example of keeping the request for Joanna anonymous. Becky, Lu, Elaine, and she had been friends since they were girls. Why the secrecy? Elaine cared about Joanna. Elaine needed to be part of the circle letter too. Becky started the circle letter so they could all share family prayer requests without saying them out loud during their quilting time. Elaine had concerns about her own family. Mandy was childless. Miriam was back in Lancaster County, unmarried. Veronica was old enough to start courting. Caleb had been working for Ike for several years now. Shouldn't he be focusing on his farm instead?

Jah, Elaine needed prayer for her family as much as any of them.

The next morning, Hiram went out to harness the horse and hitch it to the buggy. They planned to do a little visiting, starting at Elaine and Daniel's. Rhoda plucked the envelope addressed to Elaine off the table and slipped it into her apron pocket.

One of the reasons she'd agreed to move back to Strasburg Township was because of her three childhood friends. They'd welcomed her, but it wasn't the same as it had been all those years ago. The three of them had raised their kids together and volunteered at the district school and held frolics and comforted each other in times of sorrow over the years. Rhoda hadn't been a part of any of that, at least not more than making an appearance now and then.

The back door opened and Hiram said, "I'm ready when you are."

"Coming." She grabbed her black bonnet from the hook by the back door and positioned it over her Kapp.

Maybe it would be better if Lu and Joanna weren't at Elaine and Daniel's. That would give Rhoda more of a chance to interact with Elaine. She was more apt to have time for Rhoda than Becky, who was busy with work and now with Ike. And Lu had always had her head in the clouds.

Hiram waited for her by the buggy and offered her his hand. She accepted and climbed up onto the seat. Almost forty-seven years of marriage. They'd met at a livestock auction she'd gone to with her Dat when she was nineteen. It didn't seem that long ago they'd married in her parents' living room.

Rhoda had wanted to move to Maine with Nehemiah and Suzanna and their grandsons, but Hiram said the winters would be too hard on his arthritis. She missed Nehemiah more than she missed her other sons, who were all younger. The other five had left years ago and moved far away. Two to Tennessee. One to Ohio. And the last two to Wisconsin. She'd seen them and their families only a handful of times over the years.

Nehemiah had always been her favorite.

~

When they arrived at Daniel and Elaine's, Hiram jumped down and tied the reins to the hitching post. Then he came around to help Rhoda.

"Looks like Lu is here," Hiram said as they walked behind the other buggies. Rhoda wasn't sure if she hoped Joanna was with her or not. It pained her to see them together. They seemed so natural with each other.

They headed to the back door, which was open to let in the cool morning air. Through the screen, Elaine called out, "Come on in!"

Rhoda patted her apron pocket, wondering if she should give Elaine the letter now or wait until before they left. As she stepped into the kitchen, she saw Lu at the table, sitting next to Daniel. Mandy and Caleb sat on the other side. Rhoda squinted against the light coming through the windows.

"Hallo, Mammi Rhoda. Hallo, Dawdi Hiram."

"Oh, Joanna." Rhoda stepped closer. "I didn't see you there."

Joanna stood. "Sit here. I'll get you each a cup of coffee."

Elaine stepped away from the stove with a platter of doughnuts. "These are fresh." She handed the platter to Daniel, who took one and put it on a napkin. He passed it to Mandy, who did the same.

Joanna returned with full mugs.

"Where's Miriam?" Rhoda asked Mandy as she took the coffee.

"She's visiting a friend." Mandy glanced at Joanna as she spoke.

Rhoda thought that seemed a little odd but didn't say anything. "I thought our frolic at Becky's went well." Rhoda directed her comment at Elaine.

She laughed. "I was just going to say that."

The conversation shifted to another family in their district who needed help. After a while Caleb and Mandy readied to leave, saying they needed to stop by Caleb's grandparents' house in the next district over. His grandmother had been ill.

As Lu and Joanna stood and started saying their goodbyes, a middle-aged man opened the back door. "Hallo, Dat!" He was looking straight at Daniel. He stepped inside. A woman followed him and then Veronica entered. "We brought our girl."

Elaine stood. "You're early."

"Jah. A little bit."

Veronica held a suitcase in her hands. She smiled at her grandmother and then glanced around the room. Her smile faded as her eyes landed on Joanna.

"We were just leaving." Lu stepped toward the man. "It's good to see you, Jonathan."

Jonathan. Elaine's middle child. Veronica was working as a mother's helper for the Paul Byer family, and Rhoda was under the impression that Veronica had been living there. But now she was moving in with her grandparents. Had she left her job?

Interesting that Veronica moved right after Miriam came home from Berks County. There were a lot of changes going on in Elaine's family.

Hiram nudged Rhoda and whispered, "We should get going too." He stood and in a normal voice repeated what he'd just said to her.

Rhoda wasn't ready to go, but she stood anyway. Then she remembered the letter in her apron pocket. Elaine definitely needed to be part of the prayer letter. She pulled it out and extended it toward her friend. "We're doing a circle letter. Becky came up with the idea at our last meeting—the one you missed. It's all explained in the letter."

"Oh." Elaine seemed surprised as she took the letter. "Denki."

Joanna stepped toward the door with a puzzled expression directed toward Lu. Had Lu told Joanna about the circle letter?

Flustered, Rhoda said, "Elaine is part of our group."

Lu smiled in her warm way. "Jah, of course she is."

Rhoda wasn't going to exclude Elaine just because Becky thought she might gossip about Adam. Their way was to include everyone. But maybe they'd excluded Rhoda at different times too for whatever reason. Maybe Becky, who adored Joanna, had figured out how unengaged Rhoda had been in Joanna's life. Maybe Lu had figured out how critical Rhoda had always been of Suzanna. Rhoda's face grew warm.

Becky and Lu had always been the decision makers for their group when they were young. Apparently nothing had changed. They were old now—there was no reason for Becky and Lu to still be in charge.

19

Monday morning, Joanna stepped to the kitchen window at the honk of a horn. Nick stopped the van and Adam jumped down from the bench seat.

"Mammi!" Joanna called out. "They're here."

As Mammi Lu stepped into the room, Joanna asked, "Are you sure you don't want me to come?"

"Jah. We'll have Adam to help us at the hospital. You should go to work."

"All right. I'll walk you out." Joanna dried her hands on her apron. "Do you have money for lunch?"

Mammi smiled sweetly. "Jah. I do."

As they walked down the back steps, Adam started toward them. When he reached Joanna he held out the cell phone. "You should take this. I'll call from a hospital phone with an update on Dawdi."

"Denki." Joanna took it.

"Could you check on the one-story house on Garden Lane sometime today?"

"Why?"

"If they're not making enough progress," Adam said, "I'll need to work with them tomorrow."

"I can do that. I'll go in Mammi's buggy after they've had a chance to start."

"Denki."

Mammi Lu said to Joanna, "Make sure and remember to eat today."

"I will."

"And pray for Ike when you can."

"Of course," Joanna answered. "I'll be praying for all of you."

"Denki," Adam said.

Mammi Lu kept walking, so Joanna lowered her voice and asked Adam, "How is your Mammi doing?"

"All right, I think."

At the van, Joanna said hello to Nick. He gave her a wave through the open driver's window. She walked around the front to the passenger window. Becky lowered it and reached out her hand. Joanna took it. "I'll be praying for Ike. For you too."

"Denki." Becky's face was drawn.

Mammi Lu stepped to the side door, but Adam opened it before she could. Joanna felt unsettled about Ike's heart attack and Becky's fear. What if something happened to Mammi Lu? What would Joanna do? Adam gave Mammi Lu a hand as she climbed up into the van.

Joanna slipped the cell phone into her apron pocket and walked with Adam to the other side of the van. Before he could open it, she said, "Take good care of them."

"I will."

He'd been so attentive to Mammi Lu at dinner the day

before, asking her questions about her land that she currently leased out to an Amish farmer. The property had been in Mammi's family for over a hundred years—Dawdi Marcus had farmed it until ten years ago. Joanna hadn't known until yesterday that Becky and Ike had worked hard and saved every penny they could to be able to buy their acreage from Mammi Lu and Dawdi Marcus a few years after they all married. Becky and Ike had built the warehouse after their business took off.

After Nick pulled the van around and headed for the highway, Joanna took the back steps two at a time and hurried back into the kitchen. She glanced at the clock above the door. *6:15*. She had time to make the bouquets and place them in the flower shed and do the laundry. Again, her thoughts fell on Jacob. And this time on Miriam too.

On Saturday as they'd taken the wash off Becky's line, Mandy had apologized for not telling Joanna that Miriam had moved in with her and Caleb. "It's temporary," Mandy had said. "Just until she finds somewhere else." Miriam and Mandy's parents had moved to York County a couple of years ago.

Joanna assured Mandy she didn't need to apologize about anything. That Miriam had dated Jacob before he and Joanna dated didn't mean Joanna held any ill will toward Miriam. Joanna hoped Mandy understood that. Joanna wished Miriam all the best.

~

Once she had the horse harnessed and hitched, Joanna sat in the buggy and called the chimney inspector Ike worked with and scheduled an appointment for the Pequea Creek house. As she turned onto the highway, she planned out the rest of her day. She'd spend a short time in the office, go to the Garden Lane house, and then clean the apartment.

In just a few minutes she arrived at the warehouse. The coffee maker was the way she'd left it on Saturday. *Clean.* No surprise that no one on the team had made coffee that morning. It seemed to be exclusively her job. She took the percolator from the burner and moved to the sink.

That's when she saw the envelope with *Joanna* written in cursive on the front. At first she suspected it was a note from Becky, but the handwriting was better than hers, which seemed to grow shakier each year. Joanna put the kettle on the counter, picked up the envelope, and opened it. Inside was a piece of lined paper with a short note, including a verse from Isaiah. *Fear not; I will help thee.* Even if the handwriting wasn't Becky's, she wouldn't have written it. She was the one facing her husband's heart surgery. She was the one who needed not to be fearful.

Who would have written the note? Her heart skipped a beat. It was signed *Someone Who Cares.* It wouldn't be Caleb. For a minute she thought Mandy might have sent the letter with Caleb, but it wasn't Mandy's handwriting.

Adam wouldn't have written it. First of all, his handwriting was nearly impossible to read. Second of all, he wouldn't even commit to being her friend. Why would he write her a note of encouragement? She reread the letter and wrinkled her nose. The paper was the generic lined type, and the envelope was business size. Both were common.

Surely Jacob hadn't written it. That would be creepy. Why would he break up with her and then encourage her?

She slipped the note back into the envelope and shoved it into her apron pocket.

After she started the coffee, she sat at Becky's desk. As she tended to her recordkeeping, she glanced at the cell phone. No call from Adam, but they expected the surgery would take several hours. When she finished her work, she filled her travel mug and a thermos with coffee and then decided to stop by the bakery. She'd pick up pastries for Tim, Caleb, and Jacob.

When she arrived at the Garden Lane house twenty minutes later, Caleb was in the driveway using the table saw. The horse sidestepped, and Joanna pulled around by the shed. The wagon was parked off to the side, closer to the house. It was half filled with supplies. She came around to the front of the house carrying the pastries and coffee. Caleb stopped the saw. "Break time," she said.

He grinned. "Denki."

"Where are the other two?"

"Working down the hall." Caleb took off his goggles. "How is Ike?"

"I haven't heard anything," she answered. "I'm thinking no news is good news."

Caleb agreed.

As Joanna stepped through the front door, she heard voices. "Hallo!" She used as cheery a voice as she could muster.

Tim stepped out of a room down the hall. "Joanna, what are you doing here?" He grinned. Maybe he wrote the note.

She held up the thermos of coffee and the box of pastries. "I brought snacks."

Tim turned toward the doorway. "Jacob, Joanna brought coffee. That should wake you up."

She couldn't hear Jacob's response but continued to the table. Tim joined her a minute later. She poured him a cup of coffee while he opened the pastry box.

"How's it going?" She kept her voice low.

"Did Adam send you to check on us?"

She whispered, "Something like that."

Tim took a bite of a hand pie. "All right. We're almost done with the bathrooms. Then we'll focus entirely on the kitchen."

Tim asked about Ike too, and Joanna gave him the same answer she'd given Caleb. Jacob kept working, but Caleb came inside and joined them. "Show me what you're doing today so I can tell Adam," Joanna said to Caleb when they'd finished their snack.

Caleb showed her the first bath. "We just need to install the vanity and sink and hook up the plumbing." He led the way through the primary bedroom and toward another bathroom. "You can see for yourself what needs to be done."

Joanna stepped to the doorway. The team had painted the walls and installed the flooring, tub, and toilet. But that wasn't what Joanna couldn't help staring at—she couldn't take her eyes off Jacob sitting on the edge of the tub, his head in his hands.

"Are you all right?" she asked.

"Jah." He didn't raise his head. "I'm fine."

"Do you want some coffee?"

He shook his head, making his hands go back and forth too.

Joanna sensed she should turn around and leave but instead she took the envelope from her pocket. "Did you write this?"

He raised his head a little. "I don't know what that is." He dropped his head back in his hands and muttered, "Tell Adam we're doing fine. He doesn't need to worry."

Although she was puzzled by Jacob's behavior, Joanna tried to focus on driving the buggy through the tourist traffic on the way back to the warehouse. He'd been moody at times while they'd been courting but nothing like how he was acting today. Weird that he'd broken up with her, but he was the one who was acting despondent.

The other thing that seemed strange was that Veronica's Dat moved her from the Paul Byers' place to Elaine and Daniel's house. Joanna couldn't help but wonder if it had something to do with Jacob living next door. Of course, she wouldn't say anything to anyone. She wouldn't even ask Mandy about it. But it seemed odd.

As she neared the warehouse, Joanna feared she'd missed a call from Adam and fumbled the cell phone from her pocket. No calls. Was that a good sign or a bad sign? She took care of the horse, made herself a sandwich, took two bites, choked on the third, and went up to the apartment to start cleaning. When she was halfway through stripping the bed, the cell phone rang. It was Adam. After they said hello she asked, "How is your Dawdi?"

"He's in recovery, and Mammi is with him now. The surgeon did a quadruple bypass as expected. Everything went well."

A wave of relief swept through Joanna as she said, "What good news."

Adam let out a long sigh and changed the topic. His voice wavered a little as he asked, "How's work?"

"That was a quick transition." She continued to strip the bed.

"Sorry."

"It's fine. Things seem to be going well. The team is making good progress on the Garden Lane house." She wouldn't tell him about Jacob.

"Good to hear. It seems Mammi and Dawdi have finalized everything for the purchase of the Pequea Creek house. Apparently they have a foolproof system when it comes to buying houses."

Joanna was sure the system was called "cash," but she wouldn't say that. She started to gather the dirty towels.

"They want us to get started on the renovations right away. Dawdi approved all of our measurements and plans on Saturday. I'll submit everything to the draftsman they use tomorrow and apply for permits. Mammi said she'd like us to order what we'll need by Friday."

"What we'll need?" Joanna dropped the towels on top of the sheets and headed into the kitchen. "We'll need everything. She thinks we can complete a list by then?"

"Apparently."

"What about the demo work?"

"They'll pull Tim and Caleb over to help."

But not Jacob.

Adam said, "We can talk tomorrow."

"All right." Joanna gathered up the kitchen towels and dish cloths. "What time do you think you'll start home?"

"Mammi and Lu both seem tired, and Dawdi will be in the ICU overnight. So soon, once Nick gets here."

A wave of relief swept over Joanna. The sooner Mammi Lu was home the better she'd feel. "Becky and you should come over for dinner."

"I have a better idea," he said. "We have a pot of beef stew in the fridge for tonight." Joanna knew it was Mammi Rhoda's stew, one of her best dishes. "You and Lu should come to our house."

"All right. Do you still have the cornbread Elaine made?"

"Jah," Adam said. "We haven't touched it. We should use it tonight."

"I'll get your chores done on my way home." Joanna liked the idea of all of them eating together.

After she said goodbye and ended the call, she gathered up all the linens and headed downstairs to get the load started in the wringer washing machine. By the time she cleaned the kitchen and bathroom in the apartment, it would be time to put the laundry through the wringer and then hang it on the line. That would give her time to start a list of what they needed for the Pequea Creek house. She'd make the beds and hang the towels in the apartment in the morning.

Keeping busy kept her mind off Ike's health—and Jacob. And to be honest, Adam too.

20

As he led Mammi Becky, Joanna, and Lu in a longer silent prayer than usual as they all sat around the table, the smell of the beef stew kept distracting Adam. His mouth watered as he focused back on his prayers. They all had a lot to be thankful for, mainly that Dawdi had come through the surgery.

A knock on the door startled Adam. He cleared his throat to end the prayer and then stood. Both back doors were open in hopes of inviting the evening breeze into the sweltering house. Daniel stood behind the screen to the kitchen.

Adam strode toward it as he called out, "Come in." He opened the door.

"I won't intrude on your dinner." Daniel glanced down at his boots. "Besides, I don't want to track dirt into the house." He held up his hand and said, "Hallo Becky. Lu. Joanna."

They all responded.

Daniel said to Adam, "I wanted to check about Ike."

Adam quickly gave him the good news.

"Wunderbar." Daniel smiled faintly. "That's good to hear."

He turned a little and said, “One more thing. I was wondering if I might speak with Joanna. In private.”

With a puzzled expression on his face, Adam turned toward the table. “Joanna, Daniel would like to speak with you.”

She wrinkled her brow.

Adam shrugged.

She stood. “All right.”

As she reached the door, Daniel said, “I’m sorry to interrupt your dinner, but could we take a little walk? I need to ask you a few questions about Jacob.”

“Sure.” They both stepped out the back door.

Becky handed Adam a bowl of stew. “Why would he need to ask her about Jacob?”

Lu shook her head. “I have no idea, but I wonder if it has anything to do with Veronica.”

“Veronica?” Becky asked.

“She’s staying at Daniel and Elaine’s now. Joanna said Jacob gave her a ride home after the singing Sunday before last.”

Adam didn’t confirm that had happened even though he’d been there. The less he said the better.

Becky, after taking a piece, passed the cornbread to Lu. “How old is she? Sixteen? Seventeen?”

Lu said, “I think she just turned eighteen—or will soon.”

Becky spread butter on her cornbread. “Do you think Jacob is interested in Veronica?”

“It seems awfully soon if he is,” Lu answered.

“It’s a good thing we didn’t include Elaine in the circle letter.”

Adam asked, “What circle letter?” as Lu said, “About that.”

Becky ignored Adam. “What about it?”

“Rhoda did include Elaine,” Lu said. “She gave her the

letter yesterday when Joanna and I stopped by their house in the morning. Jonathan and his wife arrived with Veronica just as we were ready to leave."

Becky wrinkled her nose. "You're kidding."

"Nee."

"After we told Rhoda we wanted it to be just the three of us?"

"Why did you want it to be just the three of you?" Adam asked as he slid a piece of cornbread onto his plate.

Again Mammi Becky ignored him. "Well, including Elaine certainly complicates things, doesn't it?"

Lu nodded. "We shouldn't have excluded Elaine in the first place."

Becky shook her head. "Of course we should have."

Adam concentrated on eating, a little disturbed his grandmother was sounding like a schoolgirl. A mean one. No doubt she had a good reason. But he couldn't understand why she, Lu, and Rhoda needed a circle letter in the first place. They saw each other all the time.

Adam took a bite of stew. And then another. "Wow, this is the best stew I've had. Don't tell my Mamm." His face grew warm and then he asked Mammi Becky, "Have I had your stew before?"

"Jah. When you were little." Becky swirled her spoon around in the bowl. "But it was Rhoda's recipe—and not actually as good as this batch, which she made on Saturday." Becky lowered her voice. "I think she left out a secret ingredient in the recipe she shared."

Lu laughed. "No doubt."

Adam took a bit of the cornbread. "Elaine must have a secret ingredient for this too. It's delicious."

This time it was Lu who dropped her voice. "Sour cream—it *was* a secret. Elaine wrote down Greek yogurt when she shared the recipe, but we figured it out."

Adam laughed.

The screen door opened, and Joanna stepped into the kitchen.

Adam stood.

Mammi Becky said, "That was a short walk."

Joanna sat at her place without responding.

Adam sat back down too.

"Are you all right?" Lu's voice was full of concern.

"Jah. He wanted to know why Jacob broke up with me." Joanna picked up her fork.

Lu asked, "What did you tell him?"

"The truth. I don't know."

Adam's heart constricted. He hoped Joanna had seen his note. He'd write another one tonight and sneak over and leave it for her on the coffee counter so she'd see it in the morning.

~

The next morning, Adam worked at Dawdi Ike's desk. From the doorway to the office, Joanna said, "I started a list of what we'll need for the Pequea Creek house. Did you see it?"

He held up the legal pad. "I did. Denki."

"I'll be right back after I start the coffee."

Adam held up his mug. "I already made it."

She turned, sniffed, and faced Adam. "You did." She smiled. "I'll go get a cup."

He followed her and stopped where he could see her at

the counter. She picked up the envelope. Instead of opening it she turned toward him. "Did you write this? And the one from yesterday?"

He panicked. Why would she think he wrote it? "That handwriting is too nice to be mine."

"Jah, I agree." She held the front of the envelope toward him. "But I need to know, did you write the letters?"

"Nee." Why had he thought Joanna would just read the letters and be encouraged without wanting to know who wrote them? Of course she would want to know.

She put the envelope in her apron pocket. "Who did?"

He shrugged.

"Caleb wouldn't. I don't think Tim would." She rubbed her arm. "I can't imagine why Jacob would, but I'm running out of suspects."

He cringed and then hoped she didn't notice. He was guilty. Of what? Trying to encourage her? "Let me know if you figure it out."

"I will." Joanna's brow furrowed as she placed her hand over her apron pocket.

She kept busy with the apartment upstairs and then going to the rental house while Adam went over the list and added to it, all the while chastising himself for lying to Joanna. That was worse than declaring when he first met her that they couldn't be friends.

That evening, Mammi announced Dawdi was out of the ICU and back in the cardiac unit. "He should be home within a week," she said. "But the doctor said he can't return to work for six weeks." They wouldn't be done with the Pequea Creek project by then.

Adam spent Wednesday morning at the Garden Lane house

working with Tim, Caleb, and Jacob, trying to get done as much as possible so they could help with the demo at the Pequea Creek house. Wednesday afternoon he and Joanna sat at Dawdi Ike's desk. Joanna had a library book about Federalist-style houses in Pennsylvania and a couple of magazine articles with renovation advice.

Joanna said, "I had the chimney inspected this morning. There are a few repairs that need to be made—they'll be done by early next week."

Adam jotted down that note as he said, "There's some repair work that needs to be done on the woodwork."

"Jah, I noticed it's not just the banister too. The floorboards, mainly, need work." Joanna twirled the pencil in her hand. "The challenge is going to be keeping the integrity of the house while staying on budget, especially with all the work needed on the barn."

Adam agreed. He was beginning to think it would be an impossible task.

On Thursday morning, Mammi Becky didn't go to the hospital. She walked to the warehouse with Adam and the two sat in the office while Joanna made coffee.

"This project is really going to be a lot," he said.

"We have confidence in you."

Joanna came into the office carrying three cups of coffee and interrupted their conversation.

Mammi Becky took her cup and gave Joanna a sweet smile. "Denki."

The three went over the list and other concerns about renovating a two-hundred-year-old home. Joanna shared what she'd found at the library and opened the book, but

Mammi Becky seemed to be having a hard time concentrating.

Joanna asked her, "What do you think of stainless steel appliances?"

"Jah, I think that would be appropriate for the house." Mammi Becky yawned and pushed back her chair. "I'm going to go home and nap."

"Oh." Besides their Sunday afternoon naps, Adam hadn't known either of his grandparents to sleep during the day. Here it was still morning, and Mammi was tired. The week of being at the hospital had worn her out. Adam told her, "Don't worry about dinner. I took a casserole out of the freezer. I'll bake it when I get home."

"Denki." Mammi put her notebook in her bag. "You're doing great work. I have confidence in both of you."

"That means a lot." Joanna reached into her apron pocket and took out the envelope from yesterday. "I need to ask you something before you leave."

Adam's hand jerked involuntarily, causing his pen to fall to the floor. As he reached down for it, Joanna opened the envelope and handed the letter to Mammi Becky. "Who do you think sent this to me? I received one Monday and then again on Tuesday."

Mammi read the letter and then slipped it back into the envelope. She chuckled and then said, "The handwriting is too good for anyone that works here, except for you, Joanna."

"Jah." Joanna laughed. "I thought that too."

"It's probably from one of the ladies in the district."

"But how would she get it into the warehouse?"

"She could have asked someone else to deliver it," Mammi said. "Tim would be my guess."

"I hadn't thought of that."

Mammi Becky handed the envelope back to Joanna. "Isn't it nice to know someone is praying for you?"

"I suppose." Joanna slipped the letter into her apron. "You don't think I should be worried?"

"Of course not. Maybe it's from your Mammi Rhoda. Or Elaine—she could have given it to Caleb to deliver."

Joanna didn't exactly seem satisfied with Becky's answer, but she did seem less worried. "Denki," she said. "That makes me feel better."

It made Adam feel better too. Mammi Becky wasn't suspicious that it was him, and Joanna didn't seem to be either. After Mammi left, Joanna said in a quiet voice, "This project frightens me."

Adam sank back in Dawdi Ike's chair. "I didn't think anything scared you."

A confused expression passed over her face. "Why would you say that?"

"You're always in control. You always have a plan."

She exhaled. "Exactly. Because all sorts of things frighten me."

"Oh." That made sense. He leaned closer. "Honestly, this project scares me too."

"We're going to go order thousands and thousands of dollars' worth of appliances and fixtures and vanities and cabinets and counters and tile and everything else." Joanna slumped a little. "This project, more than any we've ever done, requires both Ike and Becky, and yet neither is available."

"Which means we have to make this work." Adam didn't feel as confident as he sounded—as he hoped he sounded. "They're trusting us."

"Jah." Joanna laughed. "That scares me even more."

Adam smiled. "Me too."

They continued going through the list, discussing each item and referencing the books and other information Joanna had from the library. In the midafternoon, Adam told Joanna she should go home. "Go see how your Mammi is doing. She must be tired too."

"Denki." Joanna stood. "I was thinking I should check on her." As she stood Joanna smiled, which lit up her eyes. "At least we'll have each other to commiserate with as we work on the house—and figure out solutions."

Adam returned the smile. "Jah. That gives me hope."

"Me too," she answered.

After she left, Adam walked around the warehouse. Even though he felt unsettled about his grandparents and the upcoming renovation project, he'd felt a sense of harmony working with Joanna. Jah, he'd court Joanna in a minute if she'd have him. But in the meantime, he'd rather be her friend—even if he wouldn't admit it to her—than lose her altogether.

And he would keep writing her letters, masquerading as a kind older woman in their district.

21

The next morning, once Joanna reached the coffee counter, she froze. There was another letter, the third in five days.

She glanced toward the warehouse door and then snatched it up quickly. After slipping it into her pocket, she poked her head into the work area. The warehouse door was locked when she arrived. But perhaps Caleb or Tim had delivered the letter yesterday afternoon. She'd left before they'd arrived back from the Garden Lane house.

She started a pot of coffee and retreated to Becky's desk.

This time the verse was from Joshua. *Be strong and of a good courage; be not afraid, neither be thou dismayed: for the Lord thy God is with thee withersoever thou goest.*

Again, the writer had signed it *Someone Who Cares.*

Be not afraid. That was certainly timely. It was sweet to think that perhaps another older woman in the district—besides Mammi Lu and Becky—cared about her. The thought that it might be Mammi Rhoda unsettled Joanna. They'd never been close, and Joanna wasn't sure that she'd ever seen her paternal grandmother's handwriting. She knew she wouldn't recognize it if she had, but Joanna hoped that Mammi Rhoda would reach out to her in person, not in secret, if she felt led to. Then again, a secret connection was better than none. Perhaps the move to Strasburg Township had made Mammi Rhoda more caring. Joanna doubted the transition had been easy for her.

She considered writing Someone Who Cares back but then decided against it. She wanted to know who she was writing to first.

A few minutes later she heard voices in the warehouse. Caleb's and Tim's and a third one soon after. *Jacob's*. Why did his voice still make her heart race? And make her sick to her stomach at the same time?

She still felt unsettled about Daniel's conversation with her earlier in the week. He'd seemed sure she should have an answer for him. Jacob had broken up with her. He'd said they wouldn't be getting back together this time. That had been it. Why did Daniel care? Unless there really was something going on between Veronica and Jacob. That made her feel even more unsettled. Not just because of her pride, but out of worry for Veronica. She was too young for a relationship with Jacob—Mandy mentioned she'd turned eighteen the week before.

She stepped to the office door just as Adam and Becky walked into the warehouse. She couldn't see Jacob.

After Becky said hello she said, "I have a few things I need to see to. Then Nick is going to take me to the hospital. Yesterday the doctor thought Ike would spend the weekend, but the nurse called this morning and said he's going to be discharged by this afternoon."

Surprised, Joanna asked, "Today?"

"Jah." Becky seemed surprised too.

She and Adam stepped into the office, and Joanna headed to the coffee counter with her mug. As she refilled it, Jacob stepped out of the work area.

She didn't speak to him.

"Is there coffee?" he asked.

Joanna pointed at the percolator on the stovetop.

"Denki."

She wanted to say, *"I didn't make it for you"* but bit her tongue, literally, instead. But then she thought of him with his head in his hands, sitting on the edge of the tub at the Garden Lane house. And of—someone—reaching out to her in kindness. Mammi Lu sometimes said, "It's better to give others a piece of your heart than a piece of your mind." That's what Jesus would do.

As Joanna asked, "How are you doing?" Jacob asked, "Are you doing okay?"

Her heart swelled a little and she answered, "I'm all right." At the same time, he said, "Not very well."

Her heart lurched.

Caleb called out, "Jacob! We need to get going."

Jacob reached for a mug and then began pouring the coffee. Caleb called out for him again, adding, "Come on!"

Jacob headed toward the door, sloshing coffee over the rim of the mug. He stopped and took a drink and then kept going. She hoped he didn't spill any in the van. That would not make Becky happy.

Adam came out of the office. "Everything okay?"

She nodded.

Adam smiled. "*Gut*. I heard Jacob's voice—was he treating you all right?"

"Jah." She stood up straight. "He was fine."

Adam grabbed two mugs from the cupboard. "Come back into the office—Mammi's going over our list. I appreciate you copying it." He grinned. "She can actually read my contributions now."

Joanna led the way, feeling a little shaky after her encounter with Jacob. On one hand, he'd asked how she was doing. But on the other, he was acting strangely. Did he expect her to feel sorry for him? She'd avoid him as much as possible from now on, although it would be impossible once they all started working on the Pequea Creek house.

~

Joanna continued to feel unsettled as she helped Adam double-check the list with occasional comments from Becky. What if Jacob, and not Mammi Rhoda or another lady in the district, had written the letters to her? She wouldn't take him back again, she was certain of that.

No, he hadn't written the letters. He wouldn't have been capable of it six months ago, let alone now. But she would like to know what was going on with him.

An hour later, Nick dropped Adam and Joanna off at the Pequea Creek house before taking Becky to the hospital. He planned to bring both Ike and Becky home later in the day.

Joanna and Adam confirmed measurements from the draftsman's changes, talked through the needed building materials one last time, measured the veranda, and then confirmed each detail on their list. Two hours later, Nick picked them up and took them to order the building materials in Lancaster.

From there, they took the city bus to the cabinet shop, and after they completed their order they walked to the appliance store. When they finished, Adam suggested they get lunch, a late one since it was already close to three o'clock. Joanna wasn't hungry, but she knew Adam needed to eat. They walked next door to a sandwich shop. She picked at a chicken salad while Adam devoured a tuna melt on rye.

She stared out the window thinking about Jacob. Was he conflicted over something? He'd taken Veronica home, but that didn't necessarily mean anything.

Adam said something.

She answered, "Pardon?" But then it registered he'd asked if she was all right. Her face grew warm and most likely red. "I'm fine, really." She dipped a piece of cucumber in the ranch dressing.

"Not hungry?"

"Not really." She nodded toward the company cell phone Adam had placed on the table. "You should probably text Nick. Maybe he can pick us up before he goes back to the hospital."

"Good idea." Adam sent a text. Then he took the last bite of his sandwich and started in on his potato chips. "Want one?"

"No, thank you." Joanna dipped a piece of lettuce in the salad dressing.

"It's going to take a long time for you to finish your salad that way."

She pushed it toward him. "Do you want some?"

Instead of answering, he said, "I'm worried about you."

Her face grew even warmer.

"What did Jacob want today?"

She speared another piece of lettuce. "Nothing."

"Joanna, you might not believe I have your best interests

in mind, but I do." His voice dropped a little. "At least I think I do."

In the past couple of weeks, he'd become her closest friend—even though he denied being her friend at all. Besides Mammi Lu, Adam seemed to be the person she could depend on most. She cared about what he thought.

Adam leaned toward her. "Let Jacob go."

She said, "I have." But her eyes grew teary. Perhaps the breakup was finally registering. It was a big loss, not just of Jacob but of all her dreams for her future too. She'd been so determined to be brave that, perhaps, she hadn't let herself grieve. That wasn't good either.

"I know you're hurt, but he's not right for you."

She bristled. "I know. We're not getting back together."

"I'm happy to hear that." He sighed and sat up straight. He seemed genuinely relieved. "Because Jacob wouldn't have broken up with you twice if he was the right man for you."

Adam's words stung. But why was she feeling defensive? She didn't want Jacob back, right? She put her fork on her plate and her napkin on top.

"Wait." Adam reached for her plate. "If you're really not going to eat that, I will."

She took her napkin off the salad and scooted the plate toward him.

~

Helping Ike and Becky check out of the hospital distracted Joanna from thinking about Jacob and the anonymous letters. She packed Ike's things, collected all of the paperwork, and used the cell phone to coordinate Nick driving to the pickup area right before they started down.

By the time Nick helped Ike into the front seat, the patient appeared to be exhausted. Adam climbed into the back. Joanna was the last one in the van and hesitated for a moment, not sure if she should sit with Becky or Adam. She decided on Becky. The last thing she wanted was for Adam to bring up Jacob again. She also didn't want to remember sitting with him in the very same van in the very same seat three years ago.

No one talked on the way home. Joanna guessed Ike had fallen asleep.

Nick slowed down when they reached Strasburg and stopped at the red light by the creamery. Joanna glanced to the left. Was that Jacob seated at an outside table? She turned her head to get a better view. Jah, it was. And Veronica sat across from him. Becky made a funny noise. She'd seen them too. So had Adam. Joanna quickly looked straight ahead.

Adam leaned forward and put his hand on her shoulder. She ignored him. Becky's head turned a few times, most likely from watching Jacob to watching Joanna.

A few minutes later, Nick turned into Mammi Lu's driveway. Joanna asked Adam if he'd taken a casserole out for dinner.

"We have leftovers from last night. Denki for asking." His voice was kind—too kind. It made her want to cry.

Joanna's eyelids felt scratchy again even though she hadn't been crying. Adam cared.

"Come over and check in with me in the morning," Becky said as Joanna opened the van door. "See what we need. Bring Lu."

"All right." Joanna jumped down and turned to close the door, holding back her tears. She met Adam's gaze for a brief minute. He was right about Jacob, of course. She called out goodbye to Ike and Nick. Then she turned toward the house, swallowing her tears. She didn't want Mammi Lu to ask her what was wrong. There was no reason to share her awkward interaction with Jacob from earlier or what she'd just seen. Jacob taking Veronica home from the singing could have been an act of kindness, but taking her to the creamery meant something more.

She thought of the first time Jacob had taken her to the creamery. How he'd opened up about his father leaving his family. How he'd smiled so genuinely she could feel it in her soul—or so she thought. Maybe she'd felt it somewhere else. He'd charmed her with his talk of how thankful he was to be living in Lancaster County and how he never wanted to live anywhere else. Of how God had led him to live with his uncle. Of how he knew God had a purpose for him in Strasburg Township.

She'd been so sure that purpose was her.

That evening Joanna kept working in the garden even after Mammi Lu had gone into the house to read before going to bed.

She began weeding, pulling the hoe between rows of zinnias. She still had ten minutes or so before the sun set—and then she could pull out her head lamp or go into the house alone and think more about Jacob.

She fought back tears as she heard the whistling. She stepped to the gate as Adam turned the corner to the tune of "You Are My Sunshine." What a fitting song for the setting sun. She hummed along.

You'll never know, dear, how much I love you.
Please don't take my sunshine away.

She couldn't remember the verses.

Joanna called out, "How is Ike doing?"

"*Gut*," Adam said. "He's sleeping, propped up on the couch in the living room. Mammi put a cot next to the couch so can she sleep close to him."

Joanna's heart swelled. Of all the couples she knew, she hoped for a marriage like Becky and Ike's the most.

"How are you?" Adam asked.

She pulled one glove off and rubbed her temple.

"Not so good?"

She tried to smile. "I didn't want him to move on so quickly." Was that her pride speaking? "It's not that I want him back."

Adam gave her a nod.

Obviously the letters weren't from Jacob, which she'd known. Becky was right—they were from some older woman she knew. She'd go back to thinking they were from Mammi Rhoda. Joanna swiped at her eyes. "Would you like a glass of lemonade?"

"Do you feel up to it?"

"Jah." She put her hoe against the gate.

He sat in Dawdi Marcus's rocking chair, and when she returned she handed him his lemonade, put a plate of oatmeal-and-butterscotch cookies down on the table, and sat in Mammi's chair.

Adam took a cookie. "Did you know butterscotch is my favorite?"

"Nee," Joanna answered.

He took a bite and then said, "That's because you've never gone out to ice cream with me."

Joanna laughed.

The sun set and the lightning bugs glimmered at the edge of the woods. A buggy went by, but Joanna didn't turn toward the road. It wasn't Ike and Becky. If it was Jacob, he most likely had Veronica with him.

For once, Adam didn't talk, which Joanna appreciated. She felt calmer sitting with him than she had working in the garden. Adam ate another cookie.

After a while, she said, "You should go home in case your grandfather needs you."

Adam drained his lemonade. "I'll see you tomorrow."

"Jah," she answered. "See you then."

22

Becky heard Adam come through the back door and stop at the doorway to the living room, where she and Ike lay. He was checking on Ike.

She hoped Adam had been over to see Joanna. She thought of the conversation she'd heard in the van on the way home from Noah and Emily's wedding three years ago, of Adam confessing his interest in Joanna after he'd only just met her. She'd wanted to turn around and tell him to stop, but of course she hadn't.

Ike had told her the night they met he'd wanted to marry her, but Becky had been a very different girl.

Joanna, after losing her childhood home to fire and then her family to Maine just just after that, wasn't ready for some boy she barely knew to rush her. Jah, Joanna had been interested in Jacob right away, according to Lu, but they didn't start courting for another seven months.

Becky mentally shook her head. *Ach, Adam. You should have waited a couple of months. At least a couple of weeks. It would have saved everyone a lot of worry.*

Under the blanket, something brushed against Becky's thigh. Her eyes flew open. By the moonlight coming through the living room window, she could see Ike's arm was stretched over the space between the couch and her cot. Tears stung as she took his hand. Every night for the last nearly forty-seven years, they'd gone to sleep holding hands. After he squeezed her hand three times, she let go, climbed out of her cot, pushed it flush against the couch, climbed back in, and reached for Ike's hand, squeezing it in return.

The next morning, Adam helped Ike dress, and then after breakfast they all took a little walk around the yard. Once they had Ike back on the couch and propped up with pillows, Adam went to the warehouse to work for a few hours.

Becky sat at the kitchen table putting Ike's medications into his pillbox. She yawned and stretched her back, trying to work out the kinks from sleeping on the cot, and then double-checked the meds. One for high blood pressure. A blood thinner. And a pain medication. Ike hated taking anything, but no doubt he'd be taking the first two for quite a while, if not for the rest of his life. The doctor said because of the surgery he could live another twenty years easily.

She shivered even though the house was warm already.

She was worried about Ike and the business and Adam and whether they could make payroll. They had a bid on the farmhouse that they'd accepted. Even if everything worked out, the money wouldn't come through for six weeks or so. And they were sinking a lot of money into the Pequea Creek house.

As she put the medication back in the cupboard, there was a quick knock on the door before it flew open. Lu smiled and lifted a loaf of bread in one hand and a basket in the other. Joanna stood behind her with a box.

Becky clapped her hands. "Wunderbar! Come in." She rose and hurried to take the bread and the basket filled with muffins from Lu. Company was just what she needed.

Joanna lifted the box. "We brought a hamburger casserole for your dinner."

"Denki," Becky said. "Ike's asleep. Do you have time for a muffin and a cup of coffee?" She desperately needed some company.

"Jah." Lu glanced at Joanna, who nodded.

"I'm not working today," Joanna said. "Unless you think I should."

"Nee." Becky turned to fill the kettle, but Joanna already had it in her hand. "There's not anything pressing for you to do."

Lu put muffins on a plate. Joanna made the coffee in Becky's big French press and then grabbed three cups out of the cupboard. Becky watched Joanna carefully. She seemed comfortable with every task she did, no matter how small or big, whether menial or creative.

Becky thought of Reuben and when he first brought Elizabeth home. She was young—just nineteen—and quiet as could be. Joanna was quiet too, but confident. Except when it came to Jacob. Becky could feel her pain the day before when they'd all seen Jacob and Veronica at the creamery.

"Becky?" Lu was staring at her.

"Sorry."

"Are you feeling all right?"

"Jah. Why?"

"You aren't looking like your wonderful *gut* self today."

Becky tried to laugh but it came out as a gasp.

"You look tired." Lu put a muffin on a plate.

Becky took a deep breath and then exhaled. "I slept on an old cot by Ike last night is all. He was on the couch." Becky rubbed her neck.

Lu pushed the plate toward her. "They're blueberry and lemon. Joanna made them this morning."

Of course Joanna had. She was so productive. Working full-time for Becky and Ike. Gardening. Helping Lu with the house. Doing the laundry and a good portion of the cooking and cleaning.

Jacob was a fool, thank the Lord. Hopefully he would continue to be. That was her prayer.

Lu asked quietly, "So how is Ike doing?"

Becky said he was as well as could be expected. "Honestly, the doctor is pleased with his progress. Hopefully we can move into our bedroom soon. I think the bed is too high for him, but he thinks he'll be fine."

"Of course he does." Lu shook her head. "What *can* he do?"

"Go on little walks." Becky paused a moment. "He can't work or drive a buggy for six weeks. He can start doing chores in a couple of weeks as long as he doesn't lift more than fifteen pounds." Which meant he couldn't even lift a bag of chicken feed, let alone a hay bale. Thank goodness Adam had come home. *Home.* Lancaster County had never really been his home, not since he was six. Becky hoped it was now. What would they do if he didn't stay?

Her grief over Reuben waxed and waned over the years, but suddenly it was back in full force. If only he were here now.

Joanna stood and stepped to the counter.

Lu reached for Becky's hand. "Are you okay?"

Becky smiled a little. "I was just thinking of Reuben. You know, missing him." It wasn't often she felt despondent. She was usually all business. Or all fun. She took a bite of muffin. Her heart began to race. She put her hand to her chest.

Lu asked, "What's the matter?"

"I feel funny."

Coffee sloshed over the third cup Joanna was pouring. "Oops." She put down the French press and moved to the sink.

Becky's heart raced faster. She stood.

"Are you in pain?" Joanna asked as she cleaned up the spill.

"Nee." Becky stretched to the right.

Joanna said, "I read heart problems appear differently in women than men."

"I'm not having heart problems." Becky stretched to the left.

"Are you anxious?" Joanna returned to the table.

"I don't think so." Becky wasn't an anxious person. Well, she had been after Reuben passed. And she did worry about Ike.

Becky pressed one hand to her chest again and grasped the chair with her other hand.

"Maybe you should lie down," Joanna suggested. "And do some deep breathing."

"Nee. I'm okay." But she wasn't.

Joanna stepped to Becky's side. "I'll help you into your room. Maybe resting will help."

Becky slumped a little. "I should stay seated." She put her arm on the table and her head on her arm. She took several deep breaths, like she did when she was in labor with Reuben all those years ago. Why did so much of life feel like labor?

After several raggedy breaths, she stood again.

"Where are you going?" Lu asked.

"Down." Becky tried to kneel as gracefully as she could and then spread her body out on the kitchen floor, thankful she'd mopped it that morning. Again she took several deep breaths, but her heart only raced more.

"I'm going to go call Adam." Joanna started toward the door.

Lu kneeled beside Becky. "Call 9-1-1."

"Nee," Becky said. "Call Nick."

"I'm going to call all three," Joanna called as she ran out the door.

"I don't need an ambulance." Becky's voice was shaky, and she couldn't get her breathing—or her heartbeat—right no matter how hard she tried.

"Becky, are you all right?" Ike's voice came from the doorway.

Becky groaned. "I'm fine. Go back to the couch."

Lu took Becky's hand and said to Ike, "Joanna went to call 9-1-1. And Adam."

"9-1-1? What's going on?" Ike's voice was closer.

"I'm fine, really. I told her to call Nick."

"Don't talk." Ike pulled a chair close to Becky. He sat and reached down toward her free hand. She took it and squeezed it three times and then let go.

Lu got her a glass of water and helped her to take a drink. Becky's heart raced more and she put her hand on her chest and closed her eyes.

Maybe she dozed or just lost track of time. The screen door

flew open and Joanna, a little out of breath, said, "Adam is coming, Nick will be here as soon as he can, and the ambulance is on its way."

Becky kept her eyes closed and said, "Joanna, take Ike back to the living room."

"Nee," he said. "I'll stay right here."

Becky's hand fluttered and she said, "It's time for his pain medication."

"I'm all right." Ike's voice shook a little.

Becky was afraid he'd have a setback because of her. "The doctor said to stay up on the meds—your pain will overwhelm you if you don't."

"Is it here on the table?" Joanna pointed to a basket of supplements.

"Nee. In the cupboard by the glasses."

A minute later—maybe longer, Joanna told Ike to open his hand.

Becky sighed and said, "Denki, Joanna."

Ike parroted, "Denki."

Adam came through the back door like a bull and then screeched to a halt. "Did she fall?"

"I was afraid I might." Becky opened her eyes. "That's why I'm on the floor."

Adam, with a frightened look, asked, "Dawdi, are you okay?"

"I'm fine."

Becky turned her head a little. What was wrong with her? Ike needed her. The business needed her. Adam needed her. Lu and Joanna needed her too.

She registered the wail of a siren. It grew closer. Adam and Joanna both stepped back outside.

Becky began to cry.

"Beck." Ike reached for her hand again. "We're going to be okay."

"I know," Becky said. "That's not why I'm crying." She couldn't explain it when she didn't even understand it herself. Was it because she didn't think this could happen to her and Ike, yet it was happening? Or because she couldn't stop it?

Or was it that Joanna and Adam had just gone out the door together to bring the paramedics back in to help her? Why would that make her cry? Because she was sure they'd get together? Or because she was so afraid they wouldn't?

23

Joanna and Adam both stood as Becky came into the waiting room. “It was a fake heart attack,” she said. She looked exhausted, even more than she had before.

Adam took a step toward his grandmother. “What do you mean?”

“Otherwise known, in my case, as a panic attack.” Becky lowered her voice. “A fake heart attack sounds better, don’t you think? I don’t want to be chastised for not trusting God enough.”

She began to laugh. Adam shook his head. “This isn’t funny.”

Becky stopped laughing. “I’m all right. I promise.” She took Adam’s arm. “I’m sorry I scared you.”

His eyes grew blurry. Joanna glanced away, but she doubted Adam cared if she saw him on the edge of crying. He’d certainly seen her in that state. He brushed away a tear. “Are you sure you’re all right?”

“Jah.” Becky pointed toward the hallway. “I need to go to the pharmacy. The doctor prescribed a medication.”

Nick had driven Joanna and Adam to the hospital while Lu stayed with Ike. Adam texted Nick they'd be ready to go in a half hour or so.

An hour later, Nick dropped them all off at Becky and Ike's. Joanna needed to make sure they were all settled and had a plan for dinner, and then she needed to get Mammi Lu home. She probably needed a nap.

Joanna took Becky's arm as they started up the back steps. As she opened the door, someone called out, "Joanna!"

She turned her head. She recognized the voice. *Jacob?*

"Joanna!" *Nee.* It was her Dat.

She let go of Becky's arm and turned all the way around. He was lumbering toward her, bouncing on his forward foot with each long stride, his graying brown beard blowing in the breeze.

Alarmed, she asked, "Dat?" Was everything all right? Had something happened to Mamm? *Nee.* He had a smile on his face.

"Is Luanna over here too?"

"Jah," Joanna said. "She's in the house with Ike."

Becky, her voice flat, said, "Hallo, Nehemiah. I hope you're doing better than we are. Ike had heart surgery on Monday, and I just got back from the emergency room."

"I'm sorry to hear that." Dat had reached the bottom step.

"Why are you here?" Joanna asked. "Did Mamm come with you?"

"Nee. Just me. I have some business I need to see to."

Dat always seemed to have some sort of business plan he was working on. But why in Lancaster County? Why now?

"I'll be staying at Luanna's." Hardly anyone but Dat called Mammi Lu by her full name. Joanna wasn't sure why.

"Does she know you're here?"

He grinned. "Nee. I wanted to surprise her."

"Nehemiah," Becky said, "this is my grandson, Adam."

A quick flash of pain passed over Dat's expression. "Hallo, Adam. It's been years since I've seen you." Dat was probably thinking of Reuben, who would have grown up with Mamm. Of course Dat had known him too.

Dat extended his hand. Adam took a step down to receive it and said, "I'm happy to meet you."

Dat clasped Adam's hand tightly.

"Come on in." Becky waved toward the door. "There's some iced tea in the fridge."

"Nee," Joanna said. "We'll get out of your way. You need to rest."

Becky shuffled past Joanna. "Just come in for a minute."

After Becky and Adam stepped into the house, Joanna's father gave her a pat on the shoulder. No one in her family showed much affection, which was normal for both their family and the larger Amish community. Mammi Lu and sometimes Mamm were the only ones who hugged Joanna.

Becky called out, "Lu. Surprise." However, her voice didn't match her words. "Nehemiah is here."

Joanna stepped into the kitchen. Mammi Lu stood at the sink with a startled expression on her face. "Nehemiah," she said. "Is Suzanna with you?"

He shook his head. "She sends her love. I caught a ride—there wasn't enough room for another passenger."

That meant Dat didn't want to pay full price for his own driver, which would allow Mamm to come too. Joanna would have liked to have seen her mother, but she wasn't surprised Dat hadn't brought her along.

Mammi Lu dried her hands on her apron. "What brings you here without Suzanna?"

"Business," he said.

Mammi Lu turned toward Becky and asked what the doctor said.

Becky waved her hand in a dismissive way and said, "I'm fine. I'll give you the details later. How is Ike?"

"He's napping. He ate well. A turkey sandwich and celery sticks."

"I'll go check on him." Becky stepped out of the kitchen.

Adam stepped to the fridge.

"Let's go over to our house," Mammi Lu said to Dat.

"It's fine if you stay," Adam said.

Mammi Lu shook her head. "I'll let Becky know we're leaving." She stepped into the hall.

Joanna gathered up the basket and box they'd brought that morning. She motioned to her Dat and stepped toward the door.

Her Dat said, "I'll wait for Luanna."

Joanna kept going. What was Dat up to?

She descended the stairs and sat on the bench by the driveway. Becky had put it in so she could sit while she waited for Ike to come around with the buggy.

Adam came down the back steps and sat beside her. "You seemed surprised to see your Dat."

"Jah. I am." Why hadn't her mother called to say he was coming? "Shocked, actually."

"Why didn't you move to Maine with them?"

That was a broad question with several answers. She chose one. "I wanted to stay here with Mammi Lu and Dawdi Marcus."

They sat silently for a long moment. Finally, Adam said, "If you need to talk, come over."

"Denki." Joanna smiled and with a little sass added, "And if you need to talk, come over to Mammi Lu's."

"All right." Adam smiled. "We can watch the lightning bugs."

"I'd like that." Joanna met his gaze.

His eyes shone. "I'd like that too."

Adam started toward the steps, just as Dat came down them. "Joanna. Why didn't you write that Jacob broke up with you?"

She didn't turn around. She didn't want to see the concerned expression on Adam's face. She sat with her back straight and stared at the barn.

"Joanna, I didn't hear your answer. Why didn't you tell me?"

That was the thing with the men in her family except for Leon—no one edited themselves. They blurted out whatever came into their heads no matter the situation or setting or who they damaged. And they were always loud about it. It hurt her ears—and her heart.

Perhaps her familiarity with this treatment was one of the reasons she'd put up with Jacob.

~

Once they reached the house, Dat asked to speak with Mammi Lu. "Make me a sandwich, would you, Jo?" he called as they stepped out onto the porch.

Jo. No one but Dat and her brothers, excluding Leon, called her that. It was as if saying her whole name was too much of a bother. And yet he called Mammi Luanna when she preferred Lu.

Come to think of it, Jacob called her Jo sometimes when he was tired. Or mad.

She made the sandwich. As she balanced the tray and opened the door, Dat said, "I wouldn't ask you if I wasn't at the end of my rope."

Joanna took a step backward and said, loudly, "Here's that sandwich." She took it to the table between the two of them and said, "And lemonade for both of you."

"Denki." Mammi Lu gave Joanna a tired smile. "Did you make a sandwich for yourself?"

"I'm not hungry."

"You need to eat anyway." Mammi Lu stood. "I'm going to go in and rest. It's been an eventful day."

"Jah, go get some rest," Dat said. "Jo and I need to talk about what went wrong with Jacob. You may need to go back to Maine with me."

Appalled, Joanna figuratively bit her tongue to keep from saying, *"I'm twenty-two years old. You can't make me go to Maine."* Dat had never tolerated back talk. She'd seen him give her older brothers tongue-lashings even after they were grown.

She kept quiet.

"There are several eligible bachelors in Maine." He chuckled. "Not a lot of young women, and from the few that are there, you would be the best pick by far."

"Dat."

"Jacob's a fool," he said. "Why did he break up with you?"

She shrugged.

"I need to speak with him."

She groaned. "Nee. That's not a good idea."

Dat didn't miss a beat. "Do you think you and Jacob will work things out again?"

She shrugged, not wanting to tell him no and make him even more set on forcing her to move to Maine.

"Give it a month. If you don't get back together, come join us."

She exhaled. "I like my job here. We've just taken on a large project—Becky and Ike need me more now than ever. And Mammi Lu needs me too."

He didn't respond. Did he think she was being impertinent? "What did you ask Mammi for?" she asked.

"Who said I asked her for something?"

"I'm just guessing."

"It's none of your business." That stung, but his words weren't surprising. It wasn't her business, and Dat had rarely shared business concerns with Joanna's mother, let alone any of his children. Except for Leon, since he was able to take on the mortgage on the second farm in Maine.

Dat took off his hat and ran his hand through his graying hair. Regardless of what he'd just said, he told her anyway. "I need a loan. We've had some setbacks. Leon's house needs some repairs."

Worried, Joanna asked, "Did something happen?"

"Jah, their house caught on fire a couple of weeks ago."

Joanna gasped. She felt as if she might be ill. Why hadn't Leon told her? Probably because he knew how much it would upset her.

"Everyone's okay. Lightning caused it."

She was relieved to hear it hadn't been negligence.

"And most of the house is fine, but there are repairs that need to be done and inspections." He took a drink of lemonade. "Plus the property next to us is for sale. We haven't found a place for Sam and Seth—" They were the twins just older than Joanna. Both had recently married.

"I'd really like to have Sam and Seth close. We can't handle another farm *and* the repairs to Leon's house. Our district's mutual fund is too lean to be used to help with the repairs."

"And you think Mammi does have the funds?"

"She has more than you'd think. Marcus was good with money." Was he implying he wasn't?

Joanna swallowed the lump in her throat. "Did you ask your parents for a loan?"

"They don't have the money." He frowned. "But speaking of, I should go call them and let them know I'm here. I'll invite them for supper."

He sauntered off as if he owned Mammi Lu's farm. And the house. And the barn. And the phone in the barn.

And apparently Mammi Lu's savings too.

~

They were all sitting around the kitchen table—her paternal grandparents, Mammi Lu, Dat, and Joanna—when a knock fell on the back door. Dat hadn't finished the prayer yet, and Joanna was doing her best to keep her eyes closed, breathing in the scent of the lavender hanging from the kitchen ceiling, willing it to keep her calm.

Another knock fell. She guessed it was Adam. If something was wrong with Ike or Becky, she hoped he'd rush inside. A third knock fell.

Dat finally ended the prayer.

Joanna stood and said, "Who could that be?"

"I invited—" Dat hesitated. "Insisted—"

Joanna turned toward the door to find Jacob standing on the other side of the screen.

He gave her a weak wave and said, "Hallo."

"—that Jacob come over." Dat exploded in his big boisterous laugh as he stood. "Jacob! Come on in!"

Mammi Rhoda beamed as Joanna followed Jacob to the table. "It's so good to see you," Mammi Rhoda said to Jacob. She caught Joanna's eye and smiled again.

Joanna hurried to collect another place setting.

"I already ate," Jacob said.

"Eat again!" Dat boomed.

After Joanna set the plate, knife, fork, napkin, and glass in front of Jacob, she slipped onto her chair and busied herself dishing up a small amount of mashed potatoes and passing the bowl to Dawdi Hiram.

Mammi Rhoda passed the roasted chicken to Jacob, who took a little.

"So." Dat leaned back in his chair. "Tell us what's going on, young man."

Young man? Did her father intend to bully Jacob into courting her again? Joanna glanced at Mammi Lu, who looked as if she might be ill.

"About?" Jacob asked.

"You and Joanna."

"There's not much to tell." He gave Joanna a furtive glance.

Mammi Lu cleared her throat and said, "Nehemiah, perhaps you could have this conversation later. Away from the table."

Dat seemed irritated by her comment for a moment, but then chuckled and said, "Good idea, Luanna. Jacob and I'll take our coffee on the porch after dinner." He glanced toward his father. "Will you join us?"

Dawdi Hiram muttered something. Mammi Rhoda nudged him. He didn't respond.

Dat dominated the conversation, telling stories about how cold the Maine winters were and how thick the mosquitoes were in the summer. "But we like it," Dat said. "We don't want to be anywhere else."

Joanna felt the same way about Mammi Lu's farm.

Dat glanced at Jacob and then Joanna. "I wish you would join us in Maine." He directed his attention to his parents and to Mammi Lu. "All of you. Then we could look after you."

Joanna squirmed in her chair, eager for her father to say the closing prayer. Clearly he was in charge.

Mammi Lu said, "I'm happy to hear Maine is treating you well."

Joanna said, "Is everyone ready for coffee? I made Mammi Lu's peach cobbler to go with it. I picked the peaches this morning."

Another flash of irritation passed over Dat's face, but then he said, "Let's pray." They all bowed their heads—but Joanna had a hard time formulating a prayer—until Dat finally said, "Amen."

Joanna shot up out of her seat and busied herself starting the coffee and then clearing the plates and food. Mammi Lu helped while the others kept talking. Once Joanna poured the coffee and served the cobbler, Dat said, "Men, let's go on out to the porch."

Dawdi Hiram cleared his throat and said, "You and Jacob go ahead. I'll stay in here with the ladies." Mammi Rhoda nudged him again, but he stood his ground. "I don't see how my input is needed."

Dat stood. "All right." He picked up his cobbler and coffee. "Come on, Jacob."

After they left, Dawdi Hiram put his hand flat on the table. "Joanna, do you want me to join them?"

She shook her head but couldn't manage to speak.

"Your Dat will have this sorted out in no time," Mammi Rhoda said. "It's a blessing he came when you needed him. It was the right thing to let him know what was going on."

Confused, Joanna spoke slowly. "You let him know?"

Rhoda smiled a little. "I sent a letter as soon as I knew Jacob had broken up with you. He's your Dat. He needs to know these sorts of things."

Joanna asked, "But is that why he came?"

"I assume so."

Joanna wasn't so sure. She guessed he already planned to come. She doubted he would have come because of her love life. Or lack of one.

She picked at her cobbler. It wasn't quite as delicious as when Mammi Lu made it, but it was still good. Mammi's secret ingredient was vanilla. When the others were done, Joanna quickly cleared the table.

"We should get going," Dawdi Hiram said. "We have church in the morning."

Mammi Rhoda yawned and pushed her chair back. "We can tell Nehemiah and Jacob goodbye as we leave."

Joanna busied herself with the dishes as Mammi Lu cleared the dessert plates. Then Dat opened the back door and said, "Joanna, go on out and have a word with Jacob."

Her face grew even warmer than it had already been as she dried her hands on her apron. *Nehemiah's Joanna*. Would she be under his thumb until she married? As she started for the door, Dat had his plate in his hand and was heading to the cobbler dish on the butcher block. No doubt he'd help himself to another piece.

Jacob stood as Joanna stepped out onto the porch. "Why did you ask your father to speak to me?"

"I didn't," Joanna said. "He acted on his own."

"He tried to talk me into us getting back together."

"I'm sorry about that." She wrapped her arms around her middle. "It wasn't my idea."

"I understand he's upset with me."

Joanna wasn't sure her father *was* upset. It seemed more as if he thought he could bully Jacob. "I don't want to get back together," Joanna said. "And I know you don't want that either, but I would like to know what happened and what's going on now."

"What are you talking about?"

"I saw you with Veronica at the creamery yesterday."

His face reddened. "She was my neighbor until recently. She's had a crush on me, and I needed to explain to her that . . ." His voice trailed off.

"That what?"

He rubbed the back of his neck. "It's none of your business." Jacob had an annoyed expression on his face.

Joanna exhaled slowly. Why had Dat asked him over? It only made things more awkward.

He put his hat on. "I'll see you tomorrow." He descended the steps and glanced back at her. "Or more likely Monday at work."

Joanna turned toward the kitchen door. Dat sat at the table, but Mammi Lu was on the other side of the screen, waiting for her.

24

Adam stood outside Dawdi Ike and Mammi Becky's bedroom door. He wished they were sleeping in the living room—at least then he could watch until he could see their chests rise and fall and know they were alive. Seeing Mammi on the kitchen floor had terrified him.

He didn't hear any movement. Hopefully they were settled. Mammi had seemed tired but fine the rest of the day, and she and Dawdi were in bed by eight. Dawdi had reassured both of them the bed wasn't too high, but Adam had put a step stool by it, just in case.

He wandered into the kitchen and checked the clock. Eight thirty. He might as well go for a little walk. He didn't remember deciding he'd walk by Lu's, but as the last of the twilight waned, that was where he found himself. At her gate.

He peered toward the house. A bit of light cast across the back porch from the kitchen. Lu was most likely already in bed. He quietly called out, "Joanna."

No one answered. He passed the garden and squinted toward the porch. Someone sat in one of the rocking chairs, a figure too small to be her Dat. "Joanna?" he asked, his volume just above a whisper.

"Jah," she answered. "It's me."

"Is it all right if I join you?"

"It's all right, although I'm not very good company."

"What happened?" Adam reached the top of the stairs.

Instead of answering, she stood. "There's one piece of cobbler left. I'll get it for you."

"Nee." He motioned toward the chairs. "Could we talk first?"

She sat and without any prompting told him about Jacob showing up at suppertime. "I'm not sure exactly what happened—but Jacob had already eaten, so I think Dat had just told him to *be* here, to talk."

"How did it go?"

"Horribly. Dat seemed to think he could force Jacob into courting me again."

Adam could only imagine how that made her feel.

"I asked him about Veronica."

"You did?" He admired her boldness.

"Jah. He said it was none of my business."

Adam shook his head. "He's a jerk."

"At one point I thought maybe he wrote those letters—you know, the ones at work."

Adam nodded, suddenly feeling cold even though the evening was still hot. And muggy.

"Jacob said he didn't write them—and, obviously, he's telling the truth. He doesn't care enough to write something so thoughtful. I don't think he ever did." She leaned forward, clasped her hands, and turned her head toward Adam. "Is there something wrong with me?"

Without hesitating, Adam said, "Nee. Absolutely not."

She stood, seemingly flustered, perhaps because she'd been vulnerable in sharing what she had. "I'll get you that cobbler," she said as she headed for the screen door.

As she stepped into the house, Adam groaned. What had he done? He couldn't fathom why she'd thought, even for a moment, the letters were from Jacob. Didn't she know his handwriting? Adam had seen Jacob's notes at work. They were barely legible. Perhaps she thought he'd spruced up his writing for the letter. Adam's face grew warm. That was exactly what he himself had done. He needed to tell her the letters were from him. He had to apologize for lying to her too.

A minute later Joanna returned with a huge piece of cobbler and a glass of water.

As she put the water on the table, a racket startled him.

"What was that?" Adam asked.

She handed him the cobbler. "My Dat." She sat and pointed to the upstairs window overlooking the porch. "He's snoring."

"He sounds like a bear."

"Jah. He acts like one too." Joanna began to rock. "All the anxiety I felt growing up came back tonight."

"What was the anxiety about?"

"How unpredictable he is. I never knew what to expect—I felt especially anxious when I answered the door and Jacob was standing there. When I was young, one week Dat would want to build a new shed. The next week he'd want to sell the farm. Then he'd want to plant wheat instead of corn. He couldn't stick to one idea for long. But he had one long-term hope—that we would all live on one humongous farm, with him and the boys all farming together."

"Lack of land is why they all moved to Maine?" Adam asked.

"Jah. After he sold most of the farm on the west side of the county, he had enough to buy one farm in Maine and put a down payment, which included Leon's savings, on the other. Now he wants to buy a third one there."

Adam had so many questions, but none of them were his business. He took a bite of the cobbler. It was delicious. After he swallowed, he told Joanna so.

"Denki," she said. "It's Mammi Lu's recipe."

He ate another bite. Then he asked, "Have you gotten back to reading, besides the gardening book? And the architecture one?"

"Nee, I haven't read a novel in a really long time." She began rocking harder. "What are you reading?"

Pleased that she asked, Adam answered, "*Persuasion*. I just finished it."

She stopped rocking. "Did Jane Austen write it?"

He grinned. "Jah. Have you read it?"

"I haven't, but I've been meaning to." She returned his smile, although hers was faint. "I'm kind of surprised you read it."

"I really like Jane Austen, thanks to you," Adam said. "I'll loan it to you. Mammi Becky won't mind." Adam felt the book would be the perfect peace offering after he confessed to her he was Someone Who Cares. "It's an old copy—small print and a little musty."

"I don't mind. What's it about?"

Adam paused a moment. He didn't want to scare her off from reading it. It was about a woman whose family had high expectations and gave minimal acknowledgment, while trying to persuade her not to marry the man she loved. And the story included well-written and transparent letters. He cringed. That was something he certainly hadn't emulated. He had to be honest with Joanna, tonight. No matter how difficult it was to tell her.

He cleared his throat. First he needed to answer her question. "*Persuasion* is about a lot of things, but mostly about a couple who get a second chance."

Without warning, Joanna started to cry. Adam put the cobbler down and reached for her hand.

She took his and sputtered, "I don't want to get back together with Jacob, honestly. I'd just like to know why he broke up with me."

Joanna's hand was surprisingly soft for how hard she worked. He held it gently, even though he wanted to hold on tight, thinking that whatever Jacob's reason, it would probably be better if Joanna didn't know. But he didn't tell her that. But maybe she couldn't move on without knowing.

"Dat wants me to move to Maine. He said I wouldn't have any trouble finding a husband there." She lifted her apron with her free hand and wiped her eyes as Adam registered what she was saying. She couldn't move to Maine. She dropped her apron. "As if being married to who-knows-who will solve my problems." She shivered, and not for the cold. The heat hadn't abated. "I don't want to move to Maine. I don't want to leave Mammi Lu. And I really like my job, plus we have the Pequea Creek house to fix."

Adam said, "I don't want you to move to Maine either."

Joanna continued to cry.

Adam waited patiently. He was comfortable with tears—he'd learned to be as a boy when his mother used to cry.

Joanna wiped her eyes on her apron again and asked, "Do you remember when you said we couldn't *just* be friends? More than once."

"Jah," Adam said.

"Can we now?" she asked. "Because I really need a friend."

"It was stupid of me to say that. And jah, we can be friends. We *are* friends." He scooted to the edge of his chair and held her hand a little tighter.

"You're the best friend I have in Lancaster County," she said. "Besides Mammi Lu."

Adam knew he needed to say the right thing. "You're the best friend I have here too." Actually she was the best friend he had anywhere, but he didn't want to scare her. "And I feel the same way about Mammi Becky and Dawdi Ike as you do about Lu."

They held hands for a what seemed like a long time. Adam couldn't tell her he'd written the letters, not now.

Finally, Joanna said, "You should finish your cobbler."

"Only if you'll share it with me." He let go of her hand and picked up the plate again. Then he cut a bite with his fork, scooped it up, and extended it toward Joanna. She hesitated but then opened her mouth. He fed her. Then he took the next bite and continued to share with her until it was all gone.

"Denki," she said. "That went down better than I thought it would."

~

Sunday morning as Dawdi walked with Adam to the edge of the pasture to water the steers, he asked, "How was Joanna last night?"

Adam gave him a questioning look. "How'd you know I saw her?"

"Lucky guess. I heard you come in late." Dawdi moved slowly. "How's she doing with her Dat around?"

Adam exhaled. "Nehemiah hopes Jacob and Joanna will get back together. He asked Jacob over for dinner."

"How did that go?"

"Not well."

When they reached the pasture, Dawdi leaned against the fence. "If you still care for Joanna, you should let her know." Had Dawdi overheard the conversation in the van three years ago too? Or was Adam just that obvious? "Don't let any more time go by."

"She's not over Jacob."

"I'm not saying you have to ask her to court you." He smiled slyly. Jah, he'd overheard the conversation. Or else Mammi had told him. "But let her know you care."

"She knows. We're friends."

This time Dawdi Ike laughed. "Well, that's progress."

Adam laughed too. Dawdi had definitely heard the conversation too—and remembered it.

Dawdi put his hand to his chest as if the laughter had hurt. "Maybe let her know you hope to be more than friends someday."

"I already tried that once."

"Son," Dawdi said, "believe me, if you want to have a future with Joanna, it's time to let her know. Give her space but be honest with her before she ends up five hundred miles away. Nehemiah is pretty headstrong."

Joanna was too, but Nehemiah would be hard to stand up to.

"You have a connection with Joanna."

Adam stared into his grandfather's blue eyes—eyes just like his own. Just like, he'd been told, his father's. "You have years of knowing each other, of friendship. Believe me, that means something. You're still young—you might not think it does. But connections that last over the years are hard to come by."

Dawdi was right. Of all the girls Adam had known over the years, Joanna was the only one he still wanted to talk with, to be close to, let alone court. Not to mention marry.

"All I'm asking is that you're honest with yourself—and her," Dawdi said.

Adam started to speak but his voice caught. He cleared his throat. "I'm afraid I'll scare her away."

"Well, at some point you'll have to choose between scaring her and losing her. Take it a step at a time, but don't be afraid to talk to her soon. You'll know when the time is right."

Adam gave his grandfather a nod. It was a lot for Dawdi to come out to the pasture and talk. Clearly, he wanted Adam to understand his message.

Adam wasn't sure what to do. Should he tell Joanna how he felt? Should he reveal he'd written the letters—and admit he'd lied to her? He couldn't confess in a letter, but he had one more verse he wanted to share. He'd head to the warehouse after he finished his chores.

~

On the way back to the house from the warehouse, Adam noticed a patch of lawn daisies. He picked several and then tore a piece of waxed paper from the roll in the kitchen, positioned them on the paper, and folded it in half. Before putting the copy of *Persuasion* in the pocket of his jacket, he slipped the daisies into the pages of the book. Once he had the horse hitched to the buggy, he pushed the book under the seat. Then he headed to the church service at Tim's parents' farm.

He searched Lu's property as he drove by, but didn't see anyone. The morning was warm, and a hot wind rustled through the trees.

Everyone had already filed into the shed when Adam slipped inside and sat on the bench with the single men, scooting in to leave a couple of open seats. The congregation was singing the second song, "Dos Loblied." The service in Pinecraft was much shorter than anywhere else Adam had ever attended church. It was a mix of Mennonite and Amish who worshipped together in a meetinghouse and not in someone's home or shed. He needed to get used to the three-hour services again. Tim slipped in next to him. After Daniel closed the singing he said, "As you pray this week, please keep Ike Slaybaugh in your prayers. He's recovering from quadruple bypass surgery. And keep Becky in your prayers too. She was in the ER yesterday and is doing better." Mammi would be embarrassed to know Daniel was asking for prayer for her too.

Next, the preacher stepped to the front and started the first sermon. It took Adam longer than it should have to register the topic was friendship. First the preacher read Proverbs 17:17, "A friend loveth at all times, and a brother is born for adversity." Next he read Ecclesiastes 4:9–10, "Two are better than one, because they have a good reward for their labour. For if they fall, the one will lift up his fellow:

but woe to him that is alone when he falleth; for he hath not another to help him up."

Adam shivered. Thank God he and Mammi and Joanna had been with Dawdi when he had his heart attack. What if Dawdi had died? As much as he loved Mammi Becky, he wasn't sure he could be the support she needed.

And as much as he hoped he could be Joanna's friend, he wasn't sure if he could give her what she needed either. Jah, if she was interested in him, he could. But what if all she ever wanted to be was *just* friends? It would be easier to leave than to spend the rest of his life being her friend when he wanted more. He'd been right all along—he couldn't *just* be her friend.

The preacher spoke about the example Jesus was of being a friend. "He always spoke the truth but in a loving way," the preacher said. "We need to follow His example in friendship."

Adam hadn't spoken the truth about the letters, but he hoped he'd spoken in a loving way to Joanna the night before. He stole a glance across the aisle. The single women were behind the single men by a row. Joanna sat by the aisle. Was she looking at him?

If he loved Joanna, wouldn't he stick around and be her friend? If he loved his grandparents, wouldn't he stick around and be the son they no longer had?

After the second sermon and a time of prayer, Daniel returned to the front. "We have a wedding to publish," he said.

Adam glanced around. It was traditional for the couple not to attend the service their wedding was announced at. Who was missing?

Jacob was missing. But that didn't mean anything. He glanced down the single men's aisle again. Adam wasn't sure if anyone else was absent.

He couldn't turn and search the row of the single women as much as he was tempted to. He did turn his head enough to see Joanna. She stared straight ahead.

25

Joanna had already noted that Jacob wasn't at the service when all of the single men filed in. At first she assumed Adam had stayed home too, with Ike and Becky. But then he came in late. She had a clear view of the row of single men. There was enough room on the end of the bench for Jacob, more than enough if Adam scooted closer to Tim.

Joanna glanced down the single women's row. Veronica was missing.

Daniel cleared his throat. "Jacob Byer and Miriam Troyer are publishing their October wedding."

Joanna froze. Miriam? Not Veronica? What was going on? She grew clammy, even in the sweltering shed. Jacob and Miriam hadn't even been dating, let alone courting, and they were marrying in three months?

None of it made sense. Why hadn't Mandy warned her?

Joanna felt eyes on her. Lots of eyes.

"Let's pray for the couple that God would bless them and that we would play our part in guiding them."

Why did Daniel seem so happy? He knew Jacob had just

dumped her. Joanna's vision began to blur. She would not cry. She could not cry.

Why hadn't she stayed home today? She should have volunteered to sit with Ike and Becky. She would have if she'd known Adam was coming to church.

"Let's close in prayer," Daniel said.

Should Joanna slip out before anyone approached her? She needed to keep busy. To keep moving. She needed to avoid everyone's questions. And opinions. But if she bolted out of the shed before Daniel ended the prayer, people would take notice. If she bolted after the prayer, people would notice that too.

Mandy, sitting in the row of young married women in front of Joanna, turned and flashed a wild look. Joanna didn't respond. She stared straight ahead. Maybe Mandy hadn't known in advance her sister was going to marry Jacob. Could that be?

Daniel ended the prayer, and the congregation began to stir. Joanna forced herself to move slowly. She stood. She smiled at Mandy. She stepped into the aisle. She glanced back at Daniel, who was now being interrogated by Dat. Joanna suppressed a groan.

The back row of congregants began filing out of the shed. Joanna shifted toward the aisle, hoping no one would speak to her. Someone took her arm. Mammi Lu. "Come with me."

Mammi Lu directed her around those who had spilled out into the aisle, and Joanna followed her grandmother's lead. How could she have been such a fool to trust Jacob a second time?

She fought back tears again.

"Lu!" Elaine came toward them with an envelope in her

hand. "Would you give this to Becky? That will save me having to put it in the mail." She, the grandmother of the bride-to-be, grinned foolishly at the grandmother of the jilted. *Jilted Joanna.*

"Jah." Mammi Lu took the letter from Elaine and quickly propelled Joanna forward.

They reached the door. Tim caught her eye and gave her a worried nod. No doubt Adam was close-by. Instead of heading toward the house and the kitchen door, Mammi swung toward the stables. And then Adam was beside Joanna. "I'll take you home."

Joanna whispered, "Denki."

"I'll go too." Mammi Lu turned. "Tim, would you let Nehemiah know Joanna and I went with Adam? Nehemiah should eat and come whenever he's ready in my buggy."

"Jah, I'll do that," Tim answered.

Joanna waited by Mammi Lu on the other side of the barn. In no time, Adam came along in his buggy. He stopped, jumped down, helped Mammi Lu in first and then Joanna. No one spoke on the way home. Joanna felt as if her already-broken heart had been jackhammered into a thousand pieces. It felt like the most violent demolition ever. Jacob had betrayed her. And Miriam had sat with her at Becky's table a week ago and hadn't said a word. The entire Troyer family seemed complicit.

How could she possibly get through the next three months? The thing with this breakup was one minute she felt fine about it—positive, in fact, as if she'd escaped a burning building. Jacob was not the right man for her. And then the next moment she felt devastated all over again, as if a burning building had collapsed on top of her. This was one of those moments.

Maybe she *should* go to Maine with her father. Maybe she'd been too prideful about her job. Too prideful about her relationship with Jacob. Too dependent on Mammi Lu instead of on her family. Too eager to avoid the chaos of her brothers.

They turned down the drive. The first book the librarian at Joanna's first library had recommended was *Anne of Green Gables*. At the sight of Mammi Lu's house, Joanna thought of a line from the book: *The best of it all was the coming home*. She felt that way all the time, but especially today.

As Adam set the brake on the buggy, he pulled something from under the seat. A book—*Persuasion*. She took it with a whispered "Denki."

He said, "I'm going to get dinner going for Dawdi and Mammi. I'll stop back by later in the day."

Joanna tried to say "Denki" again but a little gasp came out of her mouth instead.

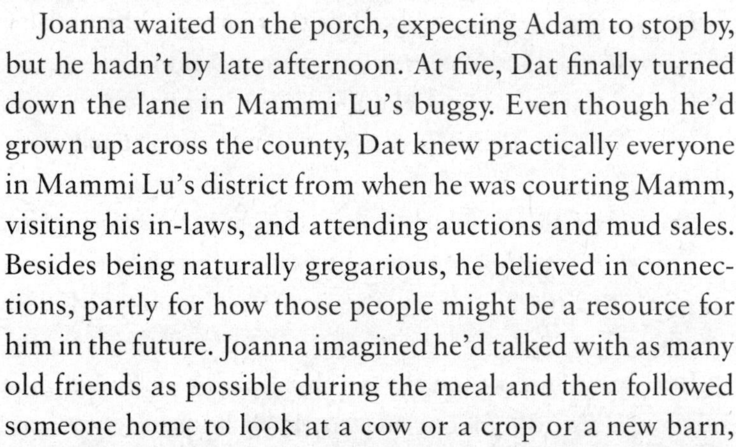

Joanna waited on the porch, expecting Adam to stop by, but he hadn't by late afternoon. At five, Dat finally turned down the lane in Mammi Lu's buggy. Even though he'd grown up across the county, Dat knew practically everyone in Mammi Lu's district from when he was courting Mamm, visiting his in-laws, and attending auctions and mud sales. Besides being naturally gregarious, he believed in connections, partly for how those people might be a resource for him in the future. Joanna imagined he'd talked with as many old friends as possible during the meal and then followed someone home to look at a cow or a crop or a new barn, perhaps to get an idea of something he could do on his own farm. She doubted he'd spent any time with his parents. In fact, she'd always felt he found Dawdi Hiram and Mammi Rhoda boring, even when they lived across the road. Maybe especially then.

After he took care of the horse, he sauntered toward the porch. "Excellent teaching today, don't you think? And the meal was good too. I went over to Daniel and Elaine's afterward to see their new shed. Have you seen it?"

Joanna nodded. "What did you say to Daniel after the service?"

"He mentioned his shed earlier. I asked if I could stop by and take a look. I'm hoping to build a new one in Maine."

Had Dat even noticed Daniel's announcement that Jacob and Miriam were getting married?

"Was anyone else at Daniel and Elaine's when you stopped by?"

"Nee." He paused a moment. "Daniel agrees with me that you should go back to Maine."

"What exactly did Daniel and you talk about?"

Dat shrugged. "Not much. Just that this is a difficult time for you. It would be easier if you were in Maine."

Easier? Easier for Daniel and Elaine? Joanna stood. "I'm going to go take a nap," she said. "I'll put out a snack when I get up."

She didn't sleep—instead she sat in her chair and stared out the window looking into the woods. It *would* be easier to go to Maine. She'd never have to see Jacob or Miriam again.

But she wouldn't have a job that she loved. She'd most likely end up going from one brother's house to another's through the years to tend nieces and nephews and help her sisters-in-law with their sewing, gardening, canning, cooking, and cleaning. She'd be *die aldi Maydel Aenti*. She shuddered.

To distract herself she picked up *Persuasion* and began reading it. She wouldn't read a novel in the rest of the house on Sunday, and she certainly wouldn't read one in front of Dat, but she didn't think God minded.

The book was, as Adam had said, a second chances story. But it was also about a community and its expectations and the demands of families and fathers—all things Joanna dealt with too, along with gossip. There were also people in authority desperately trying to persuade younger people to follow their selfish advice. That resonated with her too.

The character Anne impressed Joanna—she was composed, on the outside, and also of good character, both goals Joanna had for herself. In the first six chapters that she'd read, there wasn't much about Captain Wentworth, so she didn't have an opinion about him yet. After an hour, she put down the book, feeling more settled.

She went downstairs and put out a snack for supper. Dat was on the porch reading his Bible. She let him know the food was ready and sat in the other chair. "May I ask you a question?"

He closed his Bible. "Of course."

"Does Mamm know you asked Mammi Lu for money?"

"Jah. She sent me."

That surprised Joanna. "I have another question. Why are you staying here instead of at Mammi Rhoda and Dawdi Hiram's?"

"Because you're here." When Joanna didn't respond, he

added, "And there's something extra hospitable about Luanna. She's always been good to me. I've always felt as if I belong when I'm around her."

That was something Joanna did understand, something—maybe the only thing—she and her father had in common. "What if Mammi Lu needs her money soon?"

He put his Bible on the table. "We'll take care of her."

"In Maine?"

He nodded. "What if she doesn't want to go to Maine?"

"She'll have to, at some point."

Especially if Joanna moved. No one would be left to help Mammi Lu in Lancaster County.

~

The next morning Joanna arrived early at the warehouse and looked for another letter first thing—and found it on the counter where the previous three had been. What if it was from someone who'd known all along that Jacob and Miriam had gotten back together and felt obligated to "comfort" her before she found out? She pulled the letter from the envelope.

Dear Joanna,

You continue to be in my prayers. I hope you are able to take as good care of yourself as you do others. This verse from Philippians has encouraged me through the years, and I hope it will encourage you too: I can do all things through Christ which strengtheneth me.

Someone Who Cares

She appreciated the verse—but not the letter. In fact it was getting downright creepy. Why would an older woman in the district not sign her name? Unless it was someone close to Miriam. Was Elaine sending the letters?

Still, Joanna repeated the verse silently a few times, committing it to memory. *All things*. Including overcoming her hurt pride.

There was no reason to keep the letter. She crumpled it in one hand and the envelope in the other and tossed them both into the garbage as Adam came through the door.

Was his face red from jogging from Ike and Becky's house? Or for another reason? Perhaps because he'd stood her up the day before. In a raspy voice he said, "Guder Mariye."

Joanna didn't reply.

"We're off to the Pequea Creek house," he said.

Joanna folded her hands together. "Is Becky coming in today?"

"Nee. She said for us to take Caleb. Nick will drive Jacob and Tim to the Garden Lane house and return for the three of us. She already gave him instructions."

"How is she? How is Ike?"

"*Gut*. Tired, but both seem better."

He asked, "Any coffee?"

Joanna stared at the pot for a moment and then turned her attention back to Adam. "Feel free to make it if you want." She took a step away from him. "I'm going to pack our supplies."

Adam took a step toward her. "Joanna—"

She could walk away—or tell him what was bothering her. She lowered her voice. "You said you'd stop by and check on me yesterday."

"Jah, I did."

Chagrined, she asked, "You did?"

"Your Dat said you were taking a nap."

Her face grew warm. Why hadn't Dat told her? "I was reading," she said. "*Persuasion.*"

He smiled a little. "I should have come back, but to be honest your Dat is a little intimidating."

"He didn't tell me you came by."

Adam shrugged. "I'm not surprised, not if he wants you to move to Maine."

Was Adam implying Dat thought he wanted to court her?

Joanna's face grew warm, most likely matching the shade of Adam's. "I'm sorry I jumped to conclusions."

"Don't be," he said.

She reached for the clipboard. "We have a lot to accomplish today. We'd better start gathering our supplies."

As she packed—sledgehammers, pry bars, hammers, gloves, masks, goggles, buckets, drop cloths—Tim, Caleb, and Jacob arrived. None of them approached her. Soon, Tim and Jacob left with Nick. Caleb and Adam busied themselves taking down ladders and carting them and the crates of supplies out to the loading area.

"What about a dumpster?" Adam asked.

"I ordered one last week," Joanna answered. "If it's not there when we arrive, it will be delivered by later this morning." Joanna had a clipboard in her hands with the steps they needed to follow. "We'll need to turn off the gas and water to the kitchen. That hasn't been done yet."

A horn honked. Nick had arrived.

"You and Caleb need to make sandwiches for lunch. The cooler is by the crates."

"Oh." Adam glanced back toward the mini kitchen. "Did you make one for yourself?"

"I'm not hungry."

He gave her another smile and then said, "We'll take care of the crates. Meet you at the van."

~

Once they reached the property, unloaded their tools and supplies, and set up their work area, Joanna put on a mask and goggles and spent the next few hours slinging a sledge-hammer in the pantry while Caleb and Adam pried the cup-boards from the kitchen walls. Together they carted the debris out beside the carriage house.

When it came time to eat, Caleb and Adam took the cooler out to the veranda. Without telling them where she was going, Joanna walked along the path adjacent to the driveway toward the road. As she neared the creek, the temperature dropped a few degrees, enough to feel the difference. When she reached the creek she took a tentative step onto the footbridge. And then another. She quickly skipped across. The boards were soft and loose. She'd add the repair to the list. She picked a few of the wild roses that grew along the fence line and then looked up and down the creek. Just past the property line was the covered bridge. She kept going. The temperature dropped even more as she walked across the planks under the open beam ceiling. She stopped halfway across and leaned over the railing. The water swirled below. A duck paddled toward the shore.

Adam called out her name. She turned as he stepped out into the road.

He smiled and waved. "There you are." He held up her water bottle and a brown bag. "I made a sandwich for you."

She started to say she wasn't hungry, but her stomach growled. All that hard work had given her an appetite. "Denki."

"Stay put," he said.

She stepped back to the railing, and he met her there. She took half of the sandwich out of its plastic bag and took a bite. Then another. Without speaking, they watched the duck together and then spotted its nest by the side of the creek. Five fuzzy ducklings poked out of the reeds as the mother duck approached.

"Aww," Adam said. "They were waiting for her." He turned toward her. "I need to talk with you about something."

Joanna took the water bottle from Adam's hand. "The footbridge by the driveway needs to be repaired."

"All right." He glanced toward the property. "I'll fix it. That will be fun. So—"

"I'll show you." Joanna marched back across the bridge ahead of Adam. As they reached the driveway, a truck carrying the dumpster rumbled toward the carriage house. She pointed to the footbridge. "Take a look. I'll go tell them where to put the dumpster."

~

At the end of the day, after Joanna cleaned up the kitchen counter, she left the warehouse. Jacob had just finished hitching his horse to his buggy. Perhaps swinging a sledgehammer half the day had made her feel more powerful. Something had. She grabbed her scooter from the side of the building and decided to approach him.

He saw her coming and stepped to the side of the buggy.

"Were you going to tell me?" she asked, rather loudly.

"It doesn't concern you," he said curtly.

"It does." Anger bubbled up in her, but she managed to keep her voice calm. "Did you know, all along, I wasn't the right one for you?"

He shrugged. "Don't be like this."

Her voice rose in volume. "Like what?"

"Hurt."

She laughed wryly. "What else should I be?"

Without answering, he climbed into his buggy.

She turned away and began scootering toward the highway. Someone—Jacob—said rather loudly, "Mind your own business." Was he talking to her again? She turned but couldn't tell who he was addressing.

A few minutes later, she heard someone coming after her on foot. Her heart raced faster. Was it Jacob coming to apologize?

She didn't turn her head. Then she heard the buggy. She held her head high and kept moving. As he passed by her, Jacob called out, "It's Adam to the rescue."

She slowed the scooter and turned her head. Adam was behind her a few yards. She quickly shifted her focus ahead.

"Joanna." Adam was right behind her now, out of breath. "What do you need?"

"Nothing."

"I want to help."

"Then leave me alone." She wasn't going to go from trusting Jacob and being betrayed by him to trusting someone else. Not so soon. Not even Adam. She wouldn't be hurt again.

26

Adam slowed his pace and dropped back as Joanna increased hers. She was fast. And strong. He'd been in awe of her swinging the sledgehammer. No doubt there was more behind her energy than just wanting to get the job done.

He'd been mucking out the stalls in the stable and overheard her conversation with Jacob. If Jacob had known Adam was listening he wouldn't have responded that way. She had a right to know what had happened.

He'd intended to be the first person to the warehouse that morning, because he'd changed his mind about leaving another letter that he'd only need to apologize for. He needed to stop lying to her. He'd wanted to grab the letter he left Sunday before Joanna saw it—but she beat him to it. And tossed it in the garbage.

Over their lunch break he'd planned to confess he'd written the letters, but then she ran to meet the driver of the dumpster delivery truck before he had a chance. Well, before he'd worked up the courage to speak up. He'd missed his chance. Adam felt ill over misleading her.

After supper, he washed the dishes and then said he was going on a walk. Dawdi Ike gave him a nod as Mammi Becky gave him what looked like a knowing smile. He wasn't sure what she knew—although he guessed she assumed he was going over to Lu's. And she was right. But not for the reason his grandmother hoped for, he was sure.

When he arrived, he found Nehemiah sitting on the porch with his feet on the railing. He boomed, "Adam!" as he stood. For a moment Adam thought Nehemiah was happy to see him, but then he asked sardonically, "Did you come to tell me goodbye?"

Adam reached the bottom steps. "Are you leaving?"

Nehemiah laughed. "Soon. Jo will go with me." Adam had never heard anyone call Joanna *Jo* before.

The screen door opened and Joanna said, "Nee, I'm not going with you, Dat. I told you that."

Nehemiah winked at Adam. "She'll change her mind."

Adam said, "Hallo, Joanna."

"Hallo." She stepped onto the porch, wiping her hands on her apron. She'd changed out of her blue work dress and into a rose-colored one. "Why are you here?"

"To ask you to go on a walk."

She frowned.

So did her father, but then he said, "I'll be fine."

Joanna shook her head a little at her Dat. "I'm not worried about you."

Adam gave her a gentle smile. He wouldn't beg, but he really did hope to speak with her.

"All right," she said. "Give me just a minute."

Adam sat in the second rocking chair trying to think of a safe topic to discuss with Nehemiah, but there was no need.

"You should come visit Maine sometime. My boys remember you."

"Oh." He had vague memories of a couple of Joanna's brothers from when he was very young.

"Once you see Maine, you won't want to live anywhere else."

Adam, feeling awkward, tried to smile. He had no intention of moving to Maine.

"Lu will have to move up soon enough. Maybe we could get Ike and Becky to move too."

Adam couldn't stay silent when it came to his grandparents. No doubt Nehemiah was just talking, but he assumed too much. "Why would they move? They love it here. And all of their friends are here."

"But who will take care of them?"

Adam sat up straight and squared his shoulders. "I will."

"You will? I heard you plan to go back to Florida."

"Who told you that?"

Nehemiah rubbed his forehead. "Let me see." He paused. "Maybe Daniel."

Adam had only mentioned the idea to Caleb. Had he said something? If Nehemiah had heard that, had someone told Joanna he wanted to go back to Pinecraft too?

Joanna stepped out onto the porch again, wearing a clean apron.

Adam stood and gestured for her to lead the way.

Nehemiah called out, too loudly for how close they were, "Don't be late!"

Joanna raised her hand in response. Adam turned, met

Nehemiah's laughing eyes, and said, "We won't." Clearly Nehemiah didn't consider Adam a likely suitor for Joanna. Probably because she didn't consider him one—and never had.

As they passed the garden, Joanna pinched a sprig of lavender that had grown through the fence and twirled it between her thumb and forefinger as they walked. "What do you want to talk about?"

Of course she knew that was why he'd come over—to talk. "I need to tell you something I'm not proud of." He glanced at her.

"Oh?" She spun the lavender at her side.

"You know those letters you received at work?"

She nodded. "Jah."

"I wrote them."

She stopped walking and turned toward him. "What?" Her eyes filled with confusion.

"I wanted to encourage you."

"But you told me you didn't write them."

He nodded. "And I'm not proud of that. I'm truly sorry."

Her eyes sparked. "You lied to me." She spun the lavender faster.

"I hope you can forgive me."

She narrowed her eyes. "Why did you send them anonymously?"

"I didn't think you'd want letters from me. I figured you'd think they were from someone in the district and leave it at that." If only he could be more eloquent in explaining himself.

She crushed the sprig of lavender between her fingers and then began spinning it again. "But why did you lie? And then why didn't you tell me sooner?"

"I was embarrassed," Adam said. "It all felt a little weird."

The lavender spun out of her fingers and fell to the ground. "I don't think the letters were weird, but I think you being secretive is. Why would you let me go on trying to figure out who they were from—even wondering if they were from Jacob? That was creepy."

"I never thought you would think they were from Jacob." When she didn't respond, he added, "I wanted to be a good friend to you without—" Without what? Without letting her know how much he cared for her?

She made a gulping sound, spun around, and marched back to Lu's.

Adam called out, "Joanna!"

She said something, but he couldn't make out what it was. She began to run.

He called out her name again.

This time what she said was clear. "Leave me alone!"

~

The next day at work, Joanna spoke to Adam only when necessary. On Wednesday, Tim and Caleb worked at the Pequea Creek house and Adam helped finish up the kitchen at the Garden Lane house, working with Jacob. The two spoke only when needed.

That evening Mammi Becky sent Adam to Lu's with a letter. "I thought you saw her every day."

"Not today."

"Are you seeing her tomorrow?"

Mammi Becky rolled her eyes. "Just take the letter. Please."

He guessed she was trying to force him to see Joanna, which Adam dreaded.

When he arrived at the house, Joanna wasn't in the garden

and no one was on the porch either. The screen door was closed, but the back door was open. "Lu," he called out. "I have a letter from Mammi Becky for you."

He squinted through the screen. Joanna turned from a sink full of dirty dishes. She swiped the back of her hand across her forehead.

"It's me, Adam."

"Jah," she said, "I figured. And you have a letter for Mammi Lu?"

Adam raised the envelope. "Would you give it to her?"

Joanna's voice softened a little. "Come on in. She's in the living room."

Adam opened the screen door and stepped into the hot kitchen. A strand of hair had fallen from Joanna's bun and trailed along her cheek as she walked under the drying herbs and lavender hanging from the ceiling. She turned her attention back to the dishes.

When he stepped into the living room, Lu didn't hear him. She stared out the window, toward the woods.

"Lu," he said.

She slowly turned toward him. "Adam?" She stood. "How are you?"

"*Gut.*" He extended the letter. "Mammi sent me over with this."

She took it. "Can you stay for a glass of lemonade? We can all sit out on the porch."

He was tempted to accept her invitation, but then Joanna would be forced to spend time with him. He couldn't feel good about that.

"Denki," he said, "but I have chores to do back home. I'll stay another time."

Lu nodded and held the envelope behind her back. "Did Joanna see the letter?"

"Jah." He gave her a questioning look.

"That's all right," Lu said. "I suppose it doesn't matter."

It was odd it might matter. It was also odd Mammi Becky would send Lu a letter when they lived so close, but Mammi Becky did a lot of odd things.

On Thursday when Caleb and Adam stopped for a water break at the Pequea Creek house, Caleb told Joanna he'd heard she was going to Maine. "My Dat wants me to," she answered.

"So you're going?"

Adam listened closely for her answer, but she only shrugged. Perhaps she would have told Caleb her plans if Adam hadn't been within hearing distance.

They'd finished gutting the kitchen and pantry. They had also gutted all three-and-a-half bathrooms in the house, and all the debris had been hauled outside and loaded into the dumpster.

After their water break, Caleb and Adam headed outside to take down the shutters on the south side of the house. All the shutters needed to be repaired, painted, and rehung. Adam hesitated to ask Caleb about Miriam and Jacob, but finally he did. "How long have Miriam and Jacob been courting?"

They each carried a ladder and a drill toward the side yard. "I don't know. Daniel and Elaine haven't talked about it."

"Has Mandy talked to Joanna lately?"

"No. She's been busy with other things."

"Like what?"

"Dealing with Miriam." Caleb's face reddened. "Plus we're seeing a doctor who's doing some testing."

Adam gave him a questioning look. Caleb's voice dropped in volume. "We've been hoping for a baby since we got married."

Adam felt for his friend. "I'm sorry. That must be difficult."

"Jah, it is." Caleb stepped onto the bottom rung. "Change of topic. How are things going with Joanna?"

Adam sighed. "Is it that obvious?"

Caleb chuckled. "It's always been obvious. On your part. Not hers."

"Jah, that's my problem."

As Adam set up his ladder, he could see Joanna through the window. She was taking down the wallpaper in the dining room below the window.

He glanced upward. A branch from the maple tree brushed up against a shutter. That needed to come down. He pointed it out.

"Do we have a handsaw?" Caleb asked.

"Nee, we didn't bring one," Adam replied. "I'll go look in the barn and see if one was left behind."

As he searched, he hoped nothing would fall on him from the decaying roof. Finally, he found a few tools on a bench in what used to be a tack room. It took a minute for Adam's eyes to adjust to the dim light, but he finally found a saw. He grabbed it and hurried out of the barn.

Caleb held Adam's ladder while he climbed it and while he began sawing through the branch that was about six inches in diameter. After a few minutes, Adam climbed up another few rungs on the ladder and continued sawing. And sawing.

"Want me to take a turn?" Caleb called out.

"Nee." Adam was out of breath. He slowed a little, wanting to drop the branch straight down, but just before he completed the cut, the saw slipped. In trying to reposition it, he put more pressure on the branch. There was a snap and the branch bucked and spun, knocking Adam off the ladder. As he fell, the branch crashed through the glass.

Adam managed to toss the saw away from the house and away from Caleb as he fell, so his concern was entirely for Joanna. Was she on the other side of the window? He landed on his shoulder and rolled to his feet. The branch had missed the small panes and broken through the larger window. He tore around the side of the house, across the veranda, up the steps, and through the back door.

He slid on the drop cloth at the entryway to the dining room. Joanna stood before him, glass sprinkled on her shoulders, holding the branch.

"I'm so sorry," he said. "Did it hit you?"

"Nee," she answered. "I started working away from the window when I saw you on the ladder with the saw."

She glanced at the shattered window, which was most likely as old as the house. "We'd better clean this up," Joanna said. "And tell your grandparents what happened. In the meantime, you and Caleb need to cover the window." Adam's heart raced, but Joanna seemed to be calm. At least on the outside.

Joanna always had a contingency plan. She was composed in an emergency. She always kept a first aid kit and a fire extinguisher at the worksites, and in the midst of an emergency, she was the one in control because she was the one who was prepared.

Impressed, he took the branch from her. "I'm really glad you're all right."

Her eyes glimmered a little. She put out her hand. "If you give me the cell phone, I'll leave a message for your grandparents. We'll need to match the vintage glass if possible—the sooner we have the replacement, the better."

27

On the first day of August, Rhoda stood at the sink in the hot kitchen of her little cottage, missing the farm as she peeled potatoes until the clippity-clop of horse hooves and then the turning of wheels over the gravel driveway caught her attention. She peered out the window. It was Lu's horse. She squinted. Nehemiah drove the buggy, and it appeared he was alone.

She rinsed the potato and dried her hands. Then she braced herself. As much as she loved her oldest son, she dreaded what he might be stopping by for. His entire life, he'd had one wild idea after another. When he was a young adult, she'd been thrilled with his drive and fortitude. Then, for years, she supported as many of his ideas as she could, but the older she grew the wearier she became. She finally realized he was reckless—not visionary.

She stepped to the back door and onto the porch that had room for only two chairs. It was so much smaller than their porches—front and back—on the farm.

"Nehemiah," she called out. "Hallo."

He raised his head from where he was tying the horse to the hitching post.

"Mamm. How are you?"

"Fine." She couldn't help but think he'd stopped by to ask for something. That would be an easy answer on her part. They had nothing more to give.

"Where's Dat?"

"Running an errand. He'll be back in a little bit. How about a glass of iced tea?"

He patted the horse. "Denki."

"Let's sit on the porch. It's too hot in the house."

When Rhoda returned to the porch with the iced tea, Nehemiah was sitting down.

She extended a glass to him.

"How are you liking this place?" he asked.

"*Gut*. It serves its purpose." She sat down.

"Feels like home?"

She hesitated. Should she be honest? "I miss the old place."

"Jah, that was quite the property. I have good memories from there too."

No doubt he did. Rhoda asked, "Does the place in Maine feel like home?"

"Jah. It absolutely does. When are you and Dat joining us?"

"It's too cold for your Dat." She'd already told him that more than once.

Nehemiah chuckled. "He'll be fine. You'll need to relocate soon enough, so we can look out for the two of you."

Rhoda didn't answer. She no longer had any desire to move to Maine.

"Joanna is going to go back with me."

Rhoda gripped her glass tighter, and her voice caught in her throat. "What?"

"Jah. I told her since Jacob broke up with her there was no reason for her to stay here."

"What about Lu?" She put her glass down on the porch floor. "And her job. Joanna loves that job." And from what Becky said, Joanna was really good at it. Rhoda turned toward Nehemiah. "What about me?" She longed to get to know Joanna better. "Why would you take her away?"

Nehemiah threw back his head and laughed. "You didn't feel that way when we lived across the road."

Rhoda's face grew warm. She picked up the glass and pressed it against her cheek, mortified Nehemiah had noticed her lack of attention toward Joanna. Had everyone? She changed the topic. "Did you consider staying with us on this trip?" She'd been hurt that he hadn't.

"There's more room at Lu's. And Joanna's there."

"What did you stop by for?" Rhoda leaned back in her chair.

"We've had a couple of financial setbacks. I wondered if you and Dat could loan me some money."

"Have you asked anyone else for a loan?"

"Jah. Luanna."

She felt a jolt of embarrassment. Had he been asking Lu for money all along too?

Rhoda took a drink. "What did she say?"

"She can cover part of what we need but not all of it."

"How do you plan to pay her back?"

"Suz has been selling flowers all summer at the nearby farmers' market. We have quite a few tourists traveling through our area now. Joanna will be a big help with that. We're going to buy more cattle. We've also planted a pumpkin patch and plan to have a corn maze in October. There's not one in our area, and we're hoping it will be a success."

Rhoda finished her iced tea.

"What do you think?" Nehemiah asked. "As far as the money."

"We don't have anything to loan you," Rhoda said. "We need the savings in case we have an emergency."

"You don't have to worry about that—like I said, we'll take care of you."

Rhoda shook her head. "We're staying here."

"That's Dat's decision, right? Not yours."

"He's made it." Rhoda paused. "We're in agreement."

"I'll talk to him."

She stood. "Nee. He's having some health issues. High blood pressure, that sort of thing. I don't want you to upset him." She thought of Marcus dying when he was only sixty-nine, and Ike having a heart attack at sixty-eight. Hiram was older at seventy-four.

Nehemiah had a disappointed expression on his face. "I won't upset Dat, but he'll see things my way."

"He won't. We've given you all we can." Rhoda stood. She'd been the one who encouraged Hiram to keep supporting Nehemiah, even after her husband was done. "I need to get back to my work." She took a step toward the door but then turned back to her son. "Let Joanna make her own decision."

"She's my responsibility."

"She's twenty-two."

"We need her."

"Look at her for who she is," Rhoda said. "A sensitive,

creative, hardworking young woman. She has an important role in this community." Why hadn't she seen those same qualities in Joanna when she was a child? Instead she'd seen her as someone to tend to the chickens, hang the laundry, cook for everyone, and watch the little ones. Rhoda winced. No doubt Nehemiah had gotten his way of thinking about people from her. Lu was a source of money. Joanna was a source of labor. She and Hiram should move to Maine because it would benefit Nehemiah.

"Mamm." Nehemiah was on his feet. "Don't be like this."

"Like what?"

"Harsh."

"I'm not being harsh. I'm being realistic. We don't have the money. We already sold most of the farm for you. What we made off the remainder, we need to save." She exhaled slowly. "Joanna would be miserable in Maine."

He muttered, "And you wonder why I didn't stay here."

Rhoda bit her tongue for a moment and then said, "Have a good trip home. Tell Suzanna hello."

"What am I supposed to do?"

"It sounds as if you're taking the right steps. You need more income—you have a plan." As she stepped back into her kitchen, she felt a wave of grief. She didn't want to have conflict with Nehemiah, but she had no more to give.

But what hurt her the most was to think of him taking Joanna with him.

28

Saturday morning, while Joanna worked and Nehemiah was out and about, probably telling people goodbye before he left that evening, Lu sat at her desk in the living room determined to write her next circle letter.

Her three friends had shared far more than she had. Elaine had requested prayer for a granddaughter who longed to have a baby. It wasn't common for *anyone* to talk about fertility issues in their community.

Obviously, she was talking about Mandy. She didn't ask for prayer for anyone else, including Miriam. Of course Elaine wrote her letter before the wedding was published, which still baffled Lu. Why would Daniel allow Miriam and Jacob to marry so soon?

Elaine didn't ask for prayer for Veronica either.

Lu took out a piece of stationery paper and her pen. She wrote, *Dearest Friends—*

"Luanna?"

She quickly slipped the letters back into the envelope and tucked it into her knitting basket beside the desk.

She stood. "I'm in the living room."

Nehemiah came in, his hat in his hands. "I'm leaving today—around five. We'll drive through the night." He glanced around the room. "Where's Joanna?"

"She's working this morning."

"Do you know where at?"

Lu shook her head.

"I'll go over and ask Ike."

Lu stood. "Don't bother Joanna while she's working. I'm going to meet her at Ike and Becky's at noon. I'll tell Joanna what your plans are."

"Tell her to come home and pack. I'll meet her here after I run a few errands." Nehemiah turned back toward the kitchen. "I'll see you then."

Lu listened until the back screen door slammed, then exhaled. Surely Joanna didn't plan to go with Nehemiah.

Instead of returning to the letter, she went into the kitchen and made sandwiches, packed her basket, and added a bag of peaches from her tree that Joanna had picked that morning.

It was hot by the time she started the half mile to Becky's. The basket grew heavier and heavier as she walked, and she had to stop and put it down a few times and take a few deep—and warm—breaths. And say a few prayers. She was only halfway there when Joanna came jogging toward her.

Lu grinned. Sometimes she feared she loved the girl too much.

"Mammi." Joanna came to a stop and took the basket from her. "It's too hot for you to be walking. Why didn't you bring the buggy?"

"Your father had a few errands to run." Lu paused a moment to catch her breath. "He's leaving at five and said he wants you to be ready to go with him."

Joanna made a face but didn't say anything.

Lu choked on the words as she asked, "Do you plan to leave?"

"Nee. I have a job that I love." Joanna's voice wavered. "And I have you."

Lu's chest tightened. She couldn't speak for a long moment. Finally she asked, "Do you know your father thinks you're going with him?"

Joanna exhaled but didn't respond.

Finally, Lu asked, "How was work this morning?"

"*Gut*." Joanna kept talking as if everything was fine. "Adam and Caleb are almost done repairing the shutters and the new window was installed—it's a match. Oh, and Adam put in the new smoke alarms."

"Speaking of," Lu said, "I think we need to change the batteries in ours."

Joanna grasped the handle of the basket more tightly. "I already did."

"Good girl." It made Joanna feel better to have the battery-operated smoke alarms in the house, and Lu appreciated them too.

Nehemiah had commented a few years ago she should trust Gott to wake her up if there was a fire. Lu had told him Gott could use the fire alarms to do just that.

~

When they reached Becky's, she and Ike were standing on the front porch. It appeared they were arguing, which meant they were both feeling better. No one loved each other more than Ike and Becky, and no one argued more than they did—well, than Becky did—either.

"Nee," Becky said. "You're not going over there. Adam will be home soon. Let's talk about you going on Monday. We'll go together."

Lu and Joanna stepped around to the back door. Rhoda stood at the kitchen sink as Mandy greeted them. The younger woman seemed a little sad, making Lu think of Elaine's letter.

"Is your Mammi coming?" Lu asked.

Mandy shook her head. "Miriam isn't either."

Joanna, with concern in her voice, asked, "What about Veronica?"

Mandy stepped back toward the table. "She went back to live with her folks."

Joanna moved toward her friend. "Is she all right?"

Mandy exhaled, as if she'd been holding her breath. "I think she will be." Her voice was shaky as she said, "Look, I'm really sorry about all of this. I had no idea. I think there was some sort of mix-up as far as what my Dawdi knew, as bishop, and the decision to publish Miriam and Jacob's wedding. I think Miriam exaggerated some things. Or something."

Lu joined Rhoda at the counter, wanting to give the young women space.

"I don't hold you responsible," Joanna said. "Jah, I have questions about how all of this came about, but it's out of my control. And it's certainly not anything you're responsible for."

Mandy said, "I should have called—" as Lu asked Rhoda, "How are you doing?"

Rhoda pushed her glasses up on the bridge of her nose,

and then plunged her hand back into the sink. In a low voice she said, "I guess we all have our problems. Nehemiah said he asked you for money. I'm mortified."

"Ach, Rhoda." Lu put her hand on her friend's back. "Nehemiah and I have our own relationship." She smiled. "You're not responsible."

Rhoda leaned down and touched the top of Lu's head with her cheek. "Denki. You know, I'd be willing to talk sometime later if you wanted to. To compare notes."

"Jah, we can talk. That's probably a good idea." Lu tightened her apron as she said, "What can I do?"

"I was going to start making another batch of my stew when I finish these dishes. Do you want to peel the carrots?"

When it was time to eat, Becky made a tray for Ike to eat his sandwich in the living room. "We've had too much time together lately," she said and then laughed. "Although he wouldn't mind eating with the rest of you." After she finished the tray she said to Joanna, "You take it to him. And tell him not to come looking for chips."

Lu doubted Joanna would say that to him, and she was right. A few minutes later, Ike came into the kitchen asking for chips. Becky glared at Joanna first and then at Ike. Everyone else laughed, including Ike and Joanna. Finally Becky did too.

As they ate, Joanna said, "Becky, I've never heard how you and Ike met."

Becky grimaced. "Today might not be a good day for that story."

"Any day is good day," Lu said. "It's a sweet story."

Becky nodded. "It is." She put her sandwich down. "Ike grew up near York. We went over there for a party."

"We?" Joanna leaned forward as her eyes widened. "Party?" Her voice was playful.

"Jah." Becky grinned. "Didn't your grandmothers tell you we were all partiers?"

Rhoda harrumphed. "Speak for yourself."

Lu laughed and addressed Becky. "Jah, *you* were the partier. We sometimes tagged along for the ride."

Becky laughed. "That's true. I had an Impala. Boy, could that thing fly."

"It was too old to fly," Rhoda said with a straight face.

"Anyway, I—"

"We," Rhoda interjected.

"That's true. We—"

"Who exactly is *we*?" Joanna asked. "And what is an Impala? Some kind of car?"

"Lu, Rhoda, Elaine, and me." Becky picked up a chip. "And jah, it's a car."

"Why did you have a car?"

"Because I'd been cooped up my entire life caring for my younger siblings. I got a job waitressing when I was sixteen—it was my younger sisters' turn to take care of the little ones. I saved all my tips and somehow managed to buy a car and hide it in the woods a mile from my parents' farm." She popped the chip into her mouth.

"Because you were the best waitress around," Rhoda said, her voice droll. "You had people begging to sit in your section."

Becky sat up a little straighter. "That's true."

Lu, wanting to speed up the story, said, "We were out in the middle of nowhere west of York."

"You just took off like that?" Joanna appeared dumbfounded. "Your parents let you go that far?"

Lu met Becky's eyes and shrugged. "They didn't know," Becky said. "Well, mine didn't ask—we were on our Rumspringa."

"We all told our parents we were spending the night at each other's houses." Lu scrunched her nose. "We'd mix it up every week."

Joanna choked on a chip. "Every week?"

Rhoda cleared her throat. "Tell how you met Ike or maybe stop the story. We don't want to give Joanna any ideas."

Joanna swallowed. "Mammi Rhoda, I'm twenty-two, not fifteen."

Becky flashed Joanna her million-dollar smile. "We know, Joanna. And even so, you've always been a good girl. You were never rowdy like we were."

"Like *you* were," Rhoda retorted.

Sometimes it pained Lu that Joanna hadn't had more fun. She'd barely had a Rumspringa.

"Anyway," Becky said, "I parked my car in a field, and lo and behold, just like that this boy who was dressed Amish pulled up in a Mustang."

Joanna's eyes lit up. "I know what a Mustang is."

"They were cooler back then than now." Becky leaned toward Joanna, and her voice grew husky. "Ike climbed out of his car wearing barn pants—"

"Wait." Joanna's eyes grew wide. "Weren't *all* of you wearing Amish clothes?"

"Um," Becky said, "nee. We all wore jeans."

Lu burst out laughing. "You wore a mini skirt."

"That's right. I did." Becky grinned.

Lu turned to Joanna. "Becky was born a looker."

Joanna blurted out, "Mammi!"

"It's true." Lu shot Becky a sassy smile. "I think people would say authentic today. You were always exciting—and genuine."

Becky acted shocked. "*Were?*"

Lu laughed again and Becky waved her hand, as if to dismiss them all. "Joanna," she cooed, "read whatever you want into what your grandmother said."

Rhoda cleared her throat. "Are you going to finish your story or not?"

Becky grinned and then said, "Anyway, Ike and I took one look at each other and it was love at first sight. We sold our cars, took the membership class, joined the church, and then married." Becky brushed her hands together. "And that's that."

"Forty-seven years next month of *that's* that." Ike stood in the doorway. Was that a tear in his eye? He looked at Joanna. "She might not give me chips, but she's given me everything else I've ever wanted."

~

As Lu and Joanna walked home late in the afternoon, Lu felt anxious about the upcoming confrontation with Nehemiah. Would Joanna stand up to him? Could he somehow force her to go with him?

Joanna broke the silence. "So what makes a marriage work?"

"Liewi," Lu answered. "Love is what makes it all work. And you have to nurture that love throughout your entire relationship."

"That's interesting. It seems as if everyone focuses on commitment. Dat said once he thought any Amishman and

Amishwoman who were committed to each other and Gott could make a marriage work."

Lu's nostrils flared as she exhaled. She'd heard that sort of thing before. "When Marcus and I were courting, our bishop said essentially the same thing, but I disagreed. I couldn't have made a marriage with Daniel work."

Joanna laughed. "What about Dawdi Hiram?"

"Nee." Lu shook her head and put up one hand. "Nothing against Hiram."

"What about Ike?"

Lu chuckled. "Definitely not, as much as I care about him. Ike was absolutely made for Becky."

"Who married first?"

"Becky and Ike. Becky did everything first in our group." Lu paused for a minute before she added, "Love is what matters, but so does *Freindschaft*. You have to have both. I believe it's a solid friendship that gets you through the years. Life can be hard—marriage should make it easier." She felt the lump forming in her throat and the tears pooling in her eyes. "Marcus was my best friend."

"Wait. I thought Becky is your best friend."

"Best girlfriend. Your Dawdi Marcus was my very best best friend."

"Really?" Joanna switched the basket to her other arm. "A better friend than Becky?"

"Really. Becky is my oldest friend, but I could trust Marcus about everything. He'd tease me to make me laugh—but never to embarrass me. He always had my best interest at heart. He never competed with me. He always listened. This might sound like a given, but he took such good care of me after each of our babies was born." Lu thought for a moment. "He encouraged me to grow and sell flowers. He never minded our kitchen had flowers and herbs hanging from the ceiling. Marcus was always there for me, prioritizing my needs and interests."

"Aww," Joanna said, smiling down at her grandmother. "I love that."

Lu nodded. "Wait for a man who is a good friend first and then see if the two of you fall in love. That's the kind of man you can rely on. That's the kind of husband you want." She laughed. "Love at first sight worked for Becky and Ike, but it doesn't work for everyone."

Joanna slowed a little more to match Lu's pace. "I know my parents are committed to each other—but Dat's so wrapped up in his own ideas and dreams and projects that they don't spend as much time together as you and Dawdi did. I don't think Dat's a good partner to Mamm, a good support. I don't want that."

Lu understood what Joanna was saying, but she countered it with "You never know exactly what goes on between two people when they're alone."

"That's true." Joanna sighed. "I feel so unsettled about my life right now, about my future."

"Jah, of course you feel unsettled. But also remember you're resilient—and being resilient can feel unsettling. But eventually things will stabilize. You're strong. Right now you might not feel that way, but you will again. In fact, you will feel stronger—because you *will* be stronger."

They'd reached Lu's driveway. Two figures sat on the porch.

Lu squinted. "Can you tell who's here?"

"Dat and—" Joanna hesitated. "Is it Jacob?"

Lu bit her tongue to keep from saying she hoped not.

Joanna sounded relieved as she said, "It's Adam."

Nehemiah stood. "Jo, we only have a few minutes. Get your things!"

Joanna didn't respond and continued walking at Lu's pace.

"Hurry!" Nehemiah stepped off the porch. Adam stood and leaned against the railing.

"Our ride will be here any minute," Nehemiah said. They'd nearly reached him. "Adam came to tell you goodbye."

Lu's heart skipped a beat, and she put her hand to her chest. What did Joanna plan to do? Nehemiah was like a bundle of clean and dirty laundry all mixed together, the good and the bad. She needed Gott to sort him out—it was beyond her.

They'd reached the steps to the porch. Joanna stopped and so did Lu. Joanna, her voice firm, said, "I'm not going."

"What do you mean you're not going? Of course you're going. We already figured this out. You decided to go." Nehemiah was clearly upset.

"You decided." Joanna stood tall. "I never intended to go. I'm staying here."

Lu exhaled the pent-up breath she just realized she'd been holding.

A vehicle turned down the driveway. A van.

"Our ride is here." Nehemiah sounded frantic. "Go pack your clothes. You still have time."

Joanna shook her head. Nehemiah glared at her, but she didn't budge. He stepped back onto the porch, grabbed his bag, and brushed past Joanna as he said, "*Machs gut*, Luanna. Suz will write soon."

Lu shook her head. She'd been waiting nearly thirty years

for Nehemiah to grow up. It wasn't going to happen. "Make it good, Nehemiah," she parroted in English. "I'll write back."

Once he'd climbed into the van, Joanna turned her attention to Adam. "Did you come to see me off?"

"Nee. Of course not." He leaned toward her over the railing. "I didn't come to tell you goodbye, although your Dat assumed that. I came to give you moral support in case you decided to stay."

Gratitude filled Lu. She'd been annoyed with Becky for wanting to matchmake, but she couldn't help but agree with her friend. Adam and Joanna were good for each other. And, it seemed, they were friends. Maybe even good friends.

"Adam," Lu said, "I made meatloaf this morning. All I need to do is boil the potatoes. Will you have supper with us?"

His eyes danced as he smiled. "I will."

29

After the closing supper prayer, Mammi told Joanna that she'd clean up. "You and Adam go for a walk."

"Nee, Lu," Adam said. "Joanna and I will clean up. You've had a long day." Joanna appreciated that about Adam. He did dishes. He made coffee. He was never above a task.

Her Mamm used to tell Joanna to persevere at whatever task she was doing. "Don't give up," she'd say, even when Mamm was in bed, exhausted. "Keep trying." And Joanna did keep trying. At sewing. At cooking. At knitting. She applied her mother's advice to her work for Ike and Becky too. No doubt that was why she'd been successful.

But why had she kept trying with Jacob, even when he'd been distant? Was it because, all along, she thought she'd at least have a better relationship than her parents had? Was that her goal?

As Joanna washed the dishes, Adam dried. First he asked if she was liking *Persuasion*.

"Jah," she answered. "I'm in volume two." She laughed a little and lowered her voice. "I can relate to Anne's challenges with her father."

Adam nodded. "I really appreciated all of the complicated relationships in the story, both in the families and in the community." Joanna noted he didn't add anything about the romance.

Once he'd dried the last dish and put it away, Adam said, "How about that walk now?"

"I'll check on Mammi and see how she's doing." Joanna peered through the living room doorway. Mammi Lu sat at her desk, writing. She corresponded with all sorts of people. A sister-in-law in Ohio. A cousin in Kentucky. Joanna's family in Maine. Her three sons and their families. She often wrote letters in the evening.

Mammi didn't notice her, so Joanna stepped back into the kitchen. She met Adam's eyes. "I think I should stay here."

He gave her a faint smile. Was it a defeated one?

The truth was, she didn't want to have to talk with Adam more than she already had while they did the dishes. Even though Adam had come over in case Dat tried to bully her to leave, she was still miffed with him for writing her the anonymous letters.

~

There was no church the next day, and Joanna and Lu didn't go visiting either. Joanna intended to skip the Youngie volleyball game that evening at Mandy and Caleb's and stay home and read, but Caleb swung by in the midafternoon and asked her to come. "Mandy could use the help," he said. "We probably shouldn't have volunteered to host, but it's too late to cancel now."

"You can take the horse and buggy," Mammi Lu said from her rocker.

Caleb interjected, "Or get a ride with Adam."

She considered that for a moment, and then said, "I'll drive myself." Adam might want to stay longer.

She braced herself to see Jacob and Miriam, but they weren't there when she arrived. She joined Mandy in the kitchen, which smelled like popcorn.

Joanna asked, "How can I help?"

Mandy motioned toward a huge stainless-steel bowl that was half full. "Would you make the rest of the popcorn?" She motioned to the oil, salt, and bag of kernels.

"Of course." Joanna heated the oil, dumped in the popcorn, put the lid over the top, and slid the pan back and forth over the burner.

A girl—the one who was a friend of Veronica's that Tim had given a ride home—came into the kitchen and approached Mandy. Joanna remembered her name was Wendy. "Is Miriam here?"

"Nee," Mandy said.

"I need to speak with her."

Joanna couldn't make out Mandy's answer. Someone called out, "Joanna!"

She turned as she kept shaking the pan. Adam came toward her. "How are you?"

Tears stung her eyes. She blinked a couple of times. She turned back to the stove. "Fine." She shook the pan harder.

"Is it burning?"

She turned the burner off and yanked the pan to the middle of the stove. Smoke billowed out from under the lid.

"May I help?" Adam reached for the hot pad. "I'll take it outside."

Joanna nodded, gave him the hot pad, and stepped back.

He grasped the pan handle and hurried through the kitchen and out the back door. Joanna stepped to the window to watch him. He took it to the chopping block. Caleb yelled out, "Did you burn the popcorn?"

"Jah," Adam said.

Joanna turned to Mandy. "I'm so sorry."

The girl beside her held her nose. Mandy frowned. "Don't worry about it." She grabbed the saltshaker. "We have enough."

Joanna took the salt from Mandy and began shaking it on top of the popcorn already in the bowl.

"How is Miriam feeling?" the girl asked.

"Shh."

Joanna turned. "What's going on?"

The girl's eyes widened. "You don't know?"

"Know what?" Joanna's head began to ache.

"That's why Veronica went home. She's mortified. She thought Jacob was interested in her." Wendy paused and then said, "Miriam's—you know."

Joanna shook her head. But her stomach dropped as the girl whispered, "She's going to have a baby."

~

Joanna slipped out the back door to Mammi Lu's buggy. Caleb had just started the volleyball game, so everyone had shifted to the side yard, including Adam. He stood at the net with his back to her.

As she hitched her horse to the buggy, she turned toward the sound of hooves. Jacob came toward her. She ducked around the side of the buggy until he passed and then climbed inside, released the brake, and drove away slowly, hoping not to draw attention to herself.

She felt as if she were on fire. She fought back angry tears as she took the back roads home, taking as much time as she could. She didn't want to have to explain herself to Mammi Lu.

The sun sat on the horizon as Joanna finally turned onto the highway. Just before she turned down Mammi Lu's driveway, a buggy came toward her from the other direction. Ike and Becky. They sat closer than most courting couples she knew. Becky was driving. She waved, but without her usual grin. She had a concerned expression on her face. Joanna waved back and smiled. She didn't want Becky to worry.

Joanna took her time unhitching the horse, feeding her, and brushing her down. Then she walked to the woods and sat on a stump, staring up at the darkening sky. By the time she returned to the house, the lights were off—but someone was sitting on the porch.

She hoped it was Adam. The thought surprised her.

Then she noticed a scooter. And a second one. She squinted. Both Mandy and Miriam sat on the top porch step.

"There you are." Mandy stood. "We need to talk." She reached out toward Miriam, grabbed her arm, and pulled her up. "All of us."

Miriam appeared uncomfortable, with good reason.

"Adam was the one who noticed you were gone," Mandy said. "He started to come after you, but I said Miriam and I would. She'd just arrived." She must have been in the buggy with Jacob.

Miriam tugged her arm away from Mandy.

Joanna felt frantic, as if she were swatting at flames, but she did her best to sound composed. "Come on." Joanna motioned toward the stable. “I can take both of you home while we talk. I’m sorry you waited so long.”

“Nee. Caleb is going to come get us.” Mandy sat back down on the top step. “Come talk.”

Joanna did what her friend said, sitting on the step below. Miriam sat beside Mandy, who nudged her twin.

“I heard Wendy told you my news.” Miriam wrapped her arms around her knees. “I didn’t know you and Jacob were courting again. It’s my fault. I should have told Mandy Jacob had been coming up to see me for the last year. He’d hire a driver on Saturday afternoons.”

“I didn’t know, honestly,” Mandy said. “I’m as surprised as anyone. Miriam and I don’t talk about that sort of thing.”

“She hasn’t approved of anyone I’ve courted.”

“I’ve stopped asking,” Mandy said.

“Which makes me sound worse than I actually am—or was. I broke up with Jacob after we dated for those first few months because he assumed I was wild based on rumors he’d heard about me.”

Joanna thought of Jacob saying he’d found her the most “interesting” of all the girls at the singing on the night they first met. Perhaps he’d said the exact same thing to Miriam.

“But over time, he wore me down.”

Joanna believed her. She tried to keep her voice steady. “Do you care if I ask a few questions? Personal ones.”

Miriam’s voice was full of concern. “How personal?”

“Not *that* personal, I promise.” Joanna folded her hands. “Will you and Jacob be shunned?”

“Jah.”

“Do you love him?”

“Do you?” Miriam asked.

"Nee," Joanna answered. *Absolutely not*, but there was no need to say that out loud.

Miriam let go of her knees and slumped backward a little. "Nee, I don't either. We'd been going out, off and on, for so long that he became familiar." She grimaced. "Too familiar. But I never loved him, not really."

Joanna felt ill. Poor Miriam. "What was going on with Jacob and Veronica?"

"He wanted to court her—until I told him, you know, what's going on with me." Miriam rolled her eyes. "He didn't put it together that Veronica's our baby cousin. That really stung."

Joanna wrinkled her nose. "Jacob shouldn't have gone out with her at all," she said. "He's twenty-six."

Miriam and Mandy nodded in unison.

"I have one more question," Joanna said. "What does your grandfather say about all of this?"

"That we'll make a confession." Miriam hugged her knees again. "Then be shunned, restored, and then married. It happens all the time."

"But do you *want* to marry Jacob?" Joanna leaned toward Miriam. "This will be for the rest of your life."

Miriam's voice was barely above a whisper. Her confidence was gone. "What choice do I have? Mammi Elaine is already beside herself with shame. I think this is her worst fear come true. I spoke to our parents yesterday on the phone—they're mortified too. Honestly, Dawdi Daniel has been the most supportive."

Joanna didn't point out that rushing Miriam into marrying someone she didn't love wasn't exactly supportive. She thought of Mammi Lu's talk of love, friendship, and marriage. That was what Miriam deserved, regardless of what had happened.

"Does your Dawdi know about Veronica and Jacob?"

Miriam shook her head. "Veronica asked me not to tell him. She doesn't want anyone to know."

"He's the bishop; he needs to know." Joanna exhaled. "And he's her grandfather; he really needs to know."

Miriam glanced at Mandy, who after a long moment said, "Maybe we should think about this more."

Joanna shifted toward Miriam, putting her feet up on the step she sat on and hugging her own knees. "Don't marry him if you don't love him."

Neither Miriam nor Mandy responded. They looked at each other and then back at Joanna.

"You deserve better," Joanna said to Miriam. She'd never guessed Miriam would be the one to marry someone she didn't love. Joanna turned toward Mandy and said, "I'm sorry. I know how much you want a baby."

"About that." Mandy's hand fell to her abdomen. "It's too early to say anything." She glanced toward her twin.

Miriam grinned. "I'm shocked."

"Jah." Mandy wrapped her arms around her middle. "So am I, after all this time. I'm not very far along. Only the doctor and Caleb know. We're not telling anyone, of course—except for you two." She laughed a little. "Rather impulsively."

Joanna reached up and took Mandy's hand. "That's wonderful news." And then she took Miriam's hand. "And I'm sorry for the circumstances, but your news is wonderful too."

Again, Miriam didn't respond. After a long moment of silence, she said, "Do you remember making hollyhock dolls with Lu when we were little?"

"Jah," Joanna said. "I was thinking about that recently."

"I always loved visiting you and Lu. I only wished I'd gotten to know you better. I've been a little jealous that you and Mandy became such good friends."

"It's not too late." Maybe Joanna would have a group of friends like Mammi Lu did after all. She just hoped Miriam wouldn't throw her life away on Jacob. He clearly had problems.

Maybe Joanna was loveable after all.

~

For the first time since they were girls, Joanna hugged both Mandy and Miriam goodbye when Caleb arrived. She felt exhausted from the encounter but also relieved. Miriam had been truthful with her. She finally knew what had happened with Jacob. And Mandy valued her friendship enough to come after her and bring Miriam with her. Plus, Mandy was going to have a baby. That was good news. And Miriam was going to have a baby too, which made Joanna full of all sorts of conflicted feelings. But the baby itself wasn't the problem.

With all of that swirling around in her head, Joanna couldn't sleep. She turned her head toward the open window, hoping for a cool breeze. She listened to the crickets and katydids. She counted backward by threes from five hundred.

Finally, around midnight, she tiptoed down the stairs and poured herself a glass of water. Then she wandered into the living room and sat for a few minutes, looking out the window into the woods. Enough light came through from the nearly full moon that she decided to knit for a while. Perhaps the repetition would make her sleepy. She usually didn't knit in the summer—she was too busy gardening—but she had a stocking hat, ironically for Jacob, halfway finished. She'd give it to someone else instead. Maybe she'd mail it to Leon—he could use it in Maine.

As she pulled out her needles and yarn, an envelope and then a batch of folded papers fell out of the basket. She picked up both. The envelope said *Lu* in Becky's handwriting.

The top piece of paper read *Dear Lu*. Was it the letter Becky had written to Mammi Lu that Adam had delivered? But why was it so thick?

She glanced at the letter. Becky had asked for prayer for Ike's health and then for her grandson. She only had one. Becky asked for prayer that he would find a wife soon, someone in Lancaster County, and settle down.

Joanna flipped to the next page. It was a letter from Mammi Rhoda to Elaine. What was going on? The letter asked for prayer for Joanna, for her broken heart, and that she and Jacob would get back together. Joanna felt as if she'd just ingested a pound of sawdust. Mammi Rhoda's next letter asked for prayer for Nehemiah and his endeavors in Maine and that Joanna would find the right man to marry and soon. Joanna felt ill. She hated to be the topic of conversation, even if it was a prayerful one. Or more likely, since Elaine was involved, a gossipy one.

She flipped to the next page. It was a letter from Mammi Lu asking for prayer for someone very dear to her who was hurting. At least Mammi Lu was more discreet, but no doubt everyone knew who she was writing about.

It was obviously a circle letter among the friends for their families. She read through the letters again and as she did, she placed them in chronological order. She felt even more exposed than she had before.

Did Adam know about this? Had Becky encouraged him to write the anonymous letters to her? Was Becky, and maybe even Mammi Lu, trying to matchmake?

Joanna folded the papers and shoved them back into the basket. She didn't want to knit after all. She tiptoed back upstairs, lit her lamp, and picked up *Persuasion*. A sheath of waxed paper fell out onto her quilt. She picked it up. Inside were daisies. She opened the waxed paper. New daisies.

Did Adam remember the daisy bracelet she'd made in Pinecraft? The one he'd put on his windowsill?

Adam had been the one to drive her home from church when Jacob and Miriam's wedding was published. He was the one who came over to support her when Dat was trying to force her to move to Maine. Jah, of course he remembered the daisy chain from Pinecraft. Adam was looking out for her.

She put the sheath of waxed paper under her Bible on her bedside table and kept reading.

Finally, just after two a.m., she blew out her light. She feared everyone saw her as a problem to be solved. Her father believed she couldn't make it on her own, not even living with Mammi Lu. Becky's solution seemed to be Adam. Perhaps Mammi Lu agreed. Mammi Rhoda believed she needed divine intervention—and no doubt she did—to find a husband. Daniel wanted her to go to Maine too, and no wonder.

Did she have a genuine connection with Adam? Or did he feel she needed constant encouragement? Did she come across as that needy?

She turned to her side and pulled the quilt tightly around her. It had seemed so natural to let her concern for Miriam and her baby outweigh her concern for herself. But now she couldn't help but think maybe Maine was her best option after all. She'd be close to Leon and able to get to know his little one. And perhaps her relationship with her Mamm would be better. Maybe there was even hope things could get better with Dat, although she doubted it based on his visit.

But she had a job to do for Becky and Ike. And Mammi Lu to take care of, along with her gardens. And friendships, including Adam, even though she was miffed with him, to nurture. Jah, Maine tempted her. It seemed to be the only route of escape that could leave her pride intact. But she wouldn't do that. At least not yet.

~

Mammi Lu asked if Joanna was doing all right as they ate coffee soup—coffee with milk over bread—for breakfast because that was all Joanna felt up to fixing. "You look tired. How did you sleep?"

Joanna stirred the concoction in her bowl, making the bread even mushier. "All right."

"I heard you up during the night."

"I was thirsty." Joanna put down her spoon. She couldn't swallow another bite even though the bowl was nearly full.

"Were you looking for something in the knitting basket?"

Joanna nodded. "My knitting project."

"Did you see the letters?"

Joanna pushed the bowl toward the middle of the table. "Jah."

"Did you read them?"

"They fell out of the envelope. I'm sorry."

"Don't be. I shouldn't have left them there. Is that why you couldn't sleep?"

"Nee." Joanna rubbed her eye. "I found them because I couldn't sleep and thought knitting might help."

"Why couldn't you sleep?"

"Did you know Miriam is pregnant?"

"I found out last night while you were gone." Mammi Lu put her spoon in her bowl too. "Your Mammi Rhoda told me."

"Who told her?"

"Your Dat. He stopped by on his way out of town to tell Hiram goodbye."

Joanna swallowed the lump in her throat. "Why didn't he tell me?"

Mammi Lu smiled wryly. "It wouldn't be like him to talk about something like that—not with you. But I believe part of the reason he wanted you to go was to protect you. It seems Daniel told him."

Joanna felt as if she might retch. She put her napkin over the top of her bowl.

"I'm sorry," Mammi Lu said. "And I'm sorry about the letters too. I definitely shouldn't have left them where you could see them."

"I don't mind that you and Becky and even Mammi Rhoda were sharing prayer requests about—well, me. But Elaine?"

Mammi Lu nodded. "I understand. There was a mix-up. Rhoda passed the letters on to her."

"What do you mean?"

Mammi Lu inhaled sharply. "Becky started the circle letter so we could share prayer requests without saying them out loud during our quilting time."

"Because you didn't want Elaine to gossip?"

Mammi wrinkled her nose and nodded. It seemed Mammi Lu didn't want to say too much out loud. She didn't need to worry. Joanna wouldn't tell anyone.

Joanna stayed away from Jacob at the warehouse and stayed quiet in the van on the way to the Pequea Creek property, still feeling unsettled. Once they were there, she spent her time painting the largest of the second-floor bedrooms. Fifteen minutes before quitting time, a car turned into the driveway. Joanna watched from the landing window. She'd finished the bedroom and had washed her paintbrushes. Caleb hurried toward the car. Joanna guessed Mandy had a doctor's appointment and Caleb was going with her. She couldn't help but smile.

She continued down the stairs and put the paintbrushes and drop cloth away in a bin in the dining room. Adam stepped out of the kitchen and said, "I need to talk about last night. When we realized you'd left I was going to go after you, but Mandy insisted on going instead."

Joanna nodded.

"I'm really sorry about this new development concerning Jacob."

"Denki," she managed to say. She didn't want to talk about it, especially not with Jacob on the premises. She stepped around Adam toward the front door, longing for a breath of fresh air.

"Wait."

She turned.

Adam's eyes were full of concern. "How are you doing? Really?"

She managed to mutter, "I don't want to talk."

"That's fair, but I'm willing to listen if you change your mind."

She stepped into the foyer but then turned back. "What are your thoughts on the circle letter that our grandmothers all belong too?"

He cocked his head. "I don't know anything about a circle letter."

"Do you know anything about a matchmaking letter?"

"What?" He laughed.

Of course he'd think it was funny.

His face grew serious. "Tell me about the letters."

She gave him a brief synopsis of what she'd read.

"It doesn't sound like they are actually matchmaking. It sounds as if they're hoping we all find trustworthy spouses, like they did." His eyes filled with compassion. "But I can see why it seemed like matchmaking."

What was it about Adam that made Joanna feel both safe and frustrated at the same time? He was a good listener, but he also wasn't afraid to contradict her. Although it was always in a thoughtful way. And why did she find herself thinking about him? It had only been a month since Jacob broke up with her. She didn't want to be interested in someone else so soon, not even Adam. And yet, he was in her thoughts far more than she wanted to admit to herself.

Mammi Lu was right—above all a husband needed to be a friend. A best friend. She'd known that three years ago, which was why she thought Adam was ridiculous to bring up courting before they even knew each other.

Why hadn't she realized that Jacob, even though he'd said he wanted to be, had never been her friend? Had she been too taken with his good looks and confidence to notice he only cared about himself?

Her heart lurched. Adam had said he couldn't be her friend, and yet he had been. Jacob had said he wanted to be her friend, and yet he never was. Joanna had compared Adam's telling her he wanted to court her when they first met to her father's impulsiveness. Jacob had seemed the opposite. But as it turned out, Adam was dependable and Jacob couldn't be trusted.

Shaken, she turned away from Adam and toward the foyer. "I'm going to get some fresh air."

30

Adam wasn't sure whether he should follow Joanna as she walked out the front door. Did she want to be alone?

Follow her.

He strode through the dining room and the foyer and out onto the portico. Joanna sat on the top step, her head against the pillar, staring at the afternoon light wafting through the trees on the other side of the road. "Mind if I join you?"

She turned her head and met his gaze. "I don't mind."

He sat beside her in silence, and then put his arm around her. To his surprise, she leaned her head against his shoulder.

He froze for a minute, fearing if he said anything or even moved he might scare her. But she scooted closer to him and he tightened his grip on her shoulder, pulling her close. She turned her head toward him, her faced raised. Adam's heart raced. He leaned toward her. She lifted her face to his, and then his mouth met hers. She kissed him back. When their mouths parted she smiled up at him, and a sense of calm came over him. He kissed her again, this time more passionately.

She wrapped her arms around him and kissed him back again.

As they both pulled away, he gazed deep into her dark blue eyes. He wanted to tell her he loved her. Instead he asked, "Do you want to talk now?"

She shook her head, and then her eyes clouded. A sob tumbled out of her. She pulled away and jumped to her feet. Then she tripped down the stairs, catching herself at the bottom.

He stood and reached for her but she sped away. "Joanna! Wait!" He ran after her.

She turned and called out, her voice shaky, "I'm fine, really. I'm going home."

"I'll go with you."

She shook her head and jogged toward the footbridge. By the time she reached the other side, she was running.

Adam stopped at the road. She'd asked him not to follow her. And yet she'd kissed him back. Twice. Had he been wrong to kiss her in the first place?

He'd promised to be content with being her friend, and yet he'd asked her for more.

At least he hadn't said he loved her.

~

The next day Joanna wasn't at the warehouse in the morning. As Adam gathered supplies, Dawdi Ike and Mammi Becky arrived together for the first time since Dawdi's heart attack. They hadn't said anything at breakfast about coming in.

Mammi Becky said, "We've had a change in assignments." She motioned toward Dawdi and said, "Adam, Caleb, and Jacob, you're going with Ike to the Pequea Creek house." She glanced at Tim. "You're coming with me to the Garden Lane property."

Adam asked, "What about Joanna?"

"She's going with me to do the finishing work."

He exhaled. She was avoiding him. The last thing Adam wanted was to work with Jacob, but better for him to work with Jacob than for Joanna to have to.

It wasn't until their lunch break, while Dawdi Ike waited on the front porch for Nick to arrive to take him home, that he explained to Adam what was going on. "Joanna stopped by this morning after you left for work. She said she didn't want to work with you or Jacob—just for a day or two. She said she needed a break."

"So you accommodated her?" It hurt that she'd put him in the same category as Jacob.

"Jah, of course we did." Dawdi Ike put a hand on Adam's shoulder. "Anything you need to tell me?"

Adam shook his head. Not now. Not here. "How was she?"

"Unsettled."

Adam swallowed hard. "I'm not sure what happened." He changed his mind. Of course he needed to tell Dawdi what happened. "We had a—a moment, yesterday. And then she ran off."

Dawdi caught his beard and tugged on it. "So you upset her?"

"Jah." For that moment, they *had* connected. Even more so than they had in the van on the way home from Spartansburg.

Or when she'd visited Pinecraft. Or when they'd done dishes together that Thanksgiving he was home.

"Did you follow her? Try to find out what was the matter?"

"I started to, but she told me not to." Adam leaned against the pillar. "I thought I'd only make things worse."

The van turned down the drive and over the bridge spanning the creek. Nick waved as he stopped the vehicle. Dawdi walked toward him and, as Nick lowered the window, asked, "How are things going at the Garden Lane house?"

"Good. Becky and Joanna, with help from Tim, will have that place finished by the end of the day."

Dawdi Ike laughed. "No doubt they will." He turned back to Adam. "I'll see you after a while. Get as much done as you can this afternoon. And take another look at the barn—we need to make a decision on it."

Adam watched the van leave. He thought of sitting in the hospital waiting room with Joanna after Dawdi's heart attack. And again after Mammi Becky's panic attack. He'd had lots of moments of connection with Joanna over the years, especially over the last month.

When Adam arrived home, Dawdi was napping and Mammi Becky wasn't around.

It was obvious Mammi Becky had left in a hurry because the breakfast dishes sat in the sink. He cleaned the kitchen and then looked in the refrigerator, finding half a ham and a bowl of broccoli salad from the night before. He was setting the table when Mammi Becky walked through the back door.

He looked out the kitchen window. Joanna was in the front seat of the van, looking directly at him. His heart skipped a beat. She gave him a nod and a hint of a smile, enough to make his heart skip another beat and then race.

"Adam!" Becky clapped her hands together. "You are a dear. How's Ike?"

"*Gut*. Resting." Adam turned toward her.

"I'm right here." Dawdi stood in the doorway. "How did your day go?"

"Wunderbar." Mammi Becky swept toward him and took his hand. "We finished everything. It's all done. I did a walk-through with the owner, touched up a few places, and he signed off."

Dawdi beamed and then turned to Adam. "What about at the Pequea Creek house? What are your thoughts on the barn?"

"I think we should raze it and start over."

Mammi Becky groaned. "That's going to take time and a lot of money. We need to be looking for our next project if we're going to keep the team going."

Dawdi rubbed his arm. "About that. With all the unbudgeted expenses we're looking at, I don't know if we *can* keep this business going."

Adam's stomach dropped. "Do you plan to sell?"

Mammi Becky squeezed Dawdi's hand and then said to Adam, "We're not making any long-term plans right now. We'll talk later."

~

After supper, Adam did the dishes and then slipped out the back door to go for a walk. He turned down the lane toward the barn so he wouldn't be tempted to walk by Lu's place and hope Joanna was working in her garden.

He stopped at the barn door. When his father fell all those years ago, Adam thought he was playing until his mother came into the barn, rushed to Dat's side, and kneeled beside him. Then she stood and ran to the door, screaming, "Ike! Becky!"

Both of his grandparents came running. Mammi scooped Adam up into her arms as his mother said something to Dawdi Ike, who kneeled too and began pushing on his Dat's chest. Mammi carried Adam out of the barn to the shed, where she made a phone call. Then she took him to the swing set in the middle of the yard and explained that paramedics would come to care for his Dat. "He's ill," she said.

"When will he be better?" Adam had asked.

She choked a little as she said, "Very soon."

Of course he was never better, not on earth anyway. It took years for Adam to realize Mammi Becky probably already knew her only child was most likely dying. But she'd stayed calm for Adam. And in the days and weeks and months ahead it was Mammi Becky who bathed him and dressed him and fed him as his mother mourned. It was Dawdi Ike who pushed him in the swing and took Adam out to do the chores every afternoon and read him a story at bedtime.

That was what he'd thought about when Dawdi had his heart attack. And when he'd come into the house and Mammi was on the kitchen floor. And it had been Joanna, both times, who had seen him through.

Adam walked on the edge of the highway into town. His grandparents needed his help now, but if they sold the business they wouldn't—at least for a while. He didn't want to go back to Spartansburg. And he didn't want to stay in Lancaster County. The first time Joanna rejected him was understandable. He couldn't even say she rejected him. She didn't know him. He'd been ridiculous.

It wasn't until he spoke with an older Mennonite woman who'd had training in counseling others that he realized he had abandonment issues from his father dying. Moving to Spartansburg with his Mamm when she married Leroy added to them. Adam was six by then and completely bonded with Dawdi Ike and Mammi Becky, as much as he was to his own mother. He'd lost his father and then his grandparents. Sure, he saw them periodically, but it wasn't the same.

And his stepfather was never warm or encouraging. He competed with Adam for his mother's attention, and after Adam's younger brothers were born Leroy favored them. He was critical of Adam—nothing he did was ever good enough. Nee, Adam would never return to Spartansburg.

That left Pinecraft. He knew he could get his old job back. When his grandparents' health deteriorated more—when they truly did need help—he could return to Lancaster County again.

By the time he reached his grandparents' lane, the sun had set and twilight lingered for a few more minutes. He decided to keep walking. He stopped on the edge of the woods, wishing Joanna were with him. The lightning bugs were flitting about, but Joanna was nowhere to be seen.

He turned around and walked back home. *Home?* Probably not for long.

He didn't see Joanna until the end of the next day. She was carrying a basket of linens down the rental apartment steps. He asked if he could help her, but she shook her head.

"Joanna," he said as she brushed past him. "I'm really sorry I upset you."

She met his eyes and smiled a little. "I upset myself." That hurt. It would be easier if she were angry with him. She slipped past him into the warehouse.

He turned toward Dawdi and Mammi's house. There was a boy in the yard. Neither Dawdi nor Mammi had worked today, and he guessed they'd had friends stop by.

He strode toward the house. The boy was swinging. It was his youngest brother, Phillip. Adam began to jog. A woman waved at him. His Mamm. Was Leroy with her? He didn't see him.

Then an Amishman stepped around the corner of the house, but he didn't have a beard. It wasn't Leroy. Adam squinted. It was his other brother, Victor, all grown up.

Adam waved back to his Mamm. Mammi Becky stood beside her, and Dawdi Ike followed Victor. When Adam reached the yard, Phillip jumped out of the swing.

"Look at the two of you," Adam said. "You've both grown so much." Phillip rushed toward him, but Victor held back. "What are you doing here?"

His Mamm stepped forward. "Victor is going to work for Leroy's cousin for a while."

Adam's eyebrows shot up.

"He's seventeen," Mamm said. "We thought it would be good for him to work for someone else for a change."

"Come into the house," Mammi said. "Supper is almost ready. We can talk more at the table."

Adam waited while everyone else filed inside, and then paused a moment on the back porch to take off his work boots. As he did, Joanna scootered by the house. He waved, and she waved back, then sent him a questioning look.

"My Mamm is here," he said. "With my brothers."

"All the way from Spartansburg?"

He nodded.

"That's nice." She sounded happy for him.

Complicated was a more accurate word, but he didn't say it out loud. "See you tomorrow."

She nodded.

After a supper of a chicken pot pie, his mother said she'd do the dishes.

"Nee," Mammi Becky said. "You and Adam need a chance to talk."

"We can do the dishes together." Adam turned to his brothers. "You can help Dawdi Ike with the chores. He can't lift anything over fifteen pounds."

They hurried out the door, probably afraid they might be forced to help with the dishes too.

Mammi Becky said, "I'll go supervise."

After they cleared the table, scraped the plates, and put the food away, Mamm started running the dishwater. "Why didn't Leroy come?" Adam asked.

"There was no one else to do the chores, plus he needs to start harvest."

It must have been an emergency for Mamm to take a trip with the boys the first week of August. Adam lowered his voice. "What happened?"

"Vic's been running around, and he's gotten into some trouble." Mamm paused a moment and added, "He and two friends—Englisch kids—were arrested for vandalism. They set a play structure at the city park on fire." She exhaled. "The sheriff said to get Vic out of the area for the next year or so and make sure we put the fear of God in him."

"How did Leroy respond?"

"At first he blamed it on the Englischers' influence, but Vic is responsible for his own behavior. Leroy has come to see that. It's up to Vic what happens next."

Adam took a plate from the rinse water. "I'm sorry."

"Nee." Mamm turned toward him. "I'm sorry. You were such a good kid, yet Leroy was so hard on you while he treated Vic like a little prince. I tried to talk with Leroy, but he discounted what I had to say. I never stuck up for you like I should have." She wiped her hands on her apron and swiped at her eyes.

"Mamm, it's all right." He put his hand on her shoulder.

"Nee. It's not all right. You're my son." She reached up and squeezed his hand and then pointed out the window toward the warehouse. "We were so happy here. It makes me sad to come back." Mammi Becky and Phillip came out of the barn and headed toward the chicken coop. Both were laughing.

Mamm plunged her hands back into the dishwater. "Ike and Becky have always been good to me."

"To me too," Adam answered. "I don't know where I would be without them." For a minute he feared he'd hurt his mother's feelings, but she nodded in agreement.

They both concentrated on their work for a few minutes. Mamm broke the silence by saying, "I was used to caring men, your Dat and Ike in particular."

Adam wasn't sure what to say.

In her quietest voice, she said, "You're a lot like both of them."

Adam turned to her. "Denki." It was the nicest thing she could have said to him.

31

Joanna thought about kissing Adam as she walked along the edge of the woods that evening. She'd never felt so trusting, so real, so free—almost as free as she had felt on Siesta Beach in Florida—as she had kissing him. She'd felt it all the way down to her toes.

She'd never experienced that with Jacob. That was why she ran. Her feelings for Adam terrified her. She'd always been in control of her emotions in her relationship with Jacob—but the freedom she felt with Adam turned into fear by the time the second kiss ended.

Even though Jacob had talked about his father abandoning his family the first night they went out for ice cream, it turned out he was fairly opaque with her. He never really opened up. He was never vulnerable with her. He'd always seemed in control too—confident and in charge.

But she'd never been vulnerable with him either. She'd never told him about her childhood house catching on fire or her mother's depression. She'd never told him about her father's impulsiveness. She'd never even told him about what a caring brother Leon was.

So why did her feelings for Adam terrify her? Because she'd been vulnerable. Because she'd stopped being aware of herself. Because her heart felt as if it might explode. Because as she pulled away from Adam, she realized what she was risking. What if Adam changed his mind and left her the way Jacob had? What if it was her—what if she really wasn't loveable?

She stayed at the edge of the woods until after dark, but the lightning bugs didn't appear. She wasn't sure if she wanted Adam to appear or not but still she waited. He didn't. Finally, she trudged back to the house and on upstairs. She'd read for a while and hope sleep would come.

~

The next morning, as Joanna started toward the office door, she heard Becky say, "Ike's problems aren't the same as your Dat's. It seems those came from my side of the family and are genetic. I want you to get tested, to have an echocardiogram, and see if you have the same condition."

Adam said, "That sounds expensive."

Becky said, "We're going to pay for it."

"If I have it, will knowing make any difference?"

"Jah," Becky said. "There's medication you can take if you have HCM."

"HCM?"

"Hypertrophic cardiomyopathy, a thickening of the wall of the left ventricle. It's treatable. I already made an appointment for you, for tomorrow. Nick will take you."

"But I don't have any symptoms," Adam said.

"Just the same—"

Joanna, alarmed to be eavesdropping, retreated to the kitchen counter. She grasped the coffee percolator tightly, her palms sweaty. She wiped her hands on her apron and then picked up the percolator again. Had Adam inherited the same heart condition that killed Reuben?

What if something happened to Adam? What if he suddenly died like his father had? Her hand began to shake as she filled the coffeepot. She steadied the bottom of it with her other hand.

Of course Adam should get tested, as soon as possible. Was tomorrow soon enough? Once she started the coffee, she gathered supplies to go clean the apartment. Adam wasn't anywhere in sight.

In the afternoon, Nick drove her to the Pequea Creek house. Becky had told her Jacob and Adam would be finishing the outside trim. They'd had to strip the old paint off the south-facing window casings before painting them.

Joanna didn't see Adam when she arrived, but she did see Jacob. He was using a heat gun on the trim around a living room window. She walked through the front door and back to the kitchen. All the prep work had been done for the cabinets and appliances, and the walls and trim had been painted. She continued through the house and up the staircase. Adam stood at the window on the landing.

"Hallo," she said.

He turned around slowly, running his hand through his hair as he did. "Hi, Joanna."

"How are you?" she asked.

Adam shrugged.

Her hands tingled. She rubbed them together. "I'm just going to say what I need to say." She leaned against the railing. "I overheard your Mammi talking with you this morning."

He had a curious expression on his face. "About?"

"Getting your heart checked."

He wrinkled his nose. "I'm sorry you heard that."

"You're going to do it, right?"

He shook his head. "What is, *is*. Right?"

"Wrong. Your Mammi said there's medication if you do have the condition. You need to have the test done."

"I'm not as much of a planner as you," Adam said.

"Everyone should be a planner, especially when it comes to one's health."

He shrugged again. "We'll see."

"Do it for your grandparents."

He exhaled and swallowed, his Adam's apple bobbing up and down.

"Do it for m—"

"Joanna!" It was Jacob.

Adam sighed. "He's been looking for the extra battery for the heat gun."

Joanna turned to go.

"Wait," Adam said.

She turned back toward him. She'd almost said *"Do it for me,"* which surprised her. "Do it for your grandparents," she said again. "You're all they have." Tears pricked at the backs of her eyes and her voice wobbled as she said, "They need you."

Someone—Tim—yelled, "Feiyah!"

Joanna's knees locked. For a moment she couldn't move. Then Tim yelled, "Fire!" and she twisted around and tore down the stairs, fearing she might tumble she was moving so fast. She held on to the railing as she flew, yelling, "Adam! Call 9-1-1."

She slid to a stop in the foyer, grabbed the fire extinguisher and two fire blankets from the emergency box, and tore out the front of the house. The drop cloth and a pile of rags under the living room window where Jacob had been working were on fire. Tim had the hose and was running toward the fire—obviously he'd forgotten the plumbers had turned off the outside water the day before. Jacob was using a second drop cloth to try to beat out the fire, but it was too flimsy to do any good. Instead he was spreading the sparks.

Adam was right behind Joanna, on the phone. She turned and tossed him one of the blankets as she pulled the pin on the fire extinguisher.

She yelled at Jacob, "Use this!" as she tossed the other blanket at him and began spraying the fire that was scorching the dry azalea bushes in the flower bed and licking at the house.

An hour later the firefighters had left and everyone returned to work, except for Joanna. She sat on a bench on the back veranda, forcing herself to take deep breaths.

"You okay?" Adam stood at the kitchen door.

"Jah." Joanna took another deep breath and held it. The wail of the sirens still played in her head as she counted to ten.

"You were amazing—unflappable, really." Adam stepped onto the veranda. "All of your planning paid off. You knew exactly what to do and had the emergency box in exactly the right place. If you hadn't been working today, the fire could have spread quickly."

Joanna exhaled but didn't respond to what he said. Instead she took another couple of deep breaths and thought about how when she was little and afraid to try something new, Leon would say, "It's okay to be scared brave." *Scared brave*. When he was older he told her the definition of courage was the ability to do something even if it was frightening. "*You're courageous when you have no choice but to do the right thing, even when you're scared,*" Leon had said. That's how she felt in an emergency.

Adam sat down on the bench beside her. "You remind me of Anne in *Persuasion*. She was the one who was good in an emergency. She was the one who nursed others when they were injured."

She realized her breathing had slowed. "Did you put the daisies in the book?"

"Jah," he said. "I put them there for you."

She choked as she said, "Denki."

Adam spoke again. "Thank you for encouraging me to get tested." He paused for a long moment and then added, "I've decided to keep the appointment."

After work, Joanna was hot and sweaty and still smelled like smoke, although she guessed it was probably her imagination. Instead of working in the garden like she usually did after work, she went straight inside with the intention of showering and washing her hair. Mammi Lu sat in the living room reading. She glanced up and asked, "How was work?"

Joanna wasn't ready to talk about the fire, even though

everyone was all right and no damage had been done besides to the side of the house that needed to be cleaned and the azaleas that needed to be pruned. "Fine."

"Did you see your letters on the table?"

"Nee." Joanna turned back toward the kitchen. "Who are they from?"

"Your folks."

Joanna backtracked and grabbed the letters. The return address on one was Mamm and Dat's, while Leon's was on the second one. He hardly ever wrote anymore. She sat on her bed and opened the envelope from Leon.

Dear Joanna,

First I have to apologize for not writing more often. Life here keeps getting busier and busier. Katie delivered a baby girl—named Joanna after you, although we're calling her Jo Jo—two days ago.

Joanna's eyes filled with tears. Leon and Katie had named their baby after *her*.

Jah, she wished she'd known Katie was expecting, but it wasn't unusual for couples not to announce a pregnancy. And she wasn't surprised Dat hadn't told her.

She blinked a couple of times and continued reading.

Dat was frustrated you didn't come to Maine with him. Please don't take him seriously. There are days when I think he's getting better—and others when I think he's worse than ever when it comes to his behavior. But we're all managing. Even prospering, somehow.

Dat said he told you about our fire. It wasn't as bad as he probably made it sound, and I hope it didn't worry you. We all are doing fine. I miss you.

Your brother,
Leon

Besides bringing her joy, Leon's words also comforted her. He'd always been a strong leader and a good teacher. She knew he was a big help to their brothers as they all established themselves. He'd always been so dependable. And his advice not to take Dat too seriously confirmed that her decision to stay in Lancaster—at least for now—was the right one.

The next letter was from Mamm. She'd been busy canning the first of her tomatoes. Then, probably getting to the reason for the letter, she continued with,

Your Dat told me he ordered you to come back to Maine with him, but you refused and he ran out of time to change your mind.

It sounded as if Dat had really talked up her refusal with the rest of the family, which wasn't surprising.

I wanted to let you know we have a new doctor here, a woman who has helped me quite a bit. She ran some tests on me and found a few problems—low thyroid and other deficiencies—and I'm taking medication for the first time. Slowly, I've been feeling better than I have in years. Your father plans to

see her soon and see if she can help him too with focusing and being less impulsive. I'm hopeful.

Mamm wrote a little more about how everyone was doing, including Leon and Katie's new baby.

I'm glad you're with your Mammi. I have plenty of people here to help me—but my own mother only has you. As long as you believe it's God's will for you to stay in Lancaster County, I think you should. Not that I don't miss you—I do. But I trust you to make the decision that is best for you.

I need to close this letter and get back to my flowers and preparing for the next market.

Write soon,
Your Mamm

P. S. I'm sorry about Jacob, but—honestly—he never seemed right for you. I know God has someone better suited for you when you're ready.

Joanna held the letter to her chest as tears filled her eyes a second time. She'd never felt so hopeful for her family. Maybe, in time, her Mamm and Dat could have a good marriage after all.

32

The next day, during the lunch break, Nick arrived with Becky at the Pequea Creek house. She gathered everyone around and asked them to push to get as much done in the next few hours as possible. "Then everyone will have tomorrow off, and we'll regroup Monday morning at seven thirty. Over the weekend, Ike and I will redraft a plan to try to finish this project by the end of September."

After Jacob, Caleb, and Tim got back to work, Joanna asked Becky if everything was all right with the business.

"Jah," Becky answered. They hadn't said a word about what project was next.

But that wasn't her biggest concern. Joanna spoke quietly. "Is Adam okay?"

Becky appeared gaunt and worried. She'd lost weight, which she hadn't had to spare, in the last month. In a near whisper she said, "We haven't heard back from the doctor yet."

Saturday morning Joanna and Mammi Lu canned beans. Then Joanna spent the rest of the day weeding the garden. In the evening she mucked out the stable. That night, by the light of her lamp, she finished *Persuasion*. Of course, all along she'd known Anne and Captain Wentworth would get their second chance, but the story still resonated with her. Mostly with how composed Anne was through trial after trial, much like Elinor in *Sense and Sensibility*, and yet each character, in her own way, showed her emotions at the end.

Anne's was an "overpowering happiness." Joanna longed to feel that way.

It was a letter, a well-written letter, that changed Anne and Captain Wentworth's trajectory. But Captain Wentworth, unlike Adam, had been honest in his letter writing—and he'd also been vulnerable.

She took the daisies out from under her Bible and put them back in the book. She wouldn't return it to Adam anytime soon. Perhaps she'd reread it first.

As she blew out her lamp she wondered if she was being too hard on him. He had been honest with her eventually. And vulnerable. It had taken time for Anne and Captain Wentworth to get their second chance. Was she willing to let time work one out for her?

Sunday was a church day at Jacob's uncle's farm. Joanna would have feigned being sick, but she didn't want Mammi Lu driving the buggy along the main highway by herself. When Dawdi Marcus had grown ill, Joanna had forced herself to learn how to control his horse, and now Mammi Lu didn't venture out on her own much anymore.

They were among the last to arrive, thankfully. That meant less time to interact with others and to dodge looks and comments. When Joanna returned from seeing to the horse and buggy, Mammi Lu stood with the older women, next to Becky. Elaine and Rhoda stood a few feet away. Joanna glanced around for Ike but didn't see him. Dawdi Hiram waved and gave her a kind smile.

Adam stood with the single men. Jacob wasn't in line, and Joanna didn't see Miriam. Relieved, she joined the other single women. It appeared Jacob and Miriam would be shunned at another time, most likely in two weeks.

After the singing concluded, Caleb's father, who was a frequent preacher, gave the sermon. Joanna's mind wandered. He read Ecclesiastes 4:10 in German. *For if they fall, the one will lift up his fellow: but woe to him that is alone when he falleth; for he hath not another to help him up.* Her mind wandered again. It seemed like in no time, Caleb's father was ending the sermon with a verse from Proverbs. *A friend loveth at all times, and a brother is born for adversity.*

Did Adam love her? The thought startled her. Nee. Despite the kiss, she couldn't assume that.

After the sermon, Daniel walked to the front and said, "We have some church business to deal with."

Joanna braced herself and stared straight ahead.

"Jacob Byer and Miriam Troyer, come forward." Perhaps they had come in late or maybe even just arrived.

Jacob kept his head up and shoulders squared while Miriam mostly looked at the floor as they walked toward the front bench. Joanna had never seen her look so broken. They sat in front of Daniel.

Daniel clasped his hands and said, "As you know, Jacob and Miriam have asked permission to marry, which I announced two weeks ago. But in an ongoing conversation, it came to light that they have not been free of sin. They've confessed to God but wanted to come forward to confess in front of the church today. They will be put out of the church for six weeks and then returned to our community."

Joanna stared at the back of Jacob's head, which he held high.

"If anyone has any concerns, please speak with me," Daniel said. "Otherwise Jacob and Miriam will be married in October."

Joanna's eyes flitted to Miriam. Her head was bowed.

As the service ended, Joanna felt eyes on her. She moved along through the shed door with the other young women, holding her head up high. Once she was outside, Adam stepped to her side and whispered, "Do you want to go home?"

"Nee," she answered. She had nothing to be ashamed of. Besides, there was something she needed to do.

She headed to the driveway. Jacob was untying his horse from the hitching post, but Miriam wasn't with him. Joanna glanced toward the house. Miriam was sitting on the bench under the willow tree.

As Joanna started toward her, Miriam patted the bench and said, "Come sit."

Joanna did, saying, "I need to know if you're all right."

Miriam crossed her arms, cupping her elbows. "Jah."

"Joanna, what are you doing?" Jacob called out from his buggy, which was parked at the end of the walkway to the kitchen.

She waved her hand at him, as if dismissing him, a gesture she'd seen Becky do a hundred times.

"I'm all right," Miriam said. "But I appreciate you checking."

Joanna gave Miriam a nod. "Remember, you can still

change your mind." She gave Miriam a sympathetic smile. "Just do it soon."

Then she stood. Adam waited at the edge of the lawn. He gave her a nod. Had he been ready to step in and help, if needed, once again?

He asked, "Everything all right?"

She nodded and said, "Jah." And she meant it, at least for herself.

~

Later in the afternoon, Joanna told Mammi Lu she was going to go over to Mammi Rhoda and Dawdi Hiram's house with a plate of peanut butter cookies she'd baked the evening before. "Would you like to go with me?"

Mammi Lu shook her head. "You go along. I think I'll rest for a while and cool down." The weather had turned humid and a storm threatened.

When Joanna arrived, Mammi Rhoda sat on the porch. She stood as Joanna climbed out of the buggy. "Joanna!" Mammi Rhoda called out. "What a pleasant surprise." She sounded genuinely happy to see her.

Joanna waved, tied the reins to the hitching post, and then grabbed the plate. As she walked toward the porch, Mammi Rhoda asked, her voice full of concern, "How are you?"

"*Gut*."

Mammi Rhoda pushed her glasses up on the bridge of her nose. "Really?"

"Really." She meant it. "I brought you and Dawdi Hiram cookies."

"Denki." Mammi Rhoda leaned against the railing.

"Dawdi's napping. I'd wake him except he didn't sleep well last night. It's hard to cool this little cottage off."

"Do you have a fan?"

Mammi Rhoda shook her head.

"I'll pick up a battery-operated one for you. That might help."

"Denki." Mammi Rhoda gestured toward the chairs. "Sit. I'll go get some iced tea."

"Nee." Joanna put the cookies down on the little table. "You sit. I'll go get the tea."

A few minutes later, each ate a cookie while Joanna tried to think of a safe topic of conversation. Just as she swallowed her last bite, Mammi Rhoda said, "I need to apologize."

Joanna choked a little and began to cough. "Sorry." She took a long drink of her iced tea.

Mammi Rhoda laughed, a little ruefully. "Jah, I'm not known for my apologies."

Joanna touched her throat. "It was the cookie." But then she laughed too.

"I have a long list of things I need to address. You know, life doesn't always turn out the way we think it will. But specifically, I want to apologize to you for not spending more time with you when you were little."

Dumbfounded, Joanna wasn't sure what to say. So she said nothing.

"I had all that time to develop a relationship with you, but I squandered it. Now here you are a grown woman—" Her voice faltered a little. "I regret that now."

In her shock, it took Joanna a moment to find her voice. "I appreciate your apology. I wish I'd had more of a relationship with you as a child, but we're here, both in Strasburg

Township. I don't plan on going anywhere." She smiled at the realization. Jacob cheating on her and rejecting her would not make her abandon a life she valued in a place she loved. "We have time now to make up for the past."

Mammi Rhoda turned toward Joanna. Tears filled her faded brown eyes, amplified by her glasses. "Denki. I'd like nothing more than that. I'll never be the grandmother Lu is to you, but I promise to do my best."

"Ach," Joanna said. "Every relationship is different. It's best to focus on what we have, or can have. And the present."

"Denki for being forgiving." Mammi Rhoda took off her glasses and then dabbed at her eyes with her apron. "And for the good advice."

33

Becky stood at the bathroom sink in her white cotton nightgown, brushing her teeth. She started humming "All You Need Is Love" as she brushed. Ike, who stood next to her at his sink, joined her. She spit first and then began to sing.

Becky had an eight-track player in her car and a few cartridges, including *Magical Mystery Tour*. Selling her car, with the player and cartridges included, had been a sad moment for her. But the reward was joining the church and marrying Ike. It had been more than worth it.

Ike missed pop music the most when they joined the church. Becky missed it too, but she missed fancy clothes even more. She'd had to give up her skirts, jeans, and blouses. But no one could take away the lyrics to the songs. Of course, they'd never sing any of them with anyone but each other.

As they finished, they both giggled. Adam had gone for a walk, something he'd done every night for the last week. She'd become used to having the house to themselves over the years, but she hoped Adam never left. At sixty-seven and sixty-eight, she didn't feel as if they were old. But they did need more help than they used to and in time they would need even more.

The next morning, both Becky and Ike went to the warehouse and called the team together for a meeting. Ike announced they wouldn't be taking on another project until the Pequea Creek house was nearly finished. "We need to get it on the market."

Adam glanced at Joanna and then cleared his throat and said, "What about the barn?"

"We'll fix the roof."

"Like I said before, it definitely needs more than that," Adam said.

Ike rubbed the back of his neck. "We'll talk about it later."

As they walked home Ike looped his arm through Becky's. "Is it fair to Joanna to have Jacob still working for us?"

She pulled her arm in tightly, drawing him closer. "I asked her this morning. She doesn't want us to fire him."

"Why not?"

Becky shrugged. "She didn't say, but I think we should follow her wishes on this. She probably has Miriam's best interest at heart."

~

On Tuesday Becky caught up on paperwork in the office while Nick drove Ike to his cardiac rehab appointment. Adam had the cell phone, and when he returned from the Pequea Creek house he held up the phone as he walked into the office. "I had a message from the doctor," he said. "My heart is fine."

Becky stood but had to sit back down when her knees went

weak. "Wunderbar," she managed to say as she held out her hand. "I need to listen to it."

Adam shook his head a little as he handed her the phone. "You don't trust me?" Joanna stood behind Adam in the doorway, but then she disappeared.

"Of course I trust you," Becky said. "I just need to hear it for myself." After she listened, she handed the phone back. "Denki," she said, "for doing the testing."

He put his hand over hers. "I'm glad I did." Then he left the office. Curious about where he'd gone, Becky followed a few minutes later. Joanna and Adam stood at the counter, deep in conversation. Becky smiled as she quickly turned back toward the office, hoping Adam had shared his good news.

On Friday Becky hosted the quilting group. It had been over a month since the four of them had gathered to quilt. That morning after she tidied up, Becky lowered the quilt frame with Ike's help before he left for the warehouse. Then she arranged four kitchen chairs around it.

Lu brought her peach cobbler with whipped cream, which the women ate as they visited. The conversation started out about the muggy weather and who was canning what and moved on to Ike's health. Becky wasn't sure if it would stay surfacy or not. Elaine shared a funny story about a calf that got away. She laughed and then said, "I was out there in the middle of the lane going back and forth until the cows came home while a string of tourists' cars backed up each way. I can only imagine the photos they all took of me. It wasn't until Miriam—" Her face froze.

"It's all right," Lu said.

Elaine's eyes filled with tears.

Everyone was silent for a long moment. Then Becky said, "I need to apologize. I was the one who suggested the circle letter so we could share prayer requests about our families, but I don't know what I was thinking. It's much better for us to share face-to-face. I think we can all trust each other not to share the requests with anyone else."

"I've been thinking about this too," Lu said. "It's natural for us to want to talk about those we love. It's how we share our burdens, and it's how we bond with each other, even after all of these years. But I think we need to always be aware of our motivation. If it's ever to draw attention to ourselves, it's better not to share. Or if any of our kin, or someone else, would rather that information stay private, then we shouldn't share it either."

Elaine took a tissue from her pocket and wiped her eyes. "I know why you did the circle letter. I wasn't trustworthy." She blew her nose. "I'm sorry. I know I can be a gossip." She put her tissue in her lap and glanced around the room. "I never thought anything would happen in my family like this—like what's happened with Miriam." Elaine couldn't say it out loud, and that was all right. Becky understood. "All along people needed support, not my unkind words behind their backs. I hope you can forgive me."

Caught off guard, Becky tripped over her words. "Of course—we can."

"Jah," Lu said.

Elaine wadded the tissue in her hand. "But now I know what it feels like. I'm not sure if I'm reaping what I sowed—that will depend on how much others are talking about us—but Gott has certainly convicted me of gossiping in the past." Maybe she'd had an epiphany after all. "And it all feels so complicated. I'm worried about Miriam and I wonder if Jacob is right for her. And I worry about Joanna." Elaine leaned over the frame as if she could get closer to the other women. "How is she doing?"

"All right," Lu and Rhoda answered at the same time. Everyone laughed and the tension broke a little.

"Actually," Lu said, "she's doing well. She's worried about Miriam too, God bless her." There Lu went blessing people again. But if anyone deserved it, Joanna did.

"Ach." Elaine leaned back in her chair. "She's setting an example for me. She's a Youngie who has her house in order. I wish I'd had her maturity through the years."

Becky put her empty plate on the table beside her. "Can you believe it's been over fifty years since we started on our Rumspringa? It seems like it was last year."

Lu reached for her coffee. "The years are long, the decades short."

"Jah," Rhoda said. "Because the days fly by so quickly we can't keep track of them." She laughed. "Or remember what happened yesterday while still mulling over something from decades ago."

Elaine nodded in agreement.

They continued to quilt and talk. As they finished up the last of the stitches, Becky asked, "So who is the quilt for?"

Without hesitating Lu said, "Miriam. We'll send our prayers with it."

"Nee." Elaine reached for her tissue again. "That wouldn't be right to give it to her—and Jacob."

"I agree with Lu." Rhoda pushed her needle into her pincushion. "Miriam is going to need this."

"But what about Joanna?" Elaine asked. "Will she be hurt?"

"Nee," Lu said. "I know she won't."

"It's decided," Becky said. "The quilt is for Miriam." She grinned at Elaine. "You're outnumbered."

"What else is new?" Elaine's frown turned into a smile.

"Jah. So many things have stayed the same." Becky grinned, stood, and walked to her desk. She returned with a picture. "And yet so many things have changed." She held it up. "Remember this?" It was a photo of the four of them sitting on the hood of her Impala wearing bell-bottoms and halter tops. "It was taken the year we were nineteen, the year before we all joined the church and then married."

Elaine's mouth flew open. "Don't tell me you kept that photograph."

"Obviously I did." Becky handed it to Lu.

"Look at us." Lu sighed. "We were gorgeous." They had been. They all had long hair halfway down their backs and long legs and perfect skin.

"We're still gorgeous." Becky wanted to hug each one of her friends. What would her life have been like without them? "Pass the photo around. Remember what it was like to be young—and in love. That's what we want for our grandchildren."

~

That evening after supper while Adam did the dishes, Ike and Becky went for a walk out to the highway and down the road to Lu's and back. When they returned, the kitchen was spotless, and Adam was gone and so was the scooter they'd kept over the years. Becky hoped he was out having fun. If he and Joanna weren't going to court, then she hoped he would find someone else. And soon. He wasn't getting any younger and neither was his grandmother. More than anything, she wanted a little one around again that she could help care for.

As she and Ike got ready for bed, she asked, "What year was that old Impala I had?"

"Sixty-eight."

"That's right."

He laughed. "I'll never forget it. The day you stepped out of that thing was the happiest day of my life, up to that point in time."

"I was really something, wasn't I?"

"Was?" He reached out and gave her a pat. "You still are. You always have been."

She grabbed his hand and held it against her abdomen. "We've had a good life, haven't we? Despite the heartaches."

"Jah. The Lord has been good to us."

A little while later, after they'd crawled into bed, they both reached for the other's hand at the same time. They needed the Lord's love—and to love Him—most of all. And to keep loving each other. Becky's mind began to wander into sleep, but Ike squeezing her hand brought her back.

"You okay?" she asked.

"Jah," he whispered. "I just needed to say that I love you."

She smiled in the dark and turned her face toward him. "I love you too."

She drifted off again, holding Ike's hand. God willing, He'd give her another decade or two or even three with this man beside her. That was her hope. That was her prayer.

34

Adam kept scootering. He'd passed his grandparents strolling along on the other side of the road quite a while ago, but they were so engrossed in each other neither of them saw him. He wanted what they had someday. A love like theirs. When he was little he'd taken his grandparents' love for granted—their love pats and stolen kisses. And their hugs for him.

It wasn't until he was older that he realized other Amish couples didn't act the way his grandparents did. His mother and stepfather never showed any affection for each other in public—or even in their own house in front of their children. Nor did his stepfather ever show affection for Adam or even for his biological sons.

As he reached the Pequea Creek house, the sun was low in the sky. They couldn't sell the property without taking down the barn, and when the property included nine acres it needed some sort of large outbuilding. But Mammi Becky was right. The cost of building a barn would tank the projected profit.

That morning, Jacob had told Dawdi Ike, rather loudly in the middle of the warehouse, that he'd like to buy the business anytime Dawdi was ready to sell. Thankfully Joanna had already left to clean the rental and hadn't heard him. He guessed Jacob thought his grandparents' announcement on Monday that they wouldn't take on another project until the Pequea Creek house was almost ready to sell was an indication the business was struggling. Perhaps Jacob thought he had a chance to buy the business. Maybe his uncle planned to help him.

The thought of Jacob owning what his grandparents had built over the years made Adam cringe. On the other hand, his grandparents had said they wanted Adam to take over the business, but if they needed him to do it soon, would he be ready? Jacob had worked for them for three years. He knew the business better than Adam did. Adam didn't feel as if he was doing a great job managing the Pequea Creek house, but he didn't think he was failing at it either. But he most likely wasn't living up to his grandfather's expectations. Maybe Jacob was the right man for the job. And maybe his grandparents needed the money from the business now.

Adam parked the scooter by the barn door and then stepped inside. Swallows flew up into the rafters and out the holes in the roof. A mouse—or maybe a small rat—scurried to the back of the building. Even though the barn couldn't be repaired, much of the timber could be repurposed. It would take time to demolish the building and sort through the materials. He'd also need someone to draw up plans.

But he couldn't afford to pay for all of it from his savings and no one would give him a loan. He knew barn raisings in

Lancaster County were common, but not for an investment property. He didn't want to ask the community to help his family turn a profit, and he knew his grandparents would be mortified if he did.

The evening light filtered down through the roof. Adam turned back to the open door and then scootered back up the driveway. The sun was setting over the covered bridge and between the fir trees, shooting streaks of orange and pink both ways. Adam turned toward home.

He doubted Joanna would keep working for the business if Jacob bought it. Perhaps she'd end up going to Maine after all. Perhaps that had been her plan all along. Just because she hadn't gone when her father returned didn't mean she wouldn't eventually. Maybe she was waiting for his grandparents to retire.

There would be no reason for Adam to stay either. He could ask his grandparents to come to Florida every winter—they would love it. He could imagine them chatting with Amish and Mennonite people from all over the country in the park, playing bocce ball, kayaking on the creek, spending their mornings at the beach. He could see Dawdi buying a boat and going deep sea fishing. And Mammi organizing gatherings with her new friends. They would be the life of the party. "What happens in Pinecraft stays in Pinecraft" would take on a new meaning.

But he doubted Joanna would come down to Pinecraft from Maine. He'd most likely never see her again.

~

The next morning, Dawdi Ike gathered a few files full of paperwork at the warehouse to go over back at the house.

As Dawdi started to leave, Jacob strode to his side and said something to him, this time quietly. No doubt it was about buying the business. Dawdi replied, loud enough for Adam to hear him, "Nee, I haven't."

Jacob patted his back and said, "My offer still stands."

After Nick dropped everyone off at the Pequea Creek house, Caleb and Jacob returned to painting the outside trim once they had everything set up. Adam joined them.

Caleb asked Adam about the barn.

"I'm not sure what we're going to do," Adam answered. He didn't want to talk about it in front of Jacob.

"It needs to be razed." Jacob dipped his paintbrush in the bucket hanging from his ladder. "The sooner the better. I can probably find someone to take the wood."

"Nee." Adam concentrated on the trim. "It belongs to Dawdi and Mammi. And it's valuable."

Jacob scoffed. "Not really."

Adam bristled but didn't reply. Jacob was a cheat in more ways than one.

A voice from above called down, "Let's have a barn raising. We can incorporate the good wood from the old barn into it." It was Joanna, of course, leaning her head out the window above them.

"Mammi and Dawdi wouldn't be okay with that," Adam called up to her. "It's for their business, not their home."

"They don't have to know until it's happening." Joanna pulled her head out of the window. "I'm coming down."

Jacob yelled, "I don't think Ike and Becky would be in favor of it either. It's a bad idea."

Joanna didn't respond verbally. However, she slammed the window shut. Jacob glanced at Adam and shrugged. At least he didn't have a smirk on his face, but now Adam wanted to do whatever he could to support Joanna—not Jacob.

Joanna must have run down the stairs because immediately she came marching along the side yard. Holding up one of her ubiquitous yellow legal pads, she addressed Adam. "Do you have any idea how much your grandparents have helped people? They've paid medical bills. Bought new desks for schools. Reroofed houses for free. Loaned people money. Do you get the idea?"

Adam nodded. He knew Dawdi Ike and Mammi Becky were generous but he hadn't known the extent of their generosity.

"Everyone will want to attend a barn raising for them, even if it's on a property they're selling. I guarantee it." She gripped her notebook. "When should we do it?"

"I really don't think this is a good idea." Jacob stared down at Joanna.

She ignored him, speaking to Adam. "When?"

Adam cleared his throat. "A couple of weeks?" What exactly was he agreeing to?

"How about a month?" she answered.

He laughed. She was right. It would take a fair amount of planning and work to be ready for a barn raising.

"We'll have the cabinets in by then and the floors will be done," she explained. "We'll only have finishing work left. How about Saturday, September 20? I'll get the word out."

Adam asked, "How will we keep it a secret?

"Easy." Joanna smiled. "I'll tell everyone not to tell. And I'll make a list of everything we'll need to do to make it happen. I'll help you recruit enough men to take down the existing barn. You contact the barn builder. All we have to do is figure out how to pay him."

"I have an idea." Adam didn't want to say more in front of Jacob.

She gave him a questioning look. He shrugged. She nodded. Without saying another word, she turned and marched back into the house.

As Adam continued painting, he thought about Joanna. He longed to tell her how he felt, to talk things through with her, but he wouldn't pester her again.

He'd write her one more letter, explaining everything. There was no way he could be as eloquent as Captain Wentworth in *Persuasion*, but he'd do his best to be honest.

He wouldn't give it to her now. He didn't want to make things uncomfortable if she reacted negatively to what he had to say, not when they had over a month left to work together to finish the house. He'd wait until the barn raising, which meant he was committed to staying in Lancaster County at least until then. Evidently, so was she.

~

That evening as Adam did the chores and Dawdi Ike helped a little, Adam asked about Jacob's offer to buy the business. Dawdi said, "It's not a serious offer."

Adam wondered, regardless of Jacob's proposal, if his grandparents feared Adam wasn't the right person to run the business after all. He scooped out oats for the horses. "Do you plan to hang on to the business for a few more years?"

"Until you can take it over?"

Adam's face grew even warmer. "I need to figure out what to expect."

"At this point, it depends on my recovery, how soon the Pequea Creek house sells, what we get for it, and if we can find the right next project." Dawdi shrugged. "Sorry I don't have a solid answer for you."

"That's all right." Adam hesitated a moment. "What about my work? Do you have any pointers? Helpful criticism?" He thought of his stepfather and his constant unhelpful criticism. Dawdi hardly ever commented on Adam's work except to say he was doing a good job, but it was hard for Adam to silence the voice in his head that insisted he wasn't.

"Ach, Adam," Dawdi said. "Your work is good. I give you pointers all the time—you respond so quickly that I don't think you even notice. I haven't found any fault with your work." He patted him on the back and then said, "We do have some good news. Well, it started out as bad. The first offer on the farmhouse fell through, but we accepted the second offer last week. We don't foresee any problems."

For the next three weeks, Adam worked as hard as he could on the Pequea Creek house. A week before the barn raising, on Friday, Joanna walked toward Adam with her notebook in one hand and a pen in the other as he unloaded supplies in the warehouse. Tim, Caleb, and Jacob had just left. "Do you have a minute?" she asked Adam.

"Jah." He brushed his hands together.

"We need to confirm the details for the barn raising."

He glanced around. "Is Mammi or Dawdi here?"

"Jah," she answered. "They're in the office."

"How about if I take you out for ice cream?" It was a long time coming—if only she'd gone out with him instead of Jacob that first week after they met.

She gave him a sassy smile. "And spoil our supper?"

He flicked his hair out of his eyes. "Why not? I'll go hitch up the horse."

"Or we could ride our scooters."

He smiled again. "That sounds like fun."

She led the way to the highway and then into Strasburg. When they reached the creamery, they parked their scooters at the end of the building. "You get a table," he said. "I'll order."

"Just a scoop of chocolate," she said.

He gave her a nod. When he came out with a chocolate sundae for her and butterscotch one for him, she started to protest. But then she grinned and said, "Denki."

"Eat what you want." Adam sat down, not too close but not across the table either. A buggy went by, the clip-clop of the horse's hooves beating out a steady rhythm for his heart to emulate. Someone called out, "Adam! Joanna!"

It was Mammi Becky, no surprise, waving. Dawdi Ike was driving. He waved too. Joanna laughed. "I want to be like them when I grow up."

Adam nodded. "Me too."

Joanna seemed to be concentrating on her ice cream.

She took a few more bites and then took her notebook from her bag. "We should get to the planning."

He put his spoon down and rubbed his hands on a napkin. "We've dismantled as much of the barn as possible, thanks to the men you recruited to help. We've evaluated and stacked the wood. I told Dawdi we're doing it for safety reasons after calling in an inspector." Adam exhaled. It hadn't been easy discussing it with his grandfather. "At this point, they plan to sell the property without a barn. I met with the barn builder a couple of weeks ago and all the plans are done."

She leaned closer to him. "How did you pay for them?"

"My savings." Adam leaned toward her. "I ordered the materials, and I should be able to cover that too."

Her face softened. "I have savings too."

"I don't want to use yours."

"I'd like to help." She rested her hand on her notebook. "They might be your grandparents, but they're—"

"Your grandparents too," he said. "They adore you. But I need to pay for this. The barn builder gave me a discount and so did the lumberyard."

"I'm not surprised." She took out an envelope from her bag. "Several people contributed cash to help with the expenses."

Adam shook his head. "I can't take anyone else's money."

She slid the envelope across the table. "People gave anonymously. Dropped cash off while I was at work. That sort of thing. You have to take it—I can't keep it."

He sighed and took the money. "Denki." He had come to the end of his savings, which meant the donations would cover all the extra things he still needed to pay for.

They locked eyes for a long moment and then she glanced back down at her notebook. "Families in the district are coming, along with Englischers Ike and Becky have helped. I contacted one of your grandmother's sisters and asked her to spread the word down through the generations of the family." She made a mark on the page. "I ordered portable toilets and washing stations a while back, and I've covered the expense of those."

"Ach," Adam said, "you've already used your savings. I didn't want you to do that."

She smiled wryly and shrugged.

He doubted he could talk her out of it. "I appreciate it. And your organizational skills."

Joanna jotted something down on the notebook. "Everyone knows we're having a potluck, so that's covered." And then she asked, "When will the materials be delivered?"

"Next Friday morning, before noon. And the crane will arrive Friday afternoon."

"What will we do if your grandparents decide to come by the Pequea Creek house this week?"

"If they come before Friday, it won't matter. If they come Friday afternoon or Saturday morning, I'll have to tell them what's going on." He put his hand on the table near hers. He badly wanted to touch her, to take her hand in his.

But he didn't.

Instead he pushed his half-eaten sundae to the middle of the table and said, "I couldn't do it without you." It was true. But there was more he wasn't sure he could do without Joanna. *Life.* It was time to write that letter.

35

Saturday after her half day of work, Joanna caught a ride with Caleb to talk with Mandy, who was weeding the garden when they arrived. But then Mandy was on the back porch, calling out, "Hallo!" Joanna glanced back at the garden. Miriam was the one doing the weeding.

Mandy waved and then Miriam called out, "Hallo!" too. Hollyhocks lined the back of the garden.

After Joanna climbed down from the buggy and Caleb wrestled her scooter from the back, the twins started toward her while Caleb drove the buggy on to the barn. Miriam had a basket in her hands. As she reached Joanna, she said, "Let's make hollyhock dolls again. The blooms aren't going to last much longer."

"What about Caleb's dinner?" Joanna asked.

"He has some work to do in the barn first," Mandy said. "I have chicken noodle soup on the stove when he's ready." It had rained the night before, which dropped the temperature into the low sixties for the day.

"Jah," Joanna answered, buttoning up her sweater. "I'd

love to make hollyhock dolls." Jacob and Miriam's wedding would be at the end of October, seven weeks away. Miriam wasn't showing, not obviously, anyway.

"We'll need toothpicks." Miriam handed the basket to Joanna. "I'll go get them."

As Joanna followed Mandy around to the front porch, she asked, "Is Miriam still staying here?"

"Nee. She's living with our grandparents, but she comes over every couple of days to help me."

"How are you feeling?" Joanna asked.

"Awful." Mandy grinned. "But it's the best feeling in the world—most of the time." She sat down in one of the lawn chairs and motioned to another. "Miriam, on the other hand, is feeling fine."

"What about me?" Miriam asked as she came through the front door and joined them on the porch.

"I said you're feeling fine."

"About the baby, jah, but not . . ." Miriam's voice trailed off.

Joanna knew neither Mandy nor Miriam would be talking so openly about their pregnancies with anyone but her. And it seemed perhaps Miriam wanted to talk about something else too.

Joanna leaned toward Miriam. "But?"

She took three flowers from the basket and handed them to Joanna. "I'm not feeling so fine about Jacob."

Joanna chose three red blossoms and passed the basket to Mandy. "How so?"

Miriam met Joanna's gaze. "I've thought a lot about what you said. I don't love him." Her brown eyes sparked. "I'm not even sure I like him."

"Miriam," Mandy cooed. "The two of you just had a spat is all. Think of the baby."

"I am," Miriam said. "It's more than a spat—all we do is argue. And all I can think about is the baby. I'm this little one's mother. What kind of family will I be bringing him or her into?"

"But how would you support a child without Jacob?" Mandy asked. "Where would you live?"

Miriam put a toothpick through a flower. "Mammi Elaine said I could live with them as long as I need."

Mandy's voice squeaked a little. "Really? After your baby's born too?"

Miriam nodded. Joanna hid her surprise. That didn't sound like the Elaine she knew.

"This is all so complicated." Miriam nodded toward Mandy. "Your baby is a blessing. Mine is a—well, complication."

"Ach, Miriam," Joanna said. "Your baby is a blessing too. Truly." She would do everything she could to support Miriam and this little one.

Miriam exhaled and then said, "Denki, Joanna. I appreciate it—especially coming from you. You've been gracious. Something I don't deserve, especially not from you."

Joanna bit her tongue for a moment, but then said, "Jah. You do deserve it from me. Especially from me." She grimaced.

Miriam laughed. "I take it you didn't like him either."

"Nee, I *did*. But I've been seeing things more clearly now." Joanna threaded her hollyhocks on the toothpick. "I hope you don't mind me saying this, but I kind of feel sorry for him. I mean, he appears so put together. So confident. But he's not. He's a mess. He was courting both of us at the same time. And then he broke up with me because, it seems, he wanted to court Veronica. Didn't he realize everything would catch up with him eventually?"

"Nee." Miriam sighed. "I don't think he thought it ever would. I'm kind of surprised Becky and Ike kept him on at their business after the way he treated you."

Joanna simply said, "They're good people."

"Jah." Miriam glanced at Mandy. "Did you tell Joanna what they did for you?"

Mandy glanced around, as if someone might hear them, and then said, "Becky paid for us to go to a clinic she went to when she couldn't get pregnant again."

Joanna's heart lurched. Becky *had* wanted more children.

"I'm really sorry I repeated that rumor about Becky only wanting one child." Mandy blushed. "Mammi Elaine told it to me a long time ago. I thought it was true, but it wasn't."

Joanna winced, thankful she *hadn't* passed it on. Which she wouldn't have, no matter what.

Mandy changed the subject. "Did you know they all gave Miriam a quilt?"

Joanna shook her head.

Miriam had a peaceful expression on her face. "I can't tell you how much that means to me. And I think the other women wanting to bless me made Mammi Elaine more willing to let me live with them." Miriam took a pen out of her apron pocket and drew a face on the lime green receptacle of one of her hollyhocks. "I want to help with the barn raising, to do something to help Becky and Ike."

"What if Jacob's there?"

"He won't be," Miriam said. "He's going back to Ohio for a couple of weeks. He leaves Monday morning. I'm going to tell him tonight that I'm not going to marry him." She handed the pen to Joanna. "Honestly, he'll be relieved."

"He needs to pay child support," Joanna said.

"Jah. We'll need to figure all of that out." Miriam sighed and pushed the toothpick through her blooms. A right-side up bloom made the head, followed by two upside-down flowers, which looked like a full skirt. It was much fancier than an Amish doll. She held it up. "This is in memory of less-complicated times."

"Nee, these dolls are in hopes of all the times to come." Joanna raised hers too. "With good friends." She smiled at Miriam and then at Mandy. "I've been envying our grandmothers' friendship circle. But we have that too—more than ever now."

The twins agreed.

"Speaking of the future, how are you and Adam doing?" Miriam asked.

"What?" Joanna choked on the word.

Miriam laughed. "You two are perfect for each other." She looked at Mandy. "Right?"

Mandy smiled. "I'm not going to comment."

"It's only been a couple of months since Jacob broke up with me."

"So?" Miriam tossed her doll up in the air and then caught it. "You've known Adam for forever."

"Only three years," Joanna said.

Miriam laughed again. "That might as well be forever." She grew serious. "Adam is a good man. We all know that."

Joanna did know that. He'd given her space when she needed it. So much space that she feared he'd changed his mind about her. "He's thinking about moving back to

Florida." She looked at Mandy for confirmation. Caleb had told her that a few weeks ago. "Right?"

"He mentioned that to Caleb, but we've speculated it depends on what Becky and Ike do with the business. If they sell it to Jacob—"

"What?" Joanna almost fell off her chair.

Mandy put her hand to her mouth and then said, "Didn't you know Jacob wants to buy Ike and Becky's business?"

"He mentioned it a couple of years ago, but I didn't know he still wanted to."

Miriam rolled her eyes. "Jah, he'd like to buy it, but Ike and Becky would never sell it to him. Ike told him as much."

Relieved, Joanna changed the topic to the barn raising, not wanting to talk about Jacob anymore. Surely they would turn it over to Adam in a few years. Ike had announced that morning that they had another remodeling job lined up for October.

After she explained what she needed help with, Joanna headed toward home on her scooter, feeling more carefree than she had since, well, the day in Florida with Adam. That was the way she wanted to be, instead of worrying all the time. She knew trusting in Gott, not in herself, was key. She also knew that she felt more carefree with Adam near because she could share her burdens, and the burdens of others, with him. He was someone she could depend on.

When she reached the house, she sat on the porch with Mammi Lu and pulled out a handful of hollyhock dolls, a little wilted now, from her bag to give to her grandmother. Then she told Mammi Lu what Mandy had said about Becky.

"Jah, Becky didn't want eleven children, but she would have liked a few more. She was on birth control for a couple of years after Reuben was born because she didn't want to have one child after another. Later, she lost a couple of pregnancies and went to a special clinic. The doctor said the miscarriages had nothing to do with being on birth control previously. He recommended a couple of things, but Becky wasn't able to carry another baby. The doctor said it was no one's fault."

Joanna felt sad for Becky not being able to have more children. She was one of the most generous and loving people Joanna knew. Becky's love for Reuben must have been beyond measure, just as her love for Adam was.

Adam. What if Miriam was right? Her heart began to hammer. What if she and Adam *were* meant for each other? If only she knew how Adam felt about her now.

Over the next week Joanna thought about Adam more and more. On Thursday, she began sweeping the first floor of the Pequea Creek house, tackling the massive hearth first. It felt as if she were sweeping her heart, too, with stiff bristles. Jah, it hurt, but it felt good at the same time. She thought about Jacob less and less—and Adam more and more. She wasn't sure if the latter was a good thing or not.

"Need some help?"

Startled, she looked up. Adam stood at the open pocket doors to the living room with a broom in his hand.

"Sure." She smiled.

As they swept, Adam asked what she was looking forward to most on Saturday. She wanted to say, *Watching you build a barn*. But instead, she said, "Becky and Ike's reaction when they arrive."

"I think Mammi is going to be mad," Adam said.

Joanna agreed. "She'll get over it—and more. Not only is September twentieth our barn raising, it's also Becky and Ike's anniversary. Mammi Lu is going to bake them a cake."

Adam laughed. "That will really make her mad."

As she and Adam met in the middle of the room, he said, "I've really enjoyed working on this house *and* the barn raising with you. We make a good team."

"Denki," Joanna replied. He stopped sweeping and leaned against his broom. Did he plan to say more?

When he didn't, she said, "How about you? What are you looking forward to?"

As he opened his mouth to answer, Tim called out from the foyer, "Adam! We need your help out here."

Adam gave Joanna an apologetic look and then turned and followed Tim. Perhaps he wasn't ready to say whatever he'd started to say after all.

She thought of their kiss on the portico. Why had she run?

What if she'd stayed? What if she'd chosen to trust him?

Adam didn't come back into the house. When she left for the day, he was sitting on the foundation of the barn with a set of plans in his hands. He would be working late—he still needed to put one last coat of varnish on the banister.

Then he and Caleb and Tim would spend all of the next day seeing to the lumber delivery and the crane's arrival, as well as sorting through the hardware they needed while Joanna cleaned the vacation rentals for new arrivals Friday afternoon.

~

Saturday morning when Joanna arrived at the warehouse she decided to save time and not make coffee. After she packed the last crate, the one with paper supplies for the potluck and serving the cake, she glanced toward the coffee counter. She yawned and pushed up the sleeves of her heavy sweater, then spotted an envelope on the counter. Her heart lurched. It was the same writing as before. *Joanna*.

Adam had written her another letter.

But then she froze. After Miriam told Jacob she didn't want to marry him, he told her that was good because he wasn't coming back from Ohio. No one knew if that was his original plan or his reaction to her rejection.

Joanna assumed Adam's talk of going back to Florida had been because of the uncertainty around the business, but that seemed to be settled, at least for now. The next project was in the works. Why hadn't she asked Adam if he planned to leave? Why hadn't she told him she wanted him to stay? If he still intended to go, would he tell her in person? Or write it in a letter?

Every evening she sat on the porch and hoped he'd stop by. A few times she'd ventured back to the edge of the woods, looking for him. Sometimes she heard a scooter on the highway, but it never turned down Mammi Lu's driveway. Had she waited too long?

She picked up the envelope carefully, as if it might burn her, slipped it into her pocket, and then decided to make a pot of coffee after all.

Next she retrieved her lengthy to-do list from the office. She'd recruited a handful of Youngie boys to see to the horses and buggies and set up the tables and benches.

Mammi Lu, Mammi Rhoda, and Elaine were in charge of organizing the food and keeping the lines moving. Mandy and Miriam were in charge of the drinks and restocking the cups, napkins, and plates. When Joanna had seen them the day before, Mandy said Veronica wanted to help too. She was going to meet Tim at the barn raising. That had made Joanna smile. Perhaps Veronica would be part of their circle too.

After the coffee finished percolating, Joanna filled her travel cup and grabbed her bag, the cup, and the crate and took them to the loading area. Then she hurried out to the stable to hitch the horse to the wagon. Thankfully Ike and Becky didn't come out of their house. Next she loaded the folding tables and all of the boxes into the wagon. She glanced back toward the warehouse. She'd made enough coffee for two—she'd go fill the extra travel cup for Adam. A few minutes later, she tucked it into a box in the back and climbed onto the bench and started for the Pequea Creek house.

When she reached the highway, she pulled the wool blanket out from under the bench and spread it across her legs. Summer had turned into autumn. The yellow leaves on the big-leaf maple trees fluttered above her. Overhead, Canada geese flew south. She passed a cornfield where the farmer had started harvesting and then a pasture where two Amish boys carted sprinklers toward a shed. She turned her face up toward the blue sky and patted the letter in her apron pocket. She hoped it wasn't bad news. She felt nauseous at the thought of Adam moving back to Florida.

The smoke from a morning fire wafted from an Amish farmhouse chimney ahead. Joanna imagined the family around the kitchen table, eating their breakfast, all safe and secure and together. Jah, the last couple of months had been hard. She hadn't felt safe and secure, and yet she had been. Lancaster County was home and Strasburg Township in particular. She would stay—even if Adam returned to Florida.

Obviously Ike and Becky weren't selling their business to Jacob, but even if they sold their business to someone else she wouldn't leave. She'd trust God. He would provide other work that she loved, if needed. But above all, she hoped Adam would stay and take over the business. He was a hard worker and a good leader.

Miriam was right—Adam was a good man. A ladybug landed on her hand for a moment and then flew away. She patted the letter again, and then she pulled off the road under an oak tree. Joanna couldn't wait any longer. She had to know what Adam had written to her. She hoped he was staying. She hoped for even more than that.

The dry leaves rustled above her as she took the letter from her pocket.

~

Adam warmed as he and Caleb moved the pieces of lumber for the frame. Every few minutes Adam raised his head. He'd expected Joanna to arrive by now. Had she found his letter?

He rolled up the sleeves of his shirt as Tim called out, "Boss! Where do you want these boards?"

Adam wasn't used to having anyone call him boss, but he took it in stride. But the fact was, he would soon be the boss. The evening before, his grandparents had asked him to take over the business within the next year, and he'd said yes. He'd stopped himself from rushing over to Lu's to tell Joanna. Nee, he needed her to read the letter first.

Now he pointed toward the front of the foundation. "At the top," he instructed Caleb.

A barn raising was like a massive puzzle, and thankfully the barn builder had made an intricate plan. They'd build the frames and raise them, and then build the walls. Once the sides were up, they would start on the roof. Joanna had contacted men who had worked on Dawdi's roofing crew over the years who would lead that effort.

"Adam!"

He raised his head.

Joanna stood in the driveway next to the wagon. She held a coffee cup in her hand. As he approached, she said, "I thought you could use this."

"Denki." He took the cup from her. "How are you?"

"*Gut.*" She smiled at him. "Really *gut*. Better than I've been in a long time."

He took a drink of coffee. Was it because of his letter? Or something else? He was afraid to ask. Instead he said, "I'll help you unload the wagon."

"Denki. We're going to put the food tables on the south front lawn and then the church tables and wagons on the north lawn."

It only took a few minutes to unload the boxes and tables and cart them over to the grass. Adam helped Joanna place the tables, and just as he worked up the courage to ask if she'd read the letter, she patted the pocket of her apron. "I found your letter. We need to talk—"

Someone yelled, "Adam!"

He turned. Tim stood in the driveway. "We ended up with an extra piece."

"Not now," Joanna said. "Maybe later today, when you can get away."

"I'll unhitch the horse," he said.

"Nee. I'll do it. I have plenty of time. The men will begin arriving any minute to start putting the frame together."

He nodded and grabbed his cup from the back of the wagon. "Thank you again." He couldn't help but feel anxious about what she thought of the letter, but he'd have to wait to find out.

The boys Joanna had asked to see to the horses, buggies, and wagons arrived. They began unhitching horses, watering them, and leading them to the pasture. Men gathered around the foundation and began building the frames. By midmorning they raised them. Next Adam organized the groups to work on putting up the walls and framing the windows.

At noon, they all stopped for the meal. Adam washed up at the outside station with the others and made his way to the front yard as Nick turned the van down the driveway. Adam had asked his grandparents to meet him at the Pequea Creek house to do a walk-through because they hadn't seen it since the cabinets had been installed and the floors finished.

As the van came to a stop, Mammi Becky slid open the side door. "What in the world is going on here?"

She focused on Joanna, who walked toward the van. "Don't tell me you put all this together."

Joanna smiled. "I did." She glanced around, meeting Adam's eyes.

He stepped forward. "We did."

"You shouldn't have." Mammi Becky climbed from the van with a miffed expression on her face. "Really."

"Now, Becky." Dawdi Ike strode toward her. "I'm sure they had their reasons."

"Everyone wanted to help," Joanna said. "It was the only way to get the barn built in a hurry, so you can get the property on the market and get the price it's worth."

Lu, Rhoda, and Elaine stepped toward Mammi Becky. Lu called out, "Joanna's right. Everyone did want to help."

Mammi Becky's expression softened a little. "Are you sure?"

"Positive," Elaine answered.

Mammi Becky slipped her arm through Dawdi Ike's. Lu waved them over to the food line and said, "Get something to eat."

As the line started down the sides of the food tables, Adam saw Joanna slip into the house through the front door. He followed her. She waited, halfway up the staircase, her hand on the banister, and said, "It's lovely. You've done a beautiful job restoring it."

He started up the staircase toward her as she took an envelope from her apron pocket. "Denki."

She pulled the letter out and said, "I love that you love that I'm a planner and good in an emergency. That you love that I'm brave even when I'm afraid. That I read and share stories with you—and read what you recommend. That I love my grandparents—and yours. That I love flowers. That I do all I can to create homes for other people." She met his eyes and said, "And I love the end of your letter." She dropped her gaze again and read,

> *"I love that you were willing to be my friend from the beginning even though I wasn't willing to be yours. I'm prouder than I should be, but not too*

proud to ask again if you would be willing to court me. I love you.

Your friend,
Adam"

She stepped down a stair and reached for Adam's hand. "I love how honest you are. And patient. I love how unafraid you are. I love that you were a good friend to me, even when you didn't mean to be." She squeezed his hand. "And I love you too."

Adam stepped up one stair and leaned toward her. She held his gaze and their lips met for a sweet kiss. He grasped the banister with one hand and held Joanna with the other, pulling her close. She smelled of lavender soap and fresh air and the pine trees that bordered the house. She wrapped both arms around him, still holding the letter, and their mouths met again. When she finally pulled away he said, "I'd like my life with you to start as soon as possible."

He felt Joanna nod, but then she gasped. "The cake!"

Joanna walked out the front door of the house, across the portico, and down the front steps as she carried the double-layer chocolate cake toward Becky and Ike, who sat in lawn chairs to the right on the front lawn. Adam walked beside her, and by the time they reached his grandparents, Mammi Lu, Mammi Rhoda, and Elaine had gathered close by, with Daniel and Dawdi Hiram near them.

Becky, acting exasperated, said, "What else have you two done?"

Before Joanna could answer, Mammi Lu laughed. "Blame me. I made the cake."

Joanna said, "Happy anniversary," and extended her arms toward Becky, who took the cake.

"How many years?" someone called out.

Becky glanced at Ike, who quickly answered, "Forty-seven wunderbar years."

Several people clapped.

Becky said under her breath, "Don't ask how we met."

Joanna laughed.

"It was love at first sight." Ike gave Becky an adoring smile. Mammi Lu clasped her hands, and Mammi Rhoda stepped back to be closer to Dawdi Hiram. Daniel moved to Elaine's side.

Becky started toward the dessert table. "Dessert is served! If you don't want pie, cookies, or cupcakes, grab a slice of this." She turned toward Mammi Lu and mouthed, *Denki.*

As Joanna stepped away from the crowd, back toward the portico, Adam walked with her. When they were by themselves, he whispered in her ear, "What will we tell our grandchildren someday about how we met?"

She spoke in a normal voice. "We'll tell them we met on the way to a wedding. And you wanted to court me, but you didn't want to be friends."

Adam added, "And then we'll tell them we met again in Florida."

Joanna laughed. "And again at Thanksgiving." Her voice grew serious. "And again when I was very sad."

When she'd read his letter, she'd felt hope. Adam loved her. She could trust him. There was power in his words, and she could no longer deny the deep, deep sense of connection she felt with him. With Jacob, she'd been guarded. But with Adam she could be herself.

Adam stepped closer so their shoulders touched and said, "And we'll tell them we finally became friends, and then we courted."

Joanna leaned against him, brushing her hand against his, and whispered, "And then I'll say, 'Grandchildren, I married him.'"

Acknowledgments

First of all, I want to acknowledge each and every one of my readers. I'm eternally grateful for your support as you read my novels, review them, promote them, and share them! I couldn't do this without you.

As always, I'm thankful to my husband, Peter, for encouraging me through over twenty years of writing and publishing novels, and for loving me and caring for me through over forty years of marriage. Each of my heroes is inspired by him.

I'm also grateful to my friend Marietta Couch, who shares her knowledge and insights into Amish communities with me, answers all of my questions (even the ridiculous ones), and reads my manuscripts for accuracy. (Any mistakes are my own.)

I want to acknowledge my agent Danielle Egan-Miller, of Browne & Miller Literary Associates, for encouraging me through this project, from the initial concept to brainstorming titles. I specifically want to thank my editors Hannah Ahlfield and Rochelle Gloege for their suggestions and guidance that have definitely made this story stronger, and the entire team at Bethany House for everything they've done to make *When They Met Again* a book.

As I wrote this story, I thought of my two grandchildren, Harlow and Teza, and the joy they've brought to our entire family. My hope for them is that they will find love and community throughout their lives and know their value to God, others, and themselves.

Several sources inspired this story, including my observations of hardworking Amish people in the multiple communities I've visited. But I also had fun revisiting some of my favorite classics as I wrote the story—*Little Women* by Louisa May Alcott, *Sense and Sensibility* by Jane Austen, *Jane Eyre* by Charlotte Brontë, *Anne of Green Gables* by Lucy Maud Montgomery, and *Persuasion* by Jane Austen—and incorporating them into Joanna and Adam's reading lists and thoughts. The older I become, the more I realize the long-term, positive impact these classics (and so many more) had on my early development and on my life, along with, of course, the stories of love and redemption in Scripture. Above all, I'm thankful for God's love and faithfulness.

Discussion Questions

1. Joanna is determined to be friends first with any young man whom she might court. How important do you think it is to have a friendship with someone before falling in love with them? What romantic advice would you give to Joanna at the beginning of the story?
2. Joanna always has a plan. How do you balance having faith and planning ahead? Are you a planner, or do you take things as they come?
3. Joanna has complicated relationships with her parents. What untreated conditions might her parents have that contribute to the strained nature of their relationships? Do you think there's hope that Joanna might have a better relationship with them in the future? If so, explain.
4. Joanna's Mammi Rhoda remembers that Joanna could "prepare an entire supper by the time she was eight. By the time she was nine she could harness a horse to a buggy and run errands for Suzanna. For Rhoda too. She was doing the laundry by the time she was ten." What chores

did you do growing up? How does Joanna's growing up on an Amish farm impact her family's expectations of her?

5. Becky, Lu, Rhoda, and Elaine have been friends since they were teens over fifty years ago. Do you have a long-standing friend group? If so, what challenges has your group faced, and what do you appreciate most about them? If not, what do you miss most about a long-term friend group?
6. Joanna longs for a friend group of her own. By the end of the story, she's hopeful that she, Mandy, Miriam, and perhaps Veronica will form a circle of friends. What do you think Joanna will contribute to the group? What will she value the most?
7. Joanna is particularly close to her Mammi Lu. What were your relationships like with your own grandmothers? What do you think makes for a close relationship with a grandparent? What is your advice to grandparents looking to foster close relationships with their grandchildren?
8. By the end of the story, Miriam decides not to marry Jacob. Do you think she would have made the same decision without Joanna's support? Would she have made the same decision without the support of her grandmother, Elaine?
9. What causes Elaine to become more self-aware? What do you think motivated her to gossip in the first place?
10. Did you identify more with the grandmothers or the younger women? Why? Which character did you identify with the most?

Coming Soon:

A Second Chance to Remember

More sweet romance in book three of Letters from Lancaster County.

After losing her beloved husband, Mennonite widow Grace Conley devotes herself to her children, her Ohio farm, and the beekeeping business they started together—never expecting to fall in love again. But when a letter from a fellow widower, Amish beekeeper Michael Stoll, finds its way to her from Lancaster County, something unexpected begins to blossom. His heartfelt words echo her own grief and sleeplessness, while their phone conversations quickly become the sweetest part of her week.

Michael's quiet strength and compassion stir something Grace thought she'd buried forever. Their long-distance friendship turns tender, yet their differences—and individual grief—hold them back. Can they open their hearts to love again, without betraying the memory of those they lost?

Available everywhere books are sold,

Fall 2026

Leslie Gould is the #1 bestselling and award-winning author of fifty novels, including the COURTSHIPS OF LANCASTER COUNTY series and the AMISH MEMORIES series. She holds an MFA in creative writing and enjoys research trips, church history, and hiking, especially in the beautiful state of Oregon where she lives. She and her husband, Peter, are the parents of four adult children and have two grandchildren.

Sign Up for Leslie's Newsletter

Keep up to date with Leslie's latest news on book releases and events by signing up for her email list at the link below.

LeslieGould.com

FOLLOW LESLIE ON SOCIAL MEDIA

Leslie Gould Author

@LeslieGouldWrites